TH
BOY IN THE
DARK

By

K.McKechnie

RB

REDGATE BOOKS

First published in Great Britain in 2016 by
Redgate Books
Redgate House, Eastington
Devon EX17 6ND
books@redgate.aquiss.com

A CIP catalogue record of this book is available from
the British Library

ISBN 978-0-9955686-0-0

Printed and bound in the UK
by Short Run Press, Exeter

1

THE BAL MAIDEN

LEANING ON THE LONG SHAFT OF HER HAMMER, Grace Pascoe eyes the mound of copper ore on the dressing floor. She will break all that and earn her eight pence today. She raises the hammer, lifts it high above her shoulders then with all the force her body can muster, brings it down exactly where she has aimed. The rock shatters, quartz splinters flying, pattering on her canvas apron. Copper glitters peacock-blue in the broken rock. Rich this is, and today will be a good day for the Captain and the Adventurers. But rich ore or waste rock, Grace will earn no more than enough to buy a loaf of bread.

She swings the hammer again and again, letting her body settle to the familiar rhythm it learned so many years ago. Once more her nostrils flare at the acrid stink of struck pyrites. Its metallic taste bites at the back of her throat. This smell pervades her life: it is the smell of the dressing floor, the smell of Wheal Emma, the smell of the hillside itself, and most of all the smell of her husband's broken and grimy body when they laid him out.

He was clothed in his britches and boots, clothed just as they had found him, lying beneath a fallen timber with his ribs and chest stove in. She wept great wrenching sobs as she and Jenny Tuttle undressed him, bathed him, and her tears made runnels through the black mine dust coating his pallid skin. She washed away the blood congealed around his mouth and nose, pulled oak splinters from his body, the dead flesh lifting with the splinters. And when he was clean she kissed his forehead and they wrapped him in a winding sheet, and still Grace wept. They buried him in the dank fenced plot beside the chapel the next day, which was Saturday the fourteenth of May, eighteen fifty-nine. The sun shone. Captain Clymo stood on one side of her at the grave and her children stood on the other, their heads bowed. Amidst bird song and the Minister's word she heard the snivelling of little James her youngest who held the hand of Emily his sister, who in turn held the hand of Thomas who stood beside her. Her eyes were red-rimmed but dry by then. The Minister ceased speaking and Grace reached down, took up a clod of soil and dropped it on the linen-wrapped body of her dead husband lying in his grave.

In the quiet procession from the chapel to the mine, Captain Clymo turned to her and said, 'Grace, this here is poor John's club money, together with what the lads collected in their whip around. It will help you through.' He handed her a fist-sized leather purse, tied at the top with a leather drawstring.

'Thank you, Capun.' She took the purse, felt the weight of the coins heavy in her palm then slipped it into the pocket of her dress. She looked up at him, a long look filled with pain and resignation. 'Why, Capun? Why my John? They said no man knew the mine better than he.'

'You were a bal maiden so you know well enough that mining is a dangerous game.'

Grace bent her head, looked down at her feet in their black buttoned boots and said, 'John promised me he'd never take no risks.'

'Well, perhaps this time he did.'

'I don't believe it, Capun.'

They walked on in silence. And then he said, 'There's a place again for you on the dressing floor, if you want it.'

She nodded. 'Thank you, Capun.'

Once home in the stone built cottage she tipped the money out on the kitchen table and separated the coins, first the silver into its denominations of pounds, crowns, half-crowns, florins, shillings, sixpences and threepenny pieces, then the coppers. Her children looked on wide-eyed.

'How much is it, Ma?' Thomas asked.

'Not enough. Now get along outside.'

Once she was alone she counted the various coins, adding the totals in her head as she went. 'Twenty-four pounds, sixteen shillings and sevenpence ha'penny,' she murmured, and wondered where the halfpenny had come from. Who would think so little of dead John

Pascoe that they would give just a ha'pence to his widow? But with the club money added to the little she had saved she had near thirty pounds to her name. If she sent Thomas down the mine, this and his wage would keep the family for six months. But then what?

Grace rested her elbows on the table and her chin in her hands. Early summer light streamed in through the kitchen window. Her cottage was one of a row built by the duke for the miners and she paid but a peppercorn rent. Not that the duke was generous. It had taken a straggling ragtag of marching miners to the great gates of his estate before he took any notice of the miserable lives of the families whose labours had built his enormous wealth. Grace had marched with them. She knew that the duke took (stole more like) one twelfth of all the money that the mine produced. She put the coins back in the purse and hid it in the niche beside the kitchen fireplace.

So here she is, a week later, back with the bal maidens breaking rock. She rests again on the shaft of the hammer, deep breaths lifting her shoulders and bosom. She has chosen to return to this life, the life she endured for six long years before she married John Pascoe, breadwinner, copper miner, record breaker and dreamer, who once a month kept back pennies from his earnings to buy her trinkets from old Bill Burrows the tinker. John Pascoe, whose broad and muscled back she scrubbed each night in a tin tub before the kitchen range. Tears well in her eyes but she sniffs, shrugs and wipes her nose with the back of her hand. The time for crying is over, Grace cannot afford the luxury of grief; she must work. At least it is summer and the sun is warm and a light breeze lifts the dust of the dressing floor forming tiny whorls that fly about her feet. At the rock pile beside hers, Jenny Tuttle stops her hammering too. Jenny, her childhood friend and neighbour, is dressed as she is, round face prettily framed by a fresh white bonnet which falls to her shoulders. Her black bodice is tucked into a full black skirt covered with a canvas apron.

'You ain't forgot then?' Jenny calls.

'Hah, how'd you forget to swing a hammer? But I'll tell you

7

something, Jenny my love, there's a better life than this. I had it till my John was killed and I'll have it again. See if I don't.'

'You did that. Your John was a good miner and a better man. But at least you got summat to tide you over. Could you not have lived on the club money for a while?'

'I could have, but after it's gone I'd be back here anyway. Best keep it. I'll work thirty days this month. Thirty days at eightpence a day and I'll have just one pound. Less than a fourth of what my John earned. But Thomas starts down the mine tomorrow.' Then the image that has been lurking at the edges of her consciousness all morning leaps into her mind. It is an image that until now she has succeeded in not seeing – Thomas her eldest, just fourteen years old, working his first day fathoms deep in the mine.

It is a mystery to her, the mine, a place of men, dirt, darkness and death. She fears it and her fear is visceral, an ache in her belly, at its worst at the end of the core when the men make the long climb back to grass. And now she will send her eldest boy to take his father's place. Not that he can, not yet. It will be a many a day, if ever, before he matches his father's prowess or his earnings. John Pascoe was a tributer, free to mine as much as he could and paid not just by quantity but by quality. He had a nose for copper, they said and the ore he sent to the surface paid better than any other man's. But now he's dead and nobody can tell her why. And poor Thomas will earn no more than she on his first day deep in the candlelit darkness, holding the borer for eight hours while his two full-grown workmates drive it into the rock with sledgehammers. With a deep sigh, Grace raises her own hammer and begins again.

2

WHEAL EMMA

'LEGS ACHING, BOY?' CALEB CHAPMAN SPEAKS WITHOUT turning, his head bent low, tallow candle bobbing as he walks. It is less of a walk than a crouching trot.

'Yes sir.'

'I warrant they'll ache more, time you've climbed back up. But in a week you'll be running up and down them ladderways like a young monkey.'

Thomas thinks not. His calves hurt as they have never hurt before. One hundred and sixty fathoms he has clambered down the rickety ladders, and it will be one hundred and sixty fathoms back up at core's end. His clothes are soaked from the water that tumbles down the shaft in a steady stream. But at least he is not cold for at this great depth the mine is hot and humid. Slung across his chest he bears an oilskin satchel which contains his food and drink – a pasty made by his mother the night before and a bottle of water drawn from the village pump. The flickering yellow light of his candle is only just enough to illuminate the dripping walls of the tunnel that encloses him. Four more candles dangle by their wicks from a button of his jerkin. Running water splashes beneath his feet and squelches in his boots. His father wore good boots that he proofed with pig fat each night but it will be many a day before Thomas will fill those. Meanwhile his toes shrivel and wither in the wet.

But being a boy on his first workday in the depths of the Wheal Emma copper mine has at least one compensation – he need not adopt the crouching walk of his companions, Caleb Chapman, who is now so far ahead of him his light is but faintly visible in the gloom; and Henry Hopeful Down behind him, a giant of a man who, bent almost double, is treading on his heels. At least Thomas can walk with his head up, candle stuck on his hat with a lump of clay.

'Move it boy,' says Henry.

Thomas tries to hurry his step, stumbles, snatches at the rock wall to save himself from falling then grabs at his thick felt hat which flops over his eyes. Everything is too big for him, his boots, his hat, his sopping leather jerkin, everything except this cramped and endless tunnel. He tries to ignore the unease that wells in his mind at the dark confinement of the mine, the weight of all this rock bearing down on him. His father brought him down a year or so ago but that was only to the 20 fathom level. And his father never spoke of fear; his fireside tales were all excitement and discovery, escapes from danger and of money to be made. But in the end his escape was death.

The boys sees again the body in the grave, hears his mother's night time weeping and admits to himself that as he penetrates ever deeper into the rockbound darkness that killed his father, he is afraid – so afraid that if Henry Hopeful Down were not hard on his heels, he would turn and run, run back to the shaft and scamper up those ladders just like a monkey, in spite of the pain and shame, up to the light, the sweet air and the sunshine. But then, far ahead, it seems the fading glimmer of Caleb's candle grows stronger and the narrow arch of the tunnel is framed by increasing yellow light. The faint ring of steel on steel echoes towards him and, close to panic, Thomas runs the final hundred yards and emerges panting in a dimly lit open space – a stope, a manmade cavern where the tunnel's roof leaps upwards to a narrow cleft that disappears in darkness.

Thomas looks about him. Rubble strewn with great blocks of rock slopes from the face ahead. On one of these three men are working, one seated on the floor holding a steel bar two-handed, his wiry arms bare and his knees splayed. Thomas knows this man, Jethro Loam, who has in past times been a partner to his father. Above him and on either side his workmates, Jakeh James and Lewis Tuttle, swing their hammers, driving the steel into the rock with ringing, alternating blows. The miners are dressed in mud-stained shirts, coarse cotton trousers, boots and felted hats like his. Meanwhile Caleb Chapman has climbed the rubble to the face and takes a candle from his jacket, drips tallow onto a ledge of rock and sets the candle there. He turns sees Thomas and calls out across the gloom, 'This here is young Thomas, John Pascoe's eldest boy. He wants to be a miner.'

The two men stop their hammering and all three stare at him. 'Morning young Thomas,' says Jethro Loam and strokes his drooping moustache with a filthy hand. 'Following in your father's footsteps, eh?' Thomas does not reply. He blinks sweat and water from his eyes, and the stope falls silent save for the sound of trickling water.

Henry Hopeful Down climbs the rock pile and stands beside Caleb, sledgehammer dangling from one hand. 'Maybe not,' Caleb says, 'Isn't every boy can learn our trade. What say you, Thomas Pascoe?'

Thomas looks up at him, studies the bearded face, still saying not a word.

'Struck dumb now are you, boy? Bring that borer here, that there piece o' steel.' Caleb points to a three-foot-long steel rod, its tip ground to a flattened blade, propped up against the wall.

Thomas scrambles up the rock heap, the borer heavy in his hands. He holds it up to Henry Hopeful Down and looks from him to Caleb Chapman, far from sure that he wants to be a miner at all. He smells the sweat coming off them mingled with the animal stink of burning tallow. He thinks again of the clean air and sunlight above and wishes he were there. But like his mother he has no choice; they must work to live and this is the best, the only work, for a boy born of a miner and a bal maiden. How would he face her if he failed on this his first day underground?

'Are you ready, boy?'

'I am ready, sir,' he says in a small voice.

'Then let's set to. Stand here between us and hold the borer tight to the face, right here,' Caleb points with a finger to a crevice in the rock face where quartz glistens in the candlelight. With trembling arms the boy raises the steel and fits its point to the crevice.

'Now hold steady and turn her each time we strike.' Caleb swings, the steel and hammer ring and Thomas flinches as the shock stings his palms and runs up his arms. Before he has a chance to turn the steel, Henry Hopeful Down lands another blow and Thomas drops the borer and Caleb's next blow smashes uselessly against the face. The rock chips fly.

'Damn me, boy. That won't do. Come on now, try again.'

Once more he holds the steel against the rock. This time he manages to hold and turn the borer for five more blows before it springs from his tingling hands and clatters at his feet. The men rest on their hammers and Caleb shakes his head. 'Them skinny arms of his ain't up to this. Best you hammer Henry, and I'll drive. The boy we'll set to rolling barrows.' He grasps Thomas by the shoulder with a meaty hand and turns his body round. 'Never mind now boy, just grab that shovel there, fill that barrow by it with duds from this here pile, then roll 'n to the shaft. When you gets to the shaft dump'n and come back for more.'

Then ignoring the presence of the boy the miners turn back to their work of driving borers into rock, and the cavern rings again to the sound of hammer on steel. With a sinking heart, Thomas slithers down the rock pile past Jacob Loam and Lewis Tuttle and takes up the shovel and the barrow. The shovel's handle is as long as he is tall and his hands, already sore from the ringing steel, can barely grasp the handles of the barrow. The walk along the drive from the shaft seemed endless and now he must walk there and back alone, his way lit only by the sputtering tallow on his hat. But he wheels the barrow from its place by the wall to the rock pile, takes the shovel and tries to drive it into the rubble which looms above him. After repeated shoves he succeeds only in picking up a single piece of rock which he lifts into the barrow. He tries again and again but with each effort he only manages a stone or two or a pitiful mound of gravel shards. He is almost in tears and about to abandon the shovel and start filling the barrow with his bare hands when he realises that Caleb and Henry Hopeful Down have stopped their boring and are watching him.

'Here boy, let me show you how.' Henry Hopeful Down strides down the slope, grabs the shovel, levers it into the rock pile, shoves his whole body weight behind it, lifts and throws a shovel full of rock into the barrow. He hands the shovel back to Thomas who now, for the first time, manages to heave a half-load into the waiting barrow.

'Well done, boy,' says Henry Hopeful Down, smiling down at him. The shadowed candlelight exaggerates the pox marks on his face and Thomas remembers his father's words "Henry Hopeful Down's a good and kindly man, if a trifle short on wit. And God saved him from the pox."

'Thank you, sir,' Thomas says as Henry clambers back to Caleb Chapman and swings his hammer with increased energy.

Thomas struggles on until the barrow is almost full, then sets off along the drive to the shaft, the ring of hammers fading in his ears. By now his eyes have become accustomed to the smoky wavering light cast by the tallow on his hat and the tunnel seems not near as dark as when he came. But the barrow is heavy in his hands as he stumbles on the uneven surface of the tunnel floor. His hat keeps slipping down his brow and he must stop to right it. But finally he reaches the shaft where a lone miner shovels waste rock into a kibble.

'Well done, boy. Tip her out,' the miner says.

Panting in the hot close air, Thomas upends the barrow with a mighty heave and dumps its contents on the waiting pile. Returning, he finds to his surprise that it is easier to trot than walk and is soon back with his companions, whose ringing rhythmic blows have not ceased. With no sun, no light to mark the passing of the day, poor Thomas loses track of time. Five barrow-loads he manages until exhausted and with hands already blistered, he takes a rest, leaning on his shovel.

'Tired, boy?' Henry calls. 'Well, you're lucky for I reckon 'tis croust time.' He drops his sledgehammer and he and Caleb slide down the pile and set themselves down on a balk of timber on the floor.

The other miners join them, five men seated in a row – Henry Hopeful Down at one end and Caleb Chapman at the other. Between them sit Jethro Loam, Lewis Tuttle who lives with his wife Jenny in a cottage but two doors along from Thomas, and finally Jakeh James who says kindly, 'Come join us, Thomas Pascoe.'

Thomas takes up his satchel and sits dwarfed by Henry Hopeful Down beside him. He takes out his pasty, drinks water from his flask and thinks about his aching limbs and stinging hands. The miners eat pasties and bread and cold potatoes and swig cider from a wooden keg.

Henry, not normally a man of many words, puts an arm about Thomas's shoulder and says, 'That were a sad do, your father's death and no mistake. But he preferred to work alone and that's a danger.'

' A tributer who kept his secrets,' Jethro Loam says.

'Aye but that's the way to make money. Not tutwork like this. You know the difference don't you, boy?' Jakeh James asks.

Thomas nods. Of course he knows the difference. The miners with him will be paid by how much ground they break, so much per fathom. But his father worked the copper lodes alone and the richer the ore he mined, the more money jingled in his pockets at month's end. And like they all said, John Pascoe had a nose for copper; smell it, they said he could. Nobody speaks, the only sounds their quiet eating and the trickle of running water. Thomas is thinking of his father and his companions' silence tells him they are too.

Caleb Chapman finishes eating and with his fingers combs pastry crumbs from the great black beard that reaches to his chest. 'Tell you something I don't understand boys.' He speaks so quietly that Thomas must strain to hear. 'If John Pascoe were the best of miners and we're all agreed on that, how is it that he were in an end that he ain't made safe? John Pascoe alone and killed by falling rock – it don't make sense.'

'Nor do it,' says Henry Hopeful Down around a mouthful pasty.

'What you saying then, Caleb?' Lewis Tuttle asks. 'That it weren't no accident?' He coughs repeatedly, hauling phlegm from the depths of his chest and spitting.

'I ain't saying nothing. I'm just asking.'

Thomas finds he cannot swallow. His mother's pasty is as dry as sawdust in his mouth. He tries to wash it down with water and starts to choke.

'Easy, boy,' mutters Henry Hopeful Down and pats him on the back.

Thomas finally manages to swallow and the men lapse once more into silence. But Thomas's mind is in a turmoil. He has tried so hard to be a man and accept his father's awful death, believing it God's will, an accident, an unavoidable consequence of his father being who he was. Now, the need to howl and cry with the raw grief that rose within him when first he saw his father's battered body, surges in him once again and his shoulders shake with barely stifled sobs.

Henry leans forward and looks along the row of men. 'Whyn't you keep your big mouth shut, Caleb Chapman?'

'Things need to be said, things need to be out in the open air.'

'Tain't the open air down here. Tis the bloody mine and the boy's first day.'

'The boy must . . .' Caleb stops and cocks an ear. 'Someone's coming.'

The sound of heavy footsteps issues from the tunnel, light reflected from pools of water flickers on the roof and a tall figure emerges into the stope. He is dressed in a cotton drill shirt and waistcoat and fine serge trousers and his boots are shod with hobnails which strike sharply on the rock floor. Like the miners he wears a thick felt hat with a lighted tallow stuck on with clay. Like them he is soaked from coming down the shaft but even wet he carries an authority about him.

'Good day boys,' he calls out.

'Good day to you, Capun.' The reply is ragged, almost grumbled and the only person to get to his feet is Thomas.

'Ah, young Thomas, how goes it, boy?'

Thomas, still struck dumb, does not reply. How can he speak after what he has just heard?

'Speak up now,' Mathew Clymo says. 'Are you to be a miner?'

'Aye, sir,' Thomas says finally, head bowed.

Mathew Clymo nods and turns to Caleb. 'How many fathoms broken here this month?'

'Five fathom and some, Capun. Be seven by month's end.' The plain satisfaction in Caleb's voice is there for all to hear. For seven fathoms multiplied by four pounds a fathom makes a monthly wage of twenty-eight pounds to be divided between the five of them. There are deductions for candles and powder and the sharpening of tools at the smithy and the few shillings that Thomas himself will earn in the last week of the month. But still it is more than a living wage.

Mathew Clymo climbs up the rock pile and holds a tallow to the face. He runs his fingers over the rock and turns to look down on the men.

'I'd say we're less than two fathom from the lode. What say you, Caleb?'

'Could be Capun, could well be.' Caleb hopes that the lode is as far away as possible, even not there at all, for the rock is softish and they make good money in this ground. Once the lode is reached, it will be mined on tribute and he and his men will move to another workplace, an end where like as not the rock will be harder than Clymo's hobnails and bitter going.

'Well boys, take all due care now.' Mathew Clymo moves easily down the slope of rubble and leaves them.

'Let's set to then,' Caleb says, and the miners return to their work of boring shot holes in the rock while Thomas Pascoe wheels barrow after barrow to the shaft until his blisters weep and his arms are straining in their sockets and he is soaked anew with sweat. Possessed by both the drudgery of load and wheel, load and wheel, and hideous thoughts about his father's death, once again he loses all sense of time. He is surprised when Henry Hopeful Down takes the shovel from his hand.

'That's enough of running barrows for today now, Thomas. If you're to be a miner you need to learn. Come, watch, we're loading shot holes.'

Much relieved, Thomas joins the miners as they fill the holes they have so laboriously drilled with black powder from Caleb Chapman's flask. The boy watches as they tamp it down with an iron bar and insert the fuses made from quills already filled with powder.

'Clear out now, boys, afore I set the fire,' Caleb says, and the others pick up their bags and tools and hurry from the stope towards the shaft. Within a minute they hear behind them the sound of Caleb's running feet, then a flash and four almighty bangs and the crash of falling rock. Their candles flicker in the blast, the tunnel fills with sulphur-smelling smoke, and they run with streaming eyes and cough and choke. At the shaft they start the climb against the falling water which is now a sweet relief as rung by rung the air begins to clear.

Thomas, with Henry Hopeful Down behind him, is last but one. His hands, already raw, sting from the grit left on the ladder by the boots that step above him; his arms and calves reach and strain at every rung. He counts them – fourteen between each sollar platform, where he wishes he could rest but Henry urges him on with kindly words.

'Up you go young Thomas, up to grass. Like Caleb said afore, you'll be running ahead of all of us in a week or two.'

Thomas can only pant in answer. After what seems an endless time the men above him take a rest while he and Henry stop on a platform one stage below. 'A breather, now. We'm halfway up,' Henry says, breathless too.

All too soon they begin the climb again, slower now, falling behind the other men until, looking up, far far above him Thomas spies the glint of daylight. Much encouraged, he forces his legs and arms to work though by now his hands are bleeding.

'Well done boy,' comes the grunt of Henry Hopeful Down, 'nearly home.'

And finally at sweet last, Thomas is out in open air, the golden air of a Cornish summer afternoon, and he sits exhausted on the ground.

Henry squats in front of him. 'The first day is the worst, my boy. Take heart.'

3

AN UNEXPECTED VISIT

MATHEW CLYMO WALKS DOWN THE MAIN STREET OF the village of Penpillick. It rained earlier but the clouds have cleared away eastward over the valley leaving the cobbles glistening in the sun of a September evening. Passing the Bedford Arms he greets the group of miners spilling from the inn's front door.

'Evening boys,'

'Evenin' Capun.' Some raise their glasses, others turn away and Mathew just overhears a muttered 'Bloody Clymo, too clever by half.' He smiles to himself. A man who was once a miner needs little cleverness to catch another claiming more copper than he has really dug. Mathew knows all their tricks. He also knows that some men resent his elevation from their ranks to Captain of the Wheal Emma mine but he cares little for this. The mine is, after all, his creation.

It was he who first found green copper stones in the banks of the river below, who traced them up the valley sides and single-handed and secretly dug the first costean along the lode to expose its riches to the open air. It was Mathew Clymo who rode to London with samples in his saddlebags, and found Adventurers prepared to put their capital in this the riskiest of ventures . And he too who persuaded a reluctant Duke of Bedford to permit mining on his land.

'Ha, a twelfth you say. Ruin my pheasant shooting, sir, that's all mining will do. How do I know this is not just a shot in the dark, a wild goose chase?'

So Mathew showed the duke the diggings deep in his own woods. The duke amazed at the potential wealth beneath his lands, struck the glittering ore with Mathew's pick and avarice overcame his love of shooting birds. 'Have you the necessary funds to start this venture?' he asked.

'I do your Grace, five thousand pounds, all raised in London.'

'Indeed. A pretty fortune for a miner.' The duke gave Mathew a sideways look then said, 'Present yourself at the estate office tomorrow. I'll have my man Scoble draw up the necessary deed.'

Pursuing his walk down the street, Mathew studies the twin row of cottages that continue beyond what was once the village limit. He nods to himself, well satisfied with what he sees. The cottages are built of local stone and sturdy with roofs of Cornish slate. Five years ago most miners lived in squalor on the edge of Liskeard, two families to a two-room hovel. Until one Sunday, fuelled part with drink and part with anger, they marched with their wives and children to the mansion of the duke and duchess and stood through the afternoon shouting at the gates. Being captain of the mine, Mathew was summoned by the duke.

'This is an outrage Captain Clymo. Must I call on police or soldiers to quell this riot?'

'Neither, your Grace. The people have just cause. The mine is rich beyond our hopes. We have brought in many men and will bring more yet. They need housing but there are no more houses in the village or the town, as Mr Scoble knows too well.'

'Is this true, Scoble? Why have I not been informed?'

Mr William Scoble, agent to the duke, sat silent for a moment, eye to eye with Mathew Clymo. They liked each other not one bit. It was Mr Scoble's task to ensure the duke was paid his tithe – a twelfth of all the copper sold; he owned the land, he was the mineral lord. And Mr Scoble, meticulous to a fault, at each month's end made Mathew's life a trial with scrutinies of books and endless checks and balances.

The duke, tall, slim and dressed in black, rose from the table and rounded on his agent, 'Speak up, man, speak up. I will have the truth.'

'Your Lordship insists that economies across the whole estate are the order of the day. I merely carry out your Lordship's bidding.'

'Would you chide me, sir?' The flush suffusing his handsome face spread to include his hairless pate.

'Indeed not your Grace. I speak the truth.'

'Truth, be damned. You'll not hide things from me Mr Scoble.'

'Your Grace, might I explain?' Mathew folded his arms and looked the duke straight in the eye.

'If we build houses as the men demand and as close as possible to the mine, I assure your Lordship that every penny spent will be recouped in increased copper. The men walk five miles from the town to work and five miles home again. And there at home they have but poor rest. Families are sharing houses, and men working different cores share each other's still warm beds. Half the miners are dead tired before they start and lack the capacity for a decent day's work. And many of them are taking sick – from the lack of privies the surgeon says. He believes the wells are tainted and fears the cholera. If it strikes the town there'll be no mining, nor no copper.'

The duke sat down, leaned back and crossed his legs. 'Cholera you say. That would be unfortunate indeed. And men sleeping in each other's beds, that's not decent.' He sat silent for some time, scrutinising each man's face in turn then gazing out of the window. Finally he said, 'Scoble, get yourself down to the gates and tell that howling mob that Captain Clymo has spoken up for them. We'll build the houses, a whole damned village if needs be.'

And so it was that at Mathew Clymo's bidding, the duke built thirty cottages in Penpillick, and the miners at Wheal Emma have much to thank him for. Yet many, recalling that he once sweated with them underground, resent both his position as their master and his success. What is more, he made an enemy that day of William Scoble who could scarce hide his humiliation. Mathew shrugs. Arriving at the last cottage at the bottom of the hill he stops to watch a group of children playing by the river. He knows them all by sight and two at least by name, James and Emily, Grace Pascoe's younger son and daughter. And it is Grace he has come to see and outside whose cottage he now stands. He knocks at the open door.

'Come in.' Her voice is low-pitched but clear.

'Good evening, Grace.' Mathew ducks his head and enters the cottage. 'No, do not rise for me.'

But Grace gets up from her chair, her back to the evening light streaming through the window. In one hand she holds a shirt and in the other needle and thread. Various bits of clothing lie on the table before her. At the end of the table sits Thomas Pascoe, a book open before him.

'Good evening, Capun,' she says, 'What brings you here? No trouble I hope. Or is it my son you wish to see?'

Thomas too has got to his feet. 'Evenin' Capun,' he says.

'Evening to you too Tom.' He turns back to Grace. 'No, there's no trouble. But there is something I wish to discuss with you, in private if we may.'

Grace looks up at him, surprised. 'In private?'

Mathew nods.

'Thomas, go see to the children.'

Thomas stares unsmiling, first at his mother, then at Mathew Clymo, then leaves the cottage without a word.

Mathew picks up Thomas's book and turns it in his hands. 'The Elements of Euclid' – that's a challenge for a bal boy.'

'He was no bal boy till John died. He was at the school in Liskeard which we could bare afford. You knows that.'

He nods and puts the book down.

'Sit down, Capun. Will you take some tea?'

'I will, thank you kindly.'

Grace offers him a chair, puts a kettle on the hob and busies herself with tea things. Mathew's gaze wanders around the sparse but neatly furnished kitchen – the dresser with its plates and cups, the cast-iron range, the spotless slate-paved floor, the patterned curtains at the window where the evening light still glows. Not many miners' wives have this much. His eye is drawn back to Grace, still in her Sunday best, although without the black bonnet she wore to chapel. Her thick brown hair is drawn in a bun above the nape of her neck and unpinned wisps curl down beside her ears. He looks away, leans back in his chair and stares out through the open door listening to the children's cries. He knows her looks too well. He has watched her covertly on the dressing floor, her easy swing of the spalling-hammer, the way she rests from time to time, head back, breast out and hands pressed into the small of her back. He has seen a smile light up her face when Jenny Tuttle, resting too, sees him watching, gives him a look and makes some jest.

'Your tea, Capun Clymo.' She bends before him cup in hand, and the faintest scent of lavender mingles with that of tea. She takes her own cup to the table, turns a chair and sits to face him. 'Now tell me Capun, what do you wish to speak of?'

'Will you not call me Mathew?'

'Mathew.' She looks at him, her hands folded in her lap, his name hanging in the air between them. The china cup seems ridiculously delicate in his brawny hand.

'It's about poor John.'

Grace stiffens. It is near four months now since her husband died. The tears still soak silently into her pillow as she lies awake in the sleepless hours before dawn.

'John?'

'Aye, John. This may seem strange.' He pauses, sips his tea. 'John could read and write, yes?'

'Yes, he could. That were John's book Thomas were studying when you come in. What of it?'

'You know that John was the best miner I ever met. Not just strong and hardy – he had a second sense about the lodes. We'd lose one or t'other now and then and it was always he who found it. Almost as if he could track its whereabouts like a hunter tracks a deer.'

'Yes.' Grace puts her head on one side as if to say "and so?". But now she knows full well where Mathew Clymo's thoughts are headed.

'Did he perchance keep a journal, write anything down, make maps and suchlike of the mine?'

'He were always scribbling. Sat there he did most nights when the children were abed and he weren't underground.' She gestures towards the chair in front of which the Euclid lay. A picture of her husband comes clear into her mind. He is bent over a fat leather-bound book. A scrap of chalk-marked mine slate lies beside it. From time to time he looks up and stares into space, eyes half closed, as if recalling the detail of some feature he has seen in the shadows of the mine. 'Make our fortune this book will, Grace my love. We'll be rich one day. It's all in here.' He taps his head then adds as he bends again to his work, 'And it's all going in here' She hears again the rustle of a turning page and the scratching of his quill, sees him blowing on the ink to dry it.

Each night before they went upstairs to bed, he would erase the markings on his slate, wrap the book in oilskin, lift out the loose slab before the hearth and secrete the parcel in the cavity beneath. It lies there still, untouched since before he died. In truth she has forgotten all about the book till now. But even so, Grace is careful not to let her eyes stray towards its hiding place.

'And do you have his writings still?'

She hates to lie, it's not in her nature but suddenly she feels she must. Unable to read herself, she never set much store by her husband's writings or his dreams of riches. She had been content with his success as a simple miner who provided more for her than any miner's wife expected. But if the mighty Mathew Clymo is in her house seeking out his book, maybe what John Pascoe said is true.

'Ah, it were just scraps, ideas he said, food for thought. I burned it all after he died.' Grace drinks her tea, stands and goes to the door, looks out. 'Excuse me Capun, but I must call the children in. Tis past their bedtime.'

'But Grace, you burned it all, kept nothing?'

'Just bits o' paper with scribbling on I didn't understand. Anyways, he said it were all in his head.' She calls out, 'Thomas, James, Emily, come in now, tis past time.'

Mathew Clymo gets to his feet with cup in hand. 'Are you sure, Grace? Surely you kept some of it, some paper?'

'No Capun, nothing.' She stands hand on the door jamb still looking out, afraid to turn to face him, afraid he'll see the blush that has risen to her cheeks.

'Mama, Billy Tuttle threw mud at me.' Emily holds out her bespattered skirt.

'Never mind that, my love, get on in, it's time for bed. Upstairs and say your prayers.' She ushers in the younger boy and girl. 'You'll excuse me now, Capun.'

24

'Of course, Grace. But may I call on you again perhaps?' Mathew puts the teacup on the table and moves toward the door.

'Call?'

'As a gentleman calls on a lady.'

'I may be just a bal maiden, Capun, but I still mourn.' She turns away as Thomas comes in and looks from one to the other then sits at the table. He takes up his book without speaking.

'Good evening then Grace. Good evening, Tom.' Mathew Clymo dips his head in the vestige of a bow and leaves them.

In the fading light she sits once more and takes up her mending, puts in a stitch or two then stops, listening to the murmur of the river. Captain Mathew Clymo – tall, not handsome but well set up with the muscles of a miner, and rich of course. With him at her side she'd have no need to be breaking rocks. But would his interest in her be occasioned more by poor John's papers, or is it for her own sake? And what would that mean? She has seen him watch her and found it disconcerting; now he has declared himself. He knows that were she gentry she'd be in mourning for two years or more. She wishes she were offended at his presumption, but she is not.

'What did he want Ma?' Thomas asks.

Startled from her reverie she is confused and must collect her thoughts. She looks at Thomas without an answer. Just four months down the mine and already he acts the man.

'Mother?'

'Your father kept a book, a diary of the mine. I don't know. The capun came a-looking for it.'

'A book, what book? I never saw no book.'

'He called it "My Book". He wrote when you was all asleep.'

'You gave it to the capun?'

'No, no, it lies hidden – under there.' Grace points to the hearth.

Thomas leaps to his feet, crosses the room and squats before the hearth. 'Under here?'

'Yes.'

'We must take it out, Ma. I must read what Father wrote.'

Grace goes to the hearth, inserts a fire iron between the slabs and levers up the loosened hearthstone. 'Careful now.'

Thomas lifts the slab with ease and there the oilskin parcel nestles. Grace takes it out and Thomas lowers the slab of slate back into place. At the table Grace lights a candle and watches as her son unwraps the book and lays it unopened on the table.

'Read it then, boy. What did your father have to say?'

Reverently Thomas opens the marbled cover and as he does so a folded sheet of paper flips out. 'A letter, Mother. There's a letter.' He scans a few lines and then begins to read aloud.

My Dear Thomas,
I would write this letter to your dear Mother but being as she is not one for the reading I write it to you, my Son, that you may read my words out loud to her.

Thomas pauses and looks up at his mother. 'Go on boy, go on.' He reads again as he has been taught, in a clear and even voice.

In these past few days I have been beset by concerns that all is not as it should be in the mine and that I am in danger from some unknown person. Your Mother knows that I prefer to work my pitch alone. This is not because I dislike my comrades or that I lack friends who would work with me. In fact the opposite is the case – I have had many a request to join a pare and work with other tributers on Wheal Emma's lodes. But my knowledge of the secrets hidden in the rocks that contain so much riches is hard-won – as you will discover my Son in this here My Book – I would keep this to myself and to my heirs, namely you, your brother and your sister and of course your dear Mother. I have thought on many a day that I should take you with me once again into those dark and subterranean depths that until lately held no fears for me, that you might learn somewhat of this secret knowledge. But a miner's life is hard indeed and we deemed it better that you be schooled and who knows one day you will become a Gentleman.

Thomas glances at his mother who sits with folded arms, her face expressionless. He turns the page and begins to read once more.

But I stray from the matter in hand. Last week I was working on my accustomed pitch – its amazing rich and I have never seen the like – so much so that I do believe it is an undiscovered lode. I durst not take all I dig to grass but must conceal a part of each day's diggings under a mound of deads. Resting for an early croust I heard footsteps from the level but saw no glimmer of tallow. Thinking it must be some person come to spy on me I stays silent as a mouse. Then the footsteps stop so I douse my light and knowing by touch every inch of rock between the face at which I work and the ladderways – for have I not trod that way a hundred times or more? – I walk silently in utter darkness toward the place from whence the sound has come. Then before me I hear the steps again – of nailed boots I do believe – but this time hurrying away along the level. I calls out a great halloo. Who's there? But I hears only echoes back. I thought it might be Captain Clymo come to visit and changed his mind for he do allways wear hobnailed boots. I returns to my work and thought no more of it that day.

Next morning I discovered that thievery has been afoot the night before, for the stock of ore I have concealed against hard times is stolen. I know that there are certain Godless persons in the mine who would do this thing. But I will point no finger till I discover which of them it might be. Perhaps it is that person who came on the level in hobnailed boots and not likely to be the Captain for it is of no advantage to him to steal the fruits of a man's work.

The day after was the Lord's Day so I did not work. On Monday I changes to the evening core, leaving my pitch unattended so you and I might work the garden together during the day as maybe you will remember.

That night I bored two holes into a very rich bunch of ore which was easy going. I charges the holes and takes up my tamping bar to pack the powder hard down but the heft of the bar is strange to my hand. I hold it close to the light and see with great alarm that it is not shod with copper as mine is. Iron may strike a spark from the rock and blow the charge which has been the cause of maiming or death of many a miner. This bar is plain iron and my bar is disappeared. So I did not shoot the charge and came immediately to grass where I sought out Captain Clymo and told him that someone wishes me ill or worse.

The Captain shewed great concern and said he will look into the matter with all speed and seriousness. John says he, there are persons I have heard speak against you as a selfish man but I cannot believe that they would wish to kill you. However leave all to me and I will surely get to the root of this matter. And take all due care. Then he claps me about the shoulder.

My Son, I write this on the evening of the day of these events. I have said nothing of them to your dear Mother for I know that she worries for my safety every day that I do go down the mine and I would not give her cause for more concern. And I greatly hope that you will never read this letter but if the worst do happen you and my Dearest Grace shall know the truth of what befell me and take what measures you deem fit.

Also my Son I would urge you to study this My Book which though you might find difficult to comprehend at first will in the course of time bring you the riches which I have always promised to my sweet family.

With best love to Your Dear Mother,

Your affectionate Father JOHN PASCOE   10th day of May 1859

Thomas stops reading, looks up at his Mother and whispers, 'Ma, he wrote this three days before he died.'

Grace sits staring at her son, elbows on the table now, her hands before her mouth as if in prayer, tears welling in her eyes. She cries out, 'They killed him, they killed my poor John. What shall we do?'

With an age beyond his years Thomas replies, 'Hush Mother, I do not know, not yet. But I will think long and hard and you may be sure that I shall discover the murderer of my father.'

4

THE DRESSING FLOOR

'WHAT HOPE OF A BETTER MONTH THEN, Captain Clymo?'

'None, Mr Scoble. Worse if anything. What say you Francis?'

'A loss again, I fear,' bellows the purser.

The three men are standing high on the bob plat, a railed platform linking the engine house to the winding gear and overlooking the dressing floor. They have to shout to make themselves heard above the din of clanking machinery and the whistles and groans from the steam engine behind them. A kibble of ore comes clattering out of the shaft below. The engineman tips it into a waiting barrow and a thin armed boy wheels it away to a pile where the bal maidens are breaking rock.

'Well, it won't do,' William Scoble says. 'The duke is most unhappy and so am I.' Scoble wears a high crowned bowler hat yet is still a good head shorter than Mathew Clymo who, with his dark hair curling over his collar and a red neckerchief, cuts a fine figure.

'His Lordship's state of mind is not my worry. He is paid whether we make profit or loss. I promised my shareholders that their investment in Mr Trevithick's engine would show handsome returns And that is my first concern. As to your unhappiness, I give not a tinker's fart.'

'What?' shouts Scoble, 'I cannot hear you for this infernal din.'

'Francis, take Mr Scoble to the counthouse, show him the Cost Book. I will join you shortly.'

Mathew leans on the rail and studies the busy scene below. As always, one-eyed old Harry Rowse sits at the shaft head puffing his clay pipe and counting who comes up and who goes down. Upwards of fifty women and children are at work both outside and in open-sided sheds: boys wheeling barrows of ore, bal maidens in pairs, swinging their spall-hammers and breaking the rock into fist-sized lumps, others seated with smaller cobbing hammers, crushing the lumps into fragments to be barrowed into the sheds where boys and girls wash and sieve the ore on long sloping racks. His eye falls on Jenny Tuttle and Grace Pascoe. She is aptly named; even wielding a hammer she has grace. He cannot discern her features beneath the broad rim of her bonnet but he knows them well. Perhaps it was just a trick of the light last night but he could have sworn her pretty face blushed then hardened when he pressed her about her husband's journal. He did not believe that she would have burned it, so she must have it still and must then know its value.

Jenny Tuttle looks up from her work and catches his eye. A bold woman she is, not in the least in awe of him nor any man, he guesses. He drops his gaze, pretending to study another kibble emerging from the shaft but watching them from the corner of his eye. Grace does not turn but it is clear that they are talking about him. He turns away discomfited, leaves the bob plat, descends the stone stairway inside the engine house and strides around the corner to the counthouse. He wishes he could do something for Grace to improve her lot. She is intelligent but can neither read nor write, and for a strong young woman spalling is the best-paid job on the dressing floor. He could marry her of course, if she would have him. He could do worse for a ready made family, and marriage to Grace might solve another problem.

'Capun's watching you,' Jenny Tuttle mutters as her hammer swings down.

'Cat may look at a king.'

'I saw him come a-visitin' last evenin'.' The two women face each other across the rock pile, their hammers swinging in unison. Neither looks up from her work. 'You set your cap at him?'

'No I ain't. Nor am I likely to neither.'

'Could do a deal worse.'

Grace singles out the largest rock on her side of the pile and brings the hammer down with all her might. The rock splits clean down the middle and suddenly she is overwhelmed by the cloud of woe that settled on her the evening before. All night she tossed and turned with the words 'murder' and 'why? and 'who? repeating in her head like

30

the tolling of some awful bell, reliving again and again that dreadful afternoon and evening. He was never late. No matter how remote John's pitch, how long it took him to walk the pitch-black galleries and climb the endless fathoms up to grass, he never kept her waiting. He knew too well how much she worried for his safety every minute he was underground. So she'd be waiting at the cottage door, his dinner warming on the range until she saw him swinging down the street. And the smile that shone through the mine muck on his face made her want to laugh for joy.

But that day he did not come. By early evening she began to panic and went next door to Jenny Tuttle's.

'Lewis, you seen my John? Is he already back to grass?'

'I din't see him all day, come to think on it,' Lewis Tuttle said. 'Believe he were working his pitch at the back of 120 fathom. By hisself as usual. I'd better call the boys, we'll go down again and take a look. Now don't you worry, Grace. I 'spect he just lost track of time.'

But she knew he never lost track of time, knew even then that only injury or worse would keep him from her. So she left the children with Jenny Tuttle, trudged with the men to the shaft head and waited and waited and waited, until the early summer's night was almost fallen, and she heard them calling on the ladders, 'Easy now boys, just a few more rungs,' and they emerged panting and exhausted, and laid his broken, bloodied body on the ground before her. And she collapsed upon it, howled with grief and loss and none could comfort her.

She stops now, forehead resting on the hammer's handle and once again the tears flood down her cheeks and her shoulders heave with sobs.

Jenny Tuttle drops her hammer and running to her side puts an arm about her. 'What is it? What is it my love?'

'Is he gone?'

'Who?'

'Clymo.'

'Yes, he's gone.'

Grace straightens up and wipes her eyes with the back of her hand.

'It's nothing. He talked last night of my John, how nobody knew the mine like he did. Started me grieving for him all over again.'

'Foolish man, to come a-courting so soon after. Tain't proper.'

'I told him I was still in mourning.'

'So you are. But it'll pass.'

Grace nods and Jenny gives her a hug and they return to their labour. But she thinks her grief can never pass, cannot be assuaged now she knows that John was murdered. But what should she do? What can she do? Certainly not turn to Mathew Clymo whatever his intentions. For he pretends it was an accident when he surely knows that it was not. She is trapped, at a total loss, her only hope her eldest son, just fourteen. At six that morning she watched him join the other lads amongst the group of men assembled at the shaft. He already has the miner's pallor brought on by long hours of work in the semi-darkness but he is filling out across the chest and shoulders and holds himself as if he were a man. This morning he stood apart and looked about him with a newfound wariness. She knows he is a clever boy. Mrs Kirkpatrick told her so the day she took him out of school. 'Tis a pity he must leave. He has brains your boy.' But now he is down the mine being schooled in all its mysteries by Caleb Chapman and Henry Hopeful Down. Good men they are, John spoke well of Henry, said he would have been his partner had he wanted one. So when they offered to take him with them to their work and teach him all they knew, she trusted them, she trusts them still. She made them promise to take good care of him. She could not bear it if he were taken too.

Grace is tired now, from lack of sleep, from worry and from weeping and from this endless labour day after every weary day. She rests again and watches Jenny – Jenny the girl she played with as a child, her friend who helped her through not only her husband's death but childbirth too and like her, breaks rocks to earn a crust.

'Jenny?'

Jenny stops her hammering too and looks up.

'It's more than just my grief. I heard it said that John was murdered.'

'Who said that, the capun?'

'No, not him. Have you heard the same?'

Jenny's blue eyes stare straight at her. 'I have.'

'Who? Who was it spoke so?'

'Lewis, that day your Thomas started down the mine. When he come home he said they're saying it weren't no accident.'

'But when they brung him up that night up they said it was.'

''You know they found him under rock and timbers. Lewis said a rotten timber did give way and your John were underneath, all buried in rock and dirt.'

'So why now does the rumour run that he was murdered? And why has no one spoke to me before? Why have you not said?'

'You had enough to grieve on without listening to daft rumours. 'Sides, it were only something Caleb Chapman said. That John were too good a miner to work in an end that weren't made safe.'

'He were the best and someone killed him and I will know who and why.'

Mathew sits himself down at the counthouse table.

'It won't do, Captain Clymo, it just won't do.'

'I heard you the first time Mr Scoble. Has Mr Pryor not shown you the books?'

'Indeed I have.' The purser flips over several pages in the mine account book. 'We'll pay no dividend this quarter and the only way to stop more loss is for the price of copper to be on the up. Of course if the duke forgave his royalty until a lode turns kindly. . . '

'Absurd suggestion. Why should his Lordship pay for your incompetence?' Scoble turns again to Mathew Clymo.

'Mr Scoble, it is not a question of competence, mine or anybody else's. No man can tell where God in all his wisdom has seen fit to hide his riches.'

'Hah, I hear that John Pascoe could and what is more he kept a journal in which he hid his secrets.' William Scoble smirks.

'Nonsense. Pascoe was a simple miner. He could barely read, much less write.'

'That's not what I heard. You are incompetent Clymo. I shall inform the duke. I bid you good day.' Scoble rises from the table, jams his bowler on his head and stalks out of the door.

Mathew snorts, hard put to contain his anger.

'My, he is an unpleasant fellow,' Francis Pryor says, leaning back in his chair and clasping his hands across his ample belly. As befits a man of some financial acumen he wears a black suit, collar and bow tie. 'And tell me Mathew, did Pascoe keep a journal?'

'It's a rumour amongst the miners, just like the rumour that his death was not an accident.'

'Why did you tell Mr Scoble that John Pascoe could neither read or write?'

'He interferes too much already in business not his own. I believe he has an informant in the mine.'

'But what of this journal? Whence comes the rumour?' He speaks impatiently.

'John Pascoe came here from Botallack, in the year we sunk the first shaft. For a six month he tributed with Jethro Loam. Jethro's a man too fond of drink. On Mondays he's of little use to man nor beast – can barely lift a hammer. And after counthouse day he'll be drunk for a week. John Pascoe was a chapel-goer, his wife is still, so he split with Jethro and bid for pitches on his own. Jethro was much put out by this and spread the story that he'd done all the work while John Pascoe scratched pictures and words on scraps of slate. That part is true at least. Once underground I caught him at it, asked him what he wrote, 'Just my thoughts,' he said, 'So's I won't forget where I am tomorrow.' But he would show me nothing. Rubbed out what he had wrote. Some say that this was the secret of his success – that he could foretell the twists and turns of the lode and which rocks were kindliest for tin and copper. Others say that since his death our luck turned sour.'

'So if this journal exists it might help us out of our present difficulty?'

Mathew does not answer. Instead he gets up from the table and goes to the large desk set against one wall and takes out a map which he unrolls upon the table, weighing one end down with the mine account book and the other with a tarnished lump of copper ore.

'We lost the North Lode here on the 120 fathom level,' he stabs the map with a broad forefinger. 'We've driven twelve fathoms further and still not found it. Yet one level above it's still there. I don't understand it and I suspect that John Pascoe would. But he is dead.'

'By accident?'

Mathew sighs. 'I cannot be sure. I went down the day after. The end was completely blocked. I thought that John must have heard the collapse begin and run back from the face but was caught by falling rocks and timber. No man will go back in there to clear it, for no miner will take a dead man's pitch.'

5

THE BOOK

THAT EVENING GRACE RESTS IN THE CHAIR BESIDE THE kitchen range, her body aching from her day of labour, her mind a whirl of grief and anger and suspicion. 'Read the book Thomas. Perhaps it will tell us who killed your father and why.'

Thomas is seated at the table, his father's book before him. He turns the first page. The paper is stiff, blue-ruled with columns on the right hand side of every page. This is a book for figures, for accounts, a ledger. Yes, that is the very word, a ledger, bound in leather. But his father was not a man of figures. His hands were tough and deeply callused, the nails upon his fingers broken. Yet each night he must have held the quill that inked these lines. Thomas runs his finger beneath each word and begins to read aloud.

JOHN PASCOE HIS BOOK
Of Certain Revelations beneath the Ground and Sundry Observations at
the Wheal Emma Mine, Penpillick.

I am not what is commonly called a man of education, far less a Gentleman but before hard times befell our family I learned to read and write and figure. I had such a thirst for knowledge in them days that Reverend Dippenden the parson took pity on me and loaned me many a book. A Collector and a Scholar he was and roamed the countryside hereabouts gathering plants and animals and most particularly stones and rocks. What I thought then were bits of rock till I learned better. The Rev Dippenden taught me much, not least the rhyme and reason of how things might be beneath the earth – not random and all thrown about as folks most commonly do think, but all in order worked out by Almighty God for man to understand. He took me on his rambles, shewed me how the high and rocky moors were all of granite bleak and hard as winter weather, but shot through with mica that glitters in the sun. Shewed me too that around the granite lies the softer slate that we call killas, sometimes purple, sometimes gray and more than often rusty brown. And how between the two and on their edges there is found our tin and copper, rich and waiting to be dug.

One early summer he had a visitor to stay, a certain William Smith Esq. of Tucking Mill in Somerset, a stout bald gentleman who accompanied us on several days of rambles. I understood he was a survey man for the digging of canals and railways. Like the Rev Dippenden he collected rocks and what he said were ancient animals and plants now turned to stone. But most wonderful of all he shewed us how to make a map, not of roads and tracks and byways but how the different rocks and strata – a special word he used for different layers – must lie beneath our feet and what he called their Disposition in the ground. I tried my hand at this, along with Rev Dippenden, and found that I could see clear in my mind with greatest ease the positions of these strata in three directions – across, along and up and down. The Reverend was most surprised and passing pleased with me, for he himself had less facility. He took me to my Father and said I must become a Surveyor like Mr William Smith, once my education was complete. But twas a mere month later that my Father were cast into prison and my education ended and I began work as a pump boy in Botallack Mine. But I never did forget what I had been taught by the Reverend Dippenden and Mr. William Smith.

Thomas pauses and looks up at his Mother. 'Why was Grandfather cast into prison?'

'He was a candle maker, sold tallows to the mines. When hard times came to mining he couldn't pay his bills so he was sent to the Bodmin Gaol where he died. The shame of it killed him, your father always said. Read on Thomas, read on.'

I worked at turning pumping wheels for nigh on a year and a terrible drudgery it was for a boy used only to school work and play. Day after weary day, oftimes with water to my knees and only my tallow for company I wound that wheel till I was so tired I would cry in the dark. But all things have their

*end and after one year I was judged man enough to become a miner and put
to tutwork in the team driving out under the sea. This was a fearsome task,
for most days we could hear the moaning of the sea and the rush of shingle
above our heads and in stormy weather we heard the crash of waves and
great boulders rumbling along the sea floor. Yet despite my constant fear of
the ocean coming in upon us, it was there that I began to learn to read the
subterranean rocks.*

Thomas turns the page then draws the candle close. There is no more
writing. 'There is nought that I can read here, Mother, just the date –
November Third 1845. Come see.'

Grace rises from her chair and looks over her son's shoulder. Once
or twice she stood at her husband's side in just this fashion and watched
him trace with utmost care these wandering lines of ink across the page
with tiny symbols and lettering that even she knew were not proper
words. 'Grace,' he said, smiling up at her, 'This here is a map, a memory
of the places in the mine and the rocks that I have seen this day.' She
sighs. 'He said it were a map but what it means I do not know. But that
date is but a month after he and I were married.'

'See Mother, these are not words but a code of some sort. And
these sketches here, what could they mean? Or this number at the top,
85, what does it signify?'

'Let us look towards the end of the book. Perhaps you will find
some explanation.'

Thomas leafs through the book, page after page of sketches, maps
and figures and symbols, none of which he understands, and odd scraps
of text that he can read but that mean nothing to him.

'Nothing Mother, nothing. No treasure map, no riches as he
promised in the letter nor anything to shed light upon his death. Ah,
but here - what is this?' He flattens the book on the table a few pages
from the end and points. 'This firm line which strikes across the page
then turns on itself and turns again, and these thicker lines inked twice
over which cross it. On this side, look, he has written, *WE Sett* and on
the other, *D. Bed.* and a mark of exclamation. What could that mean?'

'I do not know, my son. But in the letter, did he not foresee that you would not understand?'

Thomas takes the letter from the inside the cover of the book and studies it. 'Yes Mother, you are right, I had forgotten. Here he says: "*my Son, I would urge you to study this My Book which though you might find difficult to comprehend at first will in the course of time bring you the riches which I have always promised to my sweet family.*"

'Good then. You must do as he desired, study the book and its secrets. But Thomas there is another task, more burdensome which I would have you do. I heard today that some miners say your father's death was not an accident. You must go to the place where he died. Perhaps you will find something, a clue, a trace of those who killed him.'

'I heard that too on my first day down the mine. I have pondered on it ever since and thought to go to that place. But how shall I find it without a guide? I durst not ask the miners lest they think I am soft in the head. There are so many galleries in the mine, cross cuts and tunnels that twist and turn on different levels, and shafts from one level to the next. How will I find my way with only candles in the dark? The only way I know is to my work place and I am always in the company of other men. I will never find the way alone.'

'You will, Thomas, if you are your father's son.'

'And I must find a way to leave my workmates, Mr Down and Mr Chapman. They are very careful of my safety. They say you made them promise.'

'I did, but none the less. . .'

Thomas looks up at his mother, his eyes wide with doubt and fear. 'When I have the chance I will do as you ask, Mother.'

Grace nods and goes back to her seat by the range. Thomas begins again to leaf through the book. 'Suppose I do discover who it was, what then? We cannot tell the capun.'

'No, not him. Perhaps I will call the Parish Constable. He will bring whoever killed your father to justice.'

6

THE FOUNTAIN HOTEL

JOSIAH HOCKING WIPES HIS MOUTH WITH HIS NAPKIN and sits back with a sigh. 'You eat well in these parts, Mr Scoble. My thanks for a splendid lunch.'

'My pleasure. Will you take coffee and then perhaps we can get to the business in hand?'

'Indeed, indeed. But we have all afternoon. The van does not leave for Plymouth till five. I will take the night train back to London.'

The two men are tucked away in a discreet corner of the dining parlour of the Fountain Hotel in Liskeard. But Josiah Hocking is anything but discreet being very fat, sporting a full set of side whiskers and wearing a loud waistcoat beneath his frock-coat. His top hat dominates the hat stand beside the parlour door. And each time the door opens William Scoble turns to see who might have come in, sees the hat and tries to sink a little lower into his chair.

'Yes, the business in hand. I take it that the purser, what did you say his name was, is co-operating following our little inducement?'

'Francis Pryor. He is most adept with numbers. I was able to spend some minutes with him going through the Cost Book. The manipulation is invisible. That fool Clymo is completely taken in, he has no idea. He thinks the losses result from bad luck and unkindly lodes.'

'"Unkindly lodes," eh. Odd ways you Cornishmen have with words.'

'It is how the miners excuse their incompetence. But it's fortunate for us. How goes the stock price?'

'I left London with the Bears in full cry at the Exchange. The rumours I put about have pushed the share price down below twenty pounds. This latest information will see Cornish Consols collapse. And then we'll buy, you and I and my special friends.'

Josiah Hocking rubs his hands. 'Girl, bring brandy.'

'Yes sir.' Maisie Tuttle puts the coffee pot and cups upon the table, bobs a curtsey and goes back to the kitchen.

'What of Clymo, if we get control?'

'Depose him. He's too soft on the miners – made the duke build them a damn village, always spending money on what he calls "improvements". But they're just to make life easier down the mine and make him popular – cuts our profit. Besides there's no shortage of captains looking for work who will do our bidding.'

William Scoble leans towards his companion. 'Another happening has gone our way. A miner, Pascoe was his name, dug more riches from that mine than ten other miners combined. Seems he knew all its secrets. Just after we began our scheme, he died – an accident they say. Clymo thinks that's what turned his luck, or so Pryor tells me.'

'I fail to see how that will help our cause.'

'There's more. Pascoe made maps and records of all he knew about the mine, some sort of journal. Clymo's searching for it so it must be worth having. My man will find it first. If we buy enough shares to make us owners, and we have this so-called journal, we will truly make our fortunes.'

'Sirs?'

'What! Don't creep up like that, girl. Pour two good glasses and leave the bottle.'

'Yes sir.' Maisie does as she is told, bobs again and leaves them.

Josiah Hocking swirls the brandy in the glass, holds it up to the light and smiles. 'Here's to our mutual fortune then, Mr Scoble.'

William Scoble raises his glass and swallows the brandy in a single gulp. He takes an envelope from the inside pocket of his riding coat and passes it to Josiah Hocking. 'A further contribution. I leave it to your judgment when to buy.'

Hocking takes out the bankers draft and reads it. 'Five hundred pounds.' He raises an eyebrow, returns the draft to the envelope and slips it inside his jacket. 'Very good. Will you take another brandy?'

'No, I must be on my way.'

'The duke calls, eh.'

'When will you return?' Scoble is impatient to be gone.

'I do not know. But I will write you.' Hocking pours himself another brandy. Scoble leaves without shaking hands.

Josiah Hocking continues to sip his brandy listening to the clip-clop of Scoble's horse upon the cobbles. 'Five hundred pounds,' he mutters to himself. 'Now I wonder where a duke's agent would find that amount of money.'

7

120 FATHOMS

IT IS THREE WEEKS SINCE THOMAS BEGAN TO STUDY HIS father's book, or 'The Book' as he always thinks of it. But he has got nowhere. He hoped that he might find a key, a clue to the code in which it must be written but every night he pores over page after page with no result. The only things he understands are the dates and that the numbers underlined in the margins of some pages refer to fathom levels in the mine, **80, 90, 105, 120** and **160,** which is where he sits at croust time with Henry Hopeful Down beside him.

He is at ease now, underground; it holds no fears. He feels secure in the flickering gloom, his eyes accustomed to the candlelight. He no longer notices the stink of burning tallow or the rank sweat of the men he works with. Each day his clothes, soaked by his descent of the shaft, dry out in the heat of the mine. His hands are callused and muscles already bulge beneath his flannel shirt. He has learned to work with his father's pick and takes pleasure in the feel of its handle, worn and polished from so many years of his father's toil. He has mastered the borer and even swings the hammer when either Caleb Chapman or Henry take a rest.

Each day and foot by foot, the three of them drill and blast towards their unseen goal, where the capun says the lode must lie. But the rock gets harder shift by shift, and every afternoon Capun Clymo studies the newly naked rock with increasing gloom. He has already set Jethro Loam, Jakeh James and Lewis Tuttle to sinking a narrow inclined shaft beneath them in further search of the errant copper lode.

And Thomas has another puzzle: how to visit the place of his father's death as his mother has instructed. He cannot leave his workplace in the middle of his shift, nor can he stay below when work is finished – he would be missed as, since the death, old Harry Rowse sits at the shaft head and counts the men as they go down and counts them up again as they emerge, weary and filthy at each core's end. Thomas will have to slip down unseen at night and descend the ladderways alone. But then, how will he find his way? He looks up at the big man beside him.

'Mr Down sir, where was my father working when he died?'

'A crosscut on the 120 fathom level.'

'Not far above us then. It's hard to think of that.'

'Don't think on it then, boy. Besides it weren't above us here. 'Twas at the east end of the mine. We're at the west end here. Your father worked an ore shoot that shouldn't have been there. Leastways, that's what Capun Clymo said.'

Thomas lapses into silence, unable to recall the entrance off the ladderways at a hundred and twenty fathoms. He'll count on the way up so at least when he descends alone he'll know where he is.

'Why does no one tribute on that lode no more?'

'Firstly boy, 'tis rotten luck to tribute on a dead man's pitch. And secondly 'tis all collapsed for twenty fathoms to the face. Ain't worth clearing and timbering all of that. And it's like a coney's warren up in there. Get lost unless you know the way. Besides they reckon your father were working a poor bunch; he weren't taking too much copper up to grass.'

Thomas sees again the words of his father's letter: *'amazing rich and I have never seen the like, so much so that I do believe I've found an undiscovered lode.'* It is on the tip of his tongue to contradict Henry who has become his friend and treats him like a son. But he says nothing. He has some understanding now of the urge which drives these men, and the disappointed hunger in Captain Clymo's eyes each day he sees just barren rock.

He will go to the crosscut on the 120 fathom level this very night and see the place where his father died.

There is no moon and a moorland wind keens in the winding gear as he slips past the sleeping engineman and begins the long climb down. The night-time core will not come up for four hours yet, but he leaves the candle in his hat unlit and goes by feel alone. He knows the very rungs by now, they are old friends, some splintered, some worn smooth and occasionally one missing where his foot feels sightlessly in the air and finds nothing. Holding out a finger or a thumb for every platform passed, he counts the levels as he goes. East and west are fixed in his mind. Four tallows tied by their wicks to a button of his shirt will give him light for many hours, enough he hopes to find the place and see all there is to see. His father's pick hangs from his belt and two lucifers are wrapped in oilskin in his pocket. Ladder by ladder he goes down into utter darkness, listening out for cries and calls from galleries on either side or from below.

Finally he stands on the 120 fathom sollar and hears nothing save the rush of falling water and the bang and rattle of a kibble rising in the shaft beside him. East to his right, west to his left. With one hand on the ladder he feels blindly for the wall then works his way around to the opening of the level. Here it is – open space, pitch-black emptiness. He takes three steps, stops and draws in breath. Each level has its smell – Henry has told him this: the wood in timbering, its age and state of rot, the type of ore and whether men have been there recently or not. Sometimes the air is stagnant, foul, thick with must and the stink of shit, barely breathable. In other galleries there is the faintest breeze, just felt on the skin, or perhaps there is the tangy smell of new-cut pine supports.

But this level seems dead, no movement in the air, no smell and deathly silent – no creaking timbers, no sounds of work; but this he has expected, indeed has hoped for. He shrugs off the fears of what befell his father and lights the candle in his hat with one of his two lucifers. He blinks in the sudden light, waits as his eyes adjust from total darkness, and sets off along the level. The tunnel twists and turns and after forty yards he finds a fork and stops, looks down at the floor to see which is the most trodden path. Before deciding, he takes his pick and scratches an arrow on the wall, pointing back the way he has come. Left, left is the way the pathway goes. He follows that but to his dismay it divides again and he must choose, left or right, once more. He marks the wall again and then turns right. The tunnel narrows and the roof gets lower until his shoulders brush the walls and he must crouch. Then there is nothing beneath his feet and he is falling, crying out. His back is raked by jagged rocks which tear his shirt until his feet jar against the bottom of the hole.

In pitch darkness once again and afraid to move, he feels for his hat but finds only rubble beneath his questing hands. He unties a candle from his shirt, lights it and holds it high. In the flaring light he sees he is in a narrow pit where tributers gouged out a block of ore. His hat and candle are at his feet, his pick beside them. Two body lengths above him he can see the edges of the hole. Hat back on his head, he clambers up, hands and boots scrabbling on the rock and heaves himself out on to the level. It is true what Henry said, this is a rabbit warren. Thomas backtracks on his footsteps, reaches the tunnel to the shaft and stops and finds his legs are shaking. He would rather turn left, give up, return to his mother and tell her that this search is not for him. Besides, what is he looking for? But with a sigh he turns right and carries on, more careful now and watching every footfall. A junction faces him, left and right – a crosscut as Henry said; and there, a mark upon the wall. He lights another candle, holds it close – a circle with a cross below. He's seen just such a symbol in the book: this is a mark his father made. Beside it, he spots a tiny arrow pointing right, and feels the hair stand up upon his neck – This way – he can hear his father's voice.

Quickly but still with care he follows down the tunnel, moving the candle from side to side in search of other marks. Now the passage opens up above him into a narrow fissure where stubby timbers keep the walls from crumbling in, and Thomas knows that this is where his father found a copper blow and mined it out. The level turns again, and there before him, rubble and timber banked up to the roof. The tunnel's blocked. He stands before it, alert and staring, waiting as if for some revelation. But there is nothing; just the sound of his breath, coming and going, and the thumping of his heart.

At his feet are rocks and two splintered timbers pulled from the rubble pile. He squats between them, holding the candle close – this must be exactly where his father died. Perhaps he should say a prayer.

He traces a dark stain on the wood with his forefinger. His father's blood. Other than this, nothing – nothing to be seen or understood, nothing to be discovered, save a blocked tunnel. But the mark, whatever it signified, pointed this way. He cannot discount the feeling that there must be something important here; important enough for his father to leave a message on the wall, a reminder either to himself or to whoever might come after. Any answers must lie beyond this barrier.

Thomas scrapes at the rubble with the pick, setting a rill of stones running down the slope, then dislodges a boulder which tumbles to the floor. He could dig his way through this, given time, but Henry said it's twenty fathoms to the face. He crawls up to the roof. It is loose and dangerous and would collapse without support. He knows how this is done, has even helped Jethro and a three-man team – wedging timbers against each wall, a beam across the top and planks laid over that. Impossible alone. The candle in his hat starts to gutter out. He takes another and lights it from the first. There is nothing he can do here, not alone. He should leave this place and go back up to grass.

But he sits for a while longer. His father was a man of truth but a dreamer, his mother says. Thomas believes those dreams. His father would not have written of promised riches in the letter if it were not true. Perhaps the answer's in the book, not here, deep underground.

He sighs, gets to his feet and sets off along the level, stopping to examine once again the mark upon the wall and fixing the image in his mind. As he nears the final turn towards the shaft he sees a glimmer of a light ahead and, without thinking, dowses his own. Feeling his way along the wall he turns the corner, stops and watches as a figure, his light flickering in the breezes of the shaft, reaches the ladderway then turns and looks into the tunnel. The figure is stooped, his face is in deep shadow, and the boy, though he knows he must be unseen, feels the man's eyes upon him and begins to tremble. He holds his breath as they stand there watching each other. Then the figure turns, steps on to the sollar and disappears.

Thomas is now in total darkness thirty yards from the shaft, both candles out and not a lucifer left to light them. Knees still shaking, he gropes his way along the wall, step by careful step. It is an age before he feels the tunnel widen out, and the sound of falling water tells him he is at the shaft. Shuffling out one foot, he feels for the timber platform, finds it and reaches out to clutch the ladder. He leans against it, lets out a single sob and then looks up. There, already far above, the faintest gleam of light still flickers. He waits until the light completely disappears and all around him, above and below, is utter darkness.

Then he begins to climb. He doesn't run up, as has become his habit, but takes it slowly wondering who would follow him and how he had known that Thomas would choose this night and time to visit the crosscut on one hundred and twenty fathoms. After half an hour of steady climbing he looks up to see a faint circle of light containing a single star. As he climbs, the circle grows and stars are scattered across it like diamond dust. On the final ladder he creeps up rung by rung and raises his eyes a fraction above the collar of the shaft. After the darkness underground, he sees quite clearly in the starlight – the glow of the engineman's brazier, the dark silhouette of the engine house hard against the sky, the sheds of the dressing floor. Slowly he turns his head, this way then that, his body twisting on the ladder. No one lurks in the shadows and the engineman is sleeping still. He hears the screech of a vixen down in the valley below the village.

Thomas steps out, breathes in the cold night air and walks down past the counthouse towards his home. A light burns in the cottage window. Inside, his mother dozes by the range. He touches her shoulder. 'Mother, I am back.'

She starts awake, hugs him and smells again the stink of the mine. 'I worried so. Get yourself washed up now.' She pours water from a pitcher into a basin and Thomas rinses his hands and face. 'What did you find?'

'I found the place where he was killed but nothing there to tell me how. And I found a marking on the wall – a mark I've seen in Father's book. But Mother, I was followed. There was another person on the level – I saw a figure at the shaft.'

'Who was it? Who would follow you? The capun?'

'No, not him. This man was tall like the capun, maybe taller, but he was stooped. I could not discern his face.'

'The man of whom your father spoke, perhaps.'

'I don't know. Mother, I am sure a secret lies in the book. I must study it until I understand.'

'The book will not tell us how your father died.' Grace stands and takes her son by the shoulders. 'Thomas, I have decided. I will go to Capun Clymo.'

'No Mother, you cannot. I beg you, do not trust him. He is seeking Father's secret. He wants the book.'

'I'll say nothing of the book. But he knew your father feared for his life, and I will say that to his face. If he lies I shall know. If he tells the truth, then I shall know that too.'

'How will you know? Capun Clymo is a clever man.'

'I am not stupid, Thomas. I am a woman and women know things that men do not always understand. And I have had another thought. You remember the Reverend Dippenden?'

'Of course. He who taught Father how to read the rocks.'

'You must go to Bodmin and find him. Show him the book. Perhaps he will help you understand it.'

'Bodmin – but I've never been beyond the moor. How shall I find the way?'

'It's simple. Go up beyond the mine and keep walking west until you meet the turnpike. From there it is but a mile or two into the town.' Grace listens for a moment head on one side. 'Hark at them foxes.'

'They'll not keep me awake. Nothing will, not after I have climbed those ladders twice in a single day. I will do as you say, Mother. I'll go to Bodmin next Sunday night.'

'And I will talk to Capun Clymo in the morning.' She snuffs out the candle and says, 'Sleep well, my son.'

8

THE COUNTHOUSE

MATHEW CLYMO SITS IN THE COUNTHOUSE, HIS booted feet up on the table listening to the scratching of pens behind him. The purser, Francis Pryor, has taken sick and his two clerks sit on high stools at a long counter filling in columns of figures in the great cost book ledgers. Mathew knows without looking at them what these figures tell : his mine has lost money for the second month in a row. It's a simple sum – the value of the copper his men have raised and he has sold to the smelters, less the cost of wages and materials. It's a minus number and there will be no payments to the Adventurers this month, no riotous counthouse dinner after the ritual examining of the books. Instead he will call on them to subscribe to the loss each according to their shareholding, and those who either cannot or will not pay will forfeit stock.

He reads again the letter from Mr William Morris, son of old Mr Morris who had been sufficiently shrewd to put up the first three hundred pounds that sunny day in the City of London in 1844. Mathew had had no letter of introduction – he simply strode into the office of the first stockbrokers he came across in Capel Court, tipped the contents of his saddlebag on the desk of the surprised gentleman behind it, and said, 'Mathew Clymo's my name and I've cut it rich in Cornwall.'

'Have you indeed.' The gentleman, who was dressed in a black-frock coat and waistcoat, bent over and peered at the dusty black mineral dirtying the tooled leather of his desk. 'Coal in Cornwall, sir, coal?'

'Copper sir, black copper, this is.' Mathew drew an envelope from his breast pocket, took out a folded sheet of paper and laid it on the desk. 'Assayed at fifty-two per cent of copper, no less.'

'And that would be rich, I suppose?' the gentleman said, scratching his beard. 'By the way, Morris is my name. I'm afraid I know nothing of mining.' He stood and grasped Mathew's hand across the desk.

'Wait, I'll fetch my partner, Mr Sanderson. He does know about these things. Do take a seat meanwhile.' He indicated one of two high-backed armchairs in a corner of the office. Mathew sat and waited, listening to the thumping of his heart, and the murmur of voices through the half open door to the inner office. Perhaps he should have asked in Liskeard for a recommendation to an honest broker, if there were such a thing. But he had dared not speak of his discovery until he had secured the rights to mine it from the duke. And the duke would never cede these to a near penniless miner. This ride to London had used up all his savings and he had funds enough for but one more night in the city. He looked down at the new worsted suit the Liskeard tailor made for two shillings, and knew he didn't cut much of a figure with these City types. But the sample of copper ore on the table would tell its own tale, if this Mr Sanderson did indeed know mines and mining. Why, only the year before one-pound shares in the Devon Mine just across the Tamar were worth five hundred and fifty pounds and paid a dividend of fifty-five pounds a share. Mathew knew that his discovery was just as rich if not even richer.

The two brokers came into the room and Mathew rose from his chair to shake the hand of the newcomer.

'Good day, sir, James Sanderson at your service.' Like his colleague he was dressed in black frock coat and waistcoat. He took a magnifying glass from a drawer and bent to study the sample on the desk. 'Well, sir, yes indeed, chalcosine unless I'm much mistaken.'

'Black copper's what we call it.'

Sanderson nodded 'And how big is the lode?'

'I've traced her for near five hundred fathom east to west and I reckon she's about two fathom wide.'

'And how deep will she go d'ye think?'

'Well, if she's like the Devon Mine she'll go down at least two hundred fathom.'

The broker scribbled some figures on a sheet of paper. ' Hmm, hmm, splendid, splendid – if it's real of course.' He looked up at Mathew, head on one side.

'I understand your doubts, sir. Maybe you'd best come see for yourself.'

'It's a long old ride to Cornwall, Mr Clymo, indeed it is. What do you say to lunch first?' Mr Sanderson chuckled and rubbed his hands.

They ate boiled mutton and onion and potatoes and Mathew drank more ale than was his wont while Sanderson regaled him with tales of mining scandals, and fortunes made and fortunes lost. At the end of it he said:

'I'll be blunt, Mr Clymo, you did well to walk in our door this morning. There's many a jobber in this city who would promise you the world, take what you have, and leave you with nothing. And you are fortunate that in London Cornish mining is still quite the rage, especially with the small investor, although some do say that when the little man speculates the wise investor sells. Nevertheless, there's plenty of interest in the genuine article – no shortage of investors large and small who get excited by the real thing. Now, I believe I'm a good judge of a mining proposition and a better judge of men. And I judge you to be an honest man, a shrewd man and a Cornish miner to boot. So if all you say is true, and I'm inclined to believe it is, you are going to make our fortunes and we will make yours.

So here is our proposal. We will issue one thousand and fifty one-pound shares. You will have one third, Mr Morris here will subscribe another third and provide you with immediate cash of three hundred pounds or thereabouts. The rest of the stock we'll sell to good friends in the City. What do you say?'

Mathew rubbed his chin. He felt comfortable with these men. Smartly dressed they were but not too slick. They had not tried to impress him with an opulent meal in a fancy establishment. He looked around: the Albion Tavern was a sensible City eating house where businessmen and merchants at other tables leaned towards each other in earnest conversation. But it would hurt to give up two-thirds of his mine, though it was no mine yet. It was a fair offer and the idea of immediate cash was more than tempting. 'Cash now, you say?'

'A draft on my bank this very afternoon,' said William Morris.

'Just on my word that this find is real? How do you know that

I am not a fraudster and a scoundrel? I could have stole the samples from another mine.'

The brokers looked at each other, smiled and nodded, and Sanderson said, 'Why, Mr Clymo, I said we trusted you and we do. Nonetheless I would be in dereliction of my professional duty if I did not accompany you on your return to Cornwall and see for myself the truth of your assertions.'

'You will be welcome, sir, and I am pleased to accept your proposal.' Mathew held out his hand across the table and both men shook it.

'Splendid, splendid,' said James Sanderson. 'Now what about a name for our little enterprise? We need a name.'

Mathew grinned. 'I've had a name in mind since first I discovered the lode. What say you to "Cornish Great Consols"?'

'Excellent, and what shall we name our first shaft? A woman's name is oft the custom, is it not? Your wife's perhaps?'

'I'm not married, sir.'

'William, how would Mrs Morris take to the idea of her name being immortalised in a Cornish copper mine?'

'I'm sure she would be flattered.'

'Wheal Emma it is then. Come, let's raise our glasses to Wheal Emma.'

And so it was that Cornish Great Consols was founded. They appointed Mr William Morris, Chairman, and Mathew Clymo, Manager, and Cornish Great Consols made them rich. Within six months of that meeting old William Morris's three-hundred pound investment grew in value to one hundred thousand pounds, though sadly he had but little time to profit from his riches for in 1847 he died.

Mathew looks up at his portrait on the wall above the clerks: the bushy beard, the shock of hair and hooded eyes looking down. How different from his son who, though not Chairman, still sits upon the board and writes letter after letter constantly interfering in the business of the mine. His latest begins:

Dear Sir, I have recently had the occasion to discuss the living and working conditions of our Cornish miners with a certain Dr Barham. In

*his studies of four mining districts (which I believe would include ours) he
has determined that out of 146 deaths of miners, 77 are from consumption
which is more than twice the normal. He tells me that few miners attain the
age of 60 years, indeed most are dead before their fortieth birthday. And
he concludes that the occupation of miners is most prejudicial to health.
We have already discussed the fearful strain on our men's hearts and lungs
of climbing up hundreds of fathoms of ladders. This will only get worse as
the depth of the mine increases. I urge you therefore without delay to set
in motion the installation of a man-machine as they have done at Fowey
Consols and the United Mine. . .*

Mathew sighs and throws the letter on the table. He knows mining is
unhealthy and dangerous, everybody knows. Half his men spit black
from breathing powder smoke and many have lost fingers or an eye in
untoward explosions. But he has done his best – at least they have a dry
in the new engine house where they can wash and change and go home
clean. And the mine is safer now, less prone to flooding. He listens to the
steady thump and hiss of the great beam engine as it sucks the water from
the depths below. Installed but two months ago, it cost the greater part
of six thousand pounds and now the mine is running at a loss.

He will announce this at the counthouse dinner in two weeks
time though he suspects that the Adventurers already know. The last
he heard, Cornish Great Consols stock was already halved in value in
just one month; less than twenty pounds a share now. Someone in the
know is talking; Pryor's clerks perhaps, scratching away behind him.
And he also knows what Mr William Morris and the Adventurers will
say. 'Reduce the wages, cut our cost, no more expenditure, we need
our dividends.' They are just as greedy as the duke. And when it gets
about amongst the City jobbers that Cornish Great Consols has failed
to pay a dividend for two months in a row, the shares will collapse even
further and Mr Morris's fortune, and his own, will be sorely dented.

He bangs his fist upon the table – they must cut it rich again, he is
sure they will; his Wheal Emma will not be a knacked bal, a worthless
mine, nothing but a hole in the ground where men's sweat trickles away

in the dust and grime and darkness. The scratching behind him ceases just as the steam engine lets off a mighty whistle. Mathew consults his fob watch – twelve o'clock and croust time. The clerks climb off their stools and go upstairs to the counthouse dining room. He stands at the clerks' counter perusing their work. The door opens and closes behind him but he doesn't turn, thinking it must be one of the counthouse women bringing his usual tea and pasty; he has never lost his taste for a miner's croust.

'Capun Clymo.'

He knows the voice and whirls around. 'Grace, Grace Pascoe.'

She stands back to the door, the rim of her felt gook framing her face. 'I need to speak with you, Capun.'

'Sit down, Grace. What is it? No trouble I hope?'

'Well, no new trouble.' Grace unlaces the ribbon beneath her chin and takes off her bonnet. The coarse stuff of her apron rustles as she sits.

Mathew sits opposite her, meets her dark eyes then looks away, resisting the desire to touch her. The memory of her rebuff a month ago still pains him.

'It's about my John.'

'Yes?' Mathew knows full well what she is about to say.

Grace is silent for a moment. Then looking down at her hands folded on the table she says, 'They say he was murdered.'

'They?'

'The miners.'

'Which miners?'

She looks him in the eye. 'Lewis Tuttle and Caleb Chapman for two.'

'Grace, I was there when we brought him up. We knew from the smell of powder he had blasted. It must have collapsed the drive all the way to the face. He was caught under falling timbers.'

'But what if somebody caused that fall – on purpose like? Maybe somebody else set the blast.'

'Why would anyone want to do that? John was well liked.'

'Not by all, Capun, not by all. And he was afeared for his life. You knows that.'

'Do I?'

'Do not play with me, Capun. I found a letter written only days before he died. Thomas read it to me. Some person interfered with his gear, his tamping bar. He came to you. You told him you would find out who done it. But he was killed.'

Mathew stares at her, remembering John Pascoe seeking him out that day, right here, in the counthouse.

'I said I would investigate the matter of his tamping bar and did that very afternoon when the core came up to grass. I asked all the men. But I discovered nothing – the men had no knowledge of it.'

'Well, whoever done it ain't going to admit it, are they?'

'True enough. But look Grace, what more could I do? If somebody did cause the collapse there's no way we can tell.'

But he admits to himself that he could do more. He could have the tunnel cleared to the face. There might just be evidence of another person there. And they never found John Pascoe's gear other than his pick which lay beside his outstretched arm. His satchel and flask, the fateful tamping bar, his bunch of tallows, all must lie buried under the rubble. It would make a difference too if John had been mining good ore, but he had brought poorly stuff to grass for two weeks before the accident. That in itself was passing strange, but it meant there was little point in diverting men to clear the tunnel to work the face, especially when Mathew was already losing money. No, when John Pascoe died he took his secrets with him – except perhaps the Journal, if indeed that did exist. 'You said you found a letter. Was that all?'

'What else would there be? I found it amongst his scribblings and I burned the rest, like I told you that night you come a-courting.' She is surprised at her own boldness but is desperate to change the subject, before he asks again about John's book. But he blushes, and Grace cannot hide her smile.

'Grace,' he pauses, and then it tumbles out, 'Grace, I want to help you, do something, I hate to see you on the dressing floor. Tis no place for you. Why not come and work here, in the counthouse? I'll pay you the same.'

'Me, here? I can't read nor write, never mind do numbers. My Thomas does all that for me. Anyway, what would I do here and what would folks think? That you're my fancy man perhaps?'

'I need another bal maid here to clean and cook. Annie's getting on. And she has the dry to look after now as well. She's late already with my croust. And the counthouse dinner's but two weeks away.'

'I won't be in your debt Capun Clymo. And what about my poor John's murder? I ain't going to see that swept under the carpet, counthouse bal maid or no.'

'If you'll take my offer I'll look further into your husband's death, I promise.'

She looks him in the eye and says, 'Then I'll take your offer if Jenny Tuttle comes with me. She's my friend and there being two of us will still the gossips' tongues.'

Mathew considers for a moment then holds out his hand. 'Agreed, Grace. You can both start here one week on Monday.' Grace takes his hand, her palm more calloused than his but even so, she feels it vulnerable in his grip.

'Right, Capun Mathew Clymo. I'll be your counthouse bal maid.' She smiles up at him for a long moment, puts on her gook and leaves the counthouse.

Mathew stands there looking out the door, aware that with the touch of her hand and her final smile his heart began to race. 'Absurd,' he says to himself. 'Absurd, to love a bal maiden.' Then he calls out, 'Grace, I'll not be here till late on Monday morning. I'm off to Redruth to a sale.' She turns and gives a little wave.

9

WHEAL VENLAND

IT IS SUNDAY MORNING AND JETHRO LOAM IS NOT IN chapel. But then, Jethro is never in chapel on Sundays. He prefers to be in his favourite corner in the tap room of the Bedford Arms with a pint mug of cider, content in the knowledge of many more mugs to follow. But this particular Sunday he is not in the Bedford Arms either, a fact which puts him in a very bad mood. In the vain hope of sheltering from the penetrating November drizzle, he huddles his skinny frame on a stone ledge in the roofless ruins of the winding house of the long abandoned Wheal Venland mine.

He is waiting for William Scoble and he wants a drink. He licks his lips but all he finds are drops of water condensed upon his moustache. Scoble won't bring drink but he will bring money, and that Jethro will then spend on drink. Money in exchange for information that Jethro has gathered listening to the gossip in the mine and loose talk in the Bedford Arms, watching unseen the comings and goings at the Pascoe cottage, and more particularly, as William Scoble has instructed him, following Thomas Pascoe.

A pair of jackdaws circle and caw about the crumbling chimney stack. Jethro gets to his feet and wanders out of the winding house and stands amongst the brambles at the open shaft, drops a stone down and waits, peering into the darkness, listening. Remote and eerie the splash echoes up. 'Twenty-five fathom,' he mutters as he goes back to his damp seat in the winding house. He waits and waits, listening to the drip of rain and is about to give up when he hears the rattle of stones as someone scrabbles up the waste dump below.

Jethro gets up and peers through a crevice in the wall. It is William Scoble, dressed in Sunday serge and bowler hat and boots. He sits again and looks up as Scoble appears around the wall.

'Good morning, Loam.' Scoble stands legs apart, looking down at the scrawny miner.

'Good mornin', though it ain't, is it? Meeting here in this rain and all.'

'Where would you rather meet? In the Bedford Arms I suppose? Let the village know you spy for me?'

Jethro shrugs.

'So what have you discovered since last we talked? What's Clymo up to?'

'The capun's carryin' on as usual – checkin' what we's doin' underground and stridin' round the village like cock robin. But I got good stuff on Thomas Pascoe, Mr Scoble. I'll have the money afore I tell.'

'No you will not. Tell me what you have and I'll judge its worth.'

'You're a hard man, Mr Scoble.' Jethro looks up, head on one side and sucks the straggled ends of his moustache. 'What if I was to tell you the boy's been down the mine in the dead o' night, by hisself?'

'So what?'

'Well, he must 'ave been looking for something, mustn't he?'

'Did you follow him down?'

'No, I had no tallows and I weren't going down there in the dark.'

Scoble snorts. 'Hah, a miner afraid of the bloody dark?'

'I ain't afraid of nothing. But that ain't all. There's more, after he come up. But you give me the money first.'

Scoble grabs Jethro by the front of his jerkin and yanks him to his feet then propels him backwards, out of the engine house to the shaft, where he holds him backwards over the edge.

'Hey, no Mr Scoble, no, please no. I'll tell you,' Jethro yells, feet scrabbling for purchase.

'You tell me all you scabrous bastard or I'll send you to the devil arse up.' Scoble pulls him forward and lets him go and Jethro slouches back into the winding house and sits. Scoble follows him and stands back against the wall looking down at Jethro. 'And so?'

'After he went down I went to the Pascoe house. There was still light in the window and I reckoned his Ma were waiting for him to come back. So I waited too. Twas a long time lying down on the cold earth underneath the back window. Colder even than this here stone.'

Jethro shifts his bottom on the granite ledge and looks up at Scoble. 'So long a time I fell asleep and only woke when I heard voices. They was talking about the book.'

'You mean Pascoe's journal?'

'Journal? I don't know about no journal. I mean the book, what I told you of already, what Pascoe wrote in all about the mine, where the good bunches of copper were and where it was poorly.'

'Yes, yes man. But what the devil were they saying?'

'I couldn't make out what she were saying. She talks quiet like. But he said that the secret lies in the book and that he must study it. Then I heard her say something about the capun and he said that the capun were after his father's secret. Then I couldn't hear nothing 'cos a vixen started up across the valley, squalling and a-yelping fit to bust. Next I heard was him sayin' he would go to Bodmin come Sunday. An' then they put out the candle and it were all quiet, save for them foxes.'

'I want that damned book, Jethro Loam.'

'So do everybody. What about my money then?'

Scoble takes a half crown from his waistcoat pocket and holds it up. 'There's more of this, if you get me that book.'

'Just give me my money and I'll think on the book.'

'The book must be in the Pascoe cottage. You'll be well rewarded.' He closes his fist on the coin. 'What say you to a guinea?'

'I don't say nothing till you give me that.' He stands holding out a hand.

Scoble shakes his head as he drops the coin into Jethro's outstretched palm. 'And don't drink that all today. I don't want gossip as to where Jethro Loam is getting money.'

Jethro pockets the coin. 'I'll drink what I like when I like. But there's somethin' I'll tell you for free.'

'And what might that be?'

'Someone else were abroad that night. As I left the Pascoe house I saw a body slide into the shadows opposite. He were watching the house too, or maybe watching me, or maybe both. Maybe he's after the book too.'

Scoble blinks and strokes his chin. 'Clymo?'

'Not him, too tall.'

'Well, keep watching, Loam.'

'I'll do that Mr Scoble.'

Scoble watches him slither down the waste dump then calls out. 'The book, Jethro Loam, don't forget the book.'

He sits on the dry patch of stone left by Jethro, folds his arms and leans back against the wall. From the inside pocket of his coat he takes the letter he received the day before from Hocking and reads with a smile. Hocking has not only bought him shares in Cornish Consols but has increased the five hundred pounds to eight hundred and eighty in the process. Scoble is not quite sure how he has done this – something to do with short selling which Scoble thinks may not quite be legal. Anyway Hocking recommends that he re-invests the eight hundred and eighty pounds in more Consols stock. He wonders if he dare do that or should he just be content with the profit and pay back the money he borrowed from his employer, the unsuspecting duke.

There is a postscript at the bottom of the letter: *What news of the Journal?*. Well, he has news but he'll keep that to himself for now. He is sure that the book exists so it is only a question of getting his hands on it. That this is likely to involve a burglary and a theft bothers him not a whit. It will not be the first time that he has been involved in crime since he fled Ireland and Viscount Abercorn's estate eight years ago. His hand goes inside his jacket to the hilt of the knife he has carried ever since the bloody days of the Irish famine. He used it more than once when gouging rents from the viscount's already starving tenants. Nor did the ever absent viscount believe his tenants' stories that Scoble would be so callous as to steal their rent. Why, he even recommended him to his friend the Duke of Bedford as the perfect conscientious agent.

He grins – his current scheme of investing a part of the duke's royalties from the mine is so much safer. The duke never checks his books and will not notice if payments to his account are two months delayed. Yes, he can risk telling Hocking to re-invest both his profits and the duke's principal in more shares. He will pay Pryor the purser to show another loss next month and the shares will be even cheaper. If he and Hocking buy enough Cornish Consols they will control the mine and he'll get rid of bloody Clymo. Then if he has the book and learns its secrets, Wheal Emma will make his fortune. He smiles at the thought, gets up from the stone slab and scrambles down the waste tip to a wind-stunted ash tree where his horse stands tethered.

Trotting towards the duke's estate, he ponders on what Loam has told him. So what was the boy doing down the mine at the dead of night? Investigating his father's death perhaps. Well that won't get him far. And who was the watcher in the night, if not Clymo? What if he too is after the book? He scratches his chin. This is a worry. What if the watcher knows that Jethro Loam is his spy? What if the watcher is watching him right now? He stops, turns in the saddle and looks back towards the crumbling engine house atop the slope of rubble but it is already obscured by drizzle.

'Walk on Nelson, walk on,' he says, turning back towards the road.

10

MAISIE TUTTLE

ONE SATURDAY EACH MONTH MAISIE TUTTLE IS allowed. A break from her duties as a serving maid at the Fountain Hotel. At two o'clock she takes the carter's van from Liskeard to Penpillick where she will stay until Sunday after chapel. Home as the sun is setting, she stands in the shadowed doorway and watches the Pascoe boy come swinging down through the village. She watches how the fabric of his shirt is stretched across his chest and shoulders, listens to the ring of his nailed boots on the cobbles. But before he sees her she slips into the dim-lit cottage. A furze fire sputters in the hearth and a black pot simmers on coals dragged to one side. She takes off her bonnet and her hair springs out in a wild red frizz about her face. 'Shall I scrub your back Ma?'

Her mother sits half dozing in a tin tub in front of the fire, exhausted from her day's work. 'You can that, maid.'

Maisie takes the rough cloth from the side of the tub, soaps it and begins to rub her mother's back with a brisk circular motion.

Jenny sighs. 'I thank the good Lord today were my last day on the dressin' floor. Come Monday me an' Grace'll be cooking and washing in the counthouse.'

'How's that, Ma?'

''Tween you and me, Capun Clymo's sweet on Grace and he wants her near him. But she won't go without me.'

'Why not?'

'Says she needs protecting.'

'Protecting from what?'

'Gossip most like. And don't you say nothing to nobody.' She rolls her shoulders under the pressure of her daughter's hand.

Maisie watches how the muscles move under the milk-white skin, feels the strength in the long back hardened by years of breaking rock, and thinks then of Tom Pascoe's chest. 'Saw Tom just now. Back to grass he is,' she says.

Jenny turns to look at her daughter. 'Is he now? You sweet on him, maid?'

Maisie blushes, is silent for a moment then says, 'Mebbe.'

'Think hard now. Marrying a miner'll just bring you grief and worry.'

'Pa's a miner.'

'And much good that done him or us. How many years have I had to break rock just to make ends meet?' She holds up her cracked and callused hands. The first two fingers of her left hand are clawed, smashed years ago by flying rock. 'This is what marrying a miner gets you. Or grief like Grace's when you must lay his broken body out. Who knows? Mayhap you'll meet a pretty farm lad in the Fountain Hotel.'

'Ain't no farm lads in the Fountain Hotel, leastways no pretty ones. Though the duke's agent were in the parlour Friday.'

'What's so special about that? He ain't pretty that Scoble, that's for sure.'

'Well, he were talking.'

'Talking to you?'

'No, Ma.' She soaps the cloth again. 'He were talking to a London gent who come in the van from Plymouth. I served them dinner. Din't take no notice of me but us were listening.'

'Too nosey for your own good, maid. Get you into trouble.'

'But Ma, they was talking about the mine. I din't understand too much but they said summat about buying Cornish Consols and when I come back with brandy I heard Mr Scoble talking about Mr Pascoe and a book and maps and things.'

Jenny sits up in the bath and turns to stare at her daughter. 'A book?'

'Mmm, a book. Mr Pascoe's book mebbe.'

'What do you know about John Pascoe's book?'

'Nothing Ma, but I heard you talking about 'un with Caleb Chapman.'

'What exactly did Scoble say?'

'Can't remember 'xactly. But I heard him say "Pascoe's journal" an' "Clymo's searching for it" an' then something about making their fortunes.'

'You told anyone about this?'

'No, Ma. I ain't said nothing to nobody till now.'

'Well maid, you got big ears, and nosey parkering'll get you into trouble one day. After supper we'll go see Grace and you can tell her what you heard. But don't go mooning no more over that Pascoe boy. I seen you watching him. Like I said, marry a miner'll just bring you grief and sorrow.'

'I like him, Ma. We played when we was kids an' we was at the dame school together. He's a man now.'

'No he ain't. He may be down the mine but he ain't a man, not yet. And you ain't no woman neither.'

'Oh Ma, I'm fifteen an' that's more'n old enough to marry.'

'That's as maybe. But you've a good position at the Fountain Hotel thanks to Capun Clymo. Otherwise you'd be on the dressing floor like I was at your age. That'd do for your good looks.'

Maisie wrings out the cloth and Jenny stands to pick up the ragged towel from the floor and wraps herself in it just as Lewis Tuttle comes in. He has washed and changed out of his mining gear at the new dry in the engine house. His pale face is lined with exhaustion. He folds his bony frame on to the single wooden chair by the fire then coughs and spits black phlegm.

'Hello Father,' Maisie says.

He looks at her, nods then stares into the fire. 'Shaft sinkin' is killin' me. Rock's as hard as the devil's arse. And there ain't scarcely a breath of air down there. Powder smoke never clears full away. And the older I get the harder the climb to grass.' He hawks and spits again.

Neither Maisie nor her mother reply. They are used to Lewis's complaints. 'I'll call the children in to supper,' Maisie says, going outside.

Jenny dresses behind the curtain that divides the room then takes a stack of plates from the rickety home made dresser and lays them on the table. 'I'm starting at the counthouse come Monday. Me and Grace.'

Lewis raises his head to look at her. 'What?'

'No more buckin' or spallin' for us. I'm going to work in the counthouse.'

'There ain't no money in that. Means I'll have to tribute or we'll starve.'

'Capun Clymo'll keep us on the same wage. And you ain't no tributer, Lewis. You ain't got the knack nor the luck.'

'Unlike some who's dead or murdered even.' He coughs a great racking cough, doubling over in the chair.

The family sits at the plain board table, six children, three and three on benches down each side, Jenny and Lewis at each end. Maisie ladles meat and potatoes from the black pot onto their plates then sits down beside her mother. Lewis mutters a grace and all but he fall on the food. He picks at the meat and scarcely sips the broth. Finally he tears a chunk from the half-eaten loaf that sits in the middle of the table, dips it in his plate and sucks at the bread. Jenny watches him. 'Lewis, you mun eat, my lover.'

'I ain't hungry. Maisie, is there tea?'

'Course there's tea.' Maisie takes the teapot from its place on the hearth and fills a china mug from the mantelshelf. She adds milk so thin it's almost blue. 'Here, father.'

'Thank you, maid.' He drinks the tea, pushes his plate away and sits again beside the fire, resting his head in his hands. Jenny sighs and the family finish the food in silence.

'Bed now children,' Jenny says and obediently and still in silence the six children who range in age from four to ten troop up the stairs.

'So the book is real then, Grace?'

'Real as us four sitting here.'

Lit only by a pair of candles that flicker in the faint draught from the half-open window behind them, they sit in front of the range drinking tea. The kettle hisses on the hob. Tom Pascoe stands, sets his teacup on his chair and begins to pace the little room. 'Capun Clymo and Mr Scoble are both after it. And they don't even know what it tells.'

'What does it tell?' Maisie asks twisting to look up at Thomas.

'Hush maid. That ain't none of our business,' her mother says.

'We must be away, Grace.'

'Well thank you for coming over to tell us. Though I'm thinking it's not good news you brung.'

'Perhaps it is, Mother,' Thomas Pascoe says. He stops his pacing at the door and opens it for Jenny and Maisie. 'Good night, Mrs Tuttle, good night, Maisie. It's a good thing you've done for us. I'll not forget.' Maisie bobs the slightest curtsey looking up at him with unmistakeable intensity. He almost blushes but she turns away and he shuts the door behind them. He crosses the room to close the window to the garden.

'Maisie's grown some since she's been away,' his mother says.

He nods then turns towards the fire. 'I will leave for Bodmin tonight. I'll take the book. We cannot wait another moment.' He pulls the casement closed.

'Both the capun and Mr Scoble believe Father's book will make their fortune. It is our book and must make ours, as Father promised.'

'Thomas, you cannot cross the moor at night. Leave it till the morning as we planned.'

'No, Mother. I must go now. Tis a clear night and you say the way is easy. We must understand Father's writings. They'll come looking for the book when I am underground and you are at your work, if they have not done so already.'

'Go then. But wait while I pack some food for you. It'll be raw on the moor tonight.'

11

TO BODMIN

AT THE TOP OF THE VILLAGE THOMAS SWINGS westward along the footpath that skirts the mine and will lead him up on to the moor. It is well past midnight and already cold. There will be a heavy frost by dawn, if not before. He wraps his coat around him feeling the weight of the book in the satchel hanging from his shoulder. There is no moon, and away to the east Wheal Emma's chimney stack is stark against the night sky. A red glow shines from the unglazed windows of the engine house. He stops, looks back the way he has come, and listens, hearing the hiss of the wind in the scrubby ash and hawthorn brakes on the slopes below, and the distant thump and clank of the great engine. He thinks of the rise and fall of the massive beam driving the pump that draws water from the bottom of the mine. Such excitement there was when the engine arrived – a team of twenty horses hauled it up through the village rocking and towering on its wagon; he hears again the shouts, the crack of whips and the squeal of wooden wheels close to shattering.

Thomas has gone carefully from home, slipping through the shadows from house to house and stopping to check that he is neither watched nor followed. He has seen not a soul. Turning again to his path, he climbs the hill past the old men's pits where tin and copper were mined in times long forgotten, until finally he is out on the open moor. The path is well marked and dry and will stay that way as he skirts the southern edge of the moor, well away from its perilous bogs. He looks over to his right and sees the Great Bear low above the northern horizon. He follows the Pointers to the Pole Star, knowing that keeping it on his right hand will lead him west to St Neot and then on to the Bodmin turnpike just north of the town. It was his father who taught him the constellations, taking him up on this very hill on clear nights such as this. It is sixteen miles to Bodmin and with the keen wind at his back he will arrive by dawn. This will give him the whole of Sunday to find and talk to the Reverend Dippenden. By midnight tomorrow he should be home again with the knowledge that will unlock the secrets of his father's book.

He pulls back his shoulders and strides out, arms swinging. How good it is to be out in the open. How clean it smells; how different from the foetid air, the stink of powder, sweat and worse that fills his working days beneath the ground. He has no need of tallows here – starlight is enough as he threads his way along the narrow path, his eyes accustomed as they are to the feeble candlelight in the mine. He draws deep breaths pulling the night air into his lungs but coughs and spits, wiping the black spittle from his mouth on his sleeve.

So Maisie Tuttle's sweet on him. He doesn't doubt his mother's word. They kissed as children in chasing games and once, hidden beneath the bridge, he held her in his arms and kissed her. But since he went down underground and she left Penpillick he has hardly thought of her. Now, suddenly he sees her face, green eyes and mop of red hair and something stirs within him. He shakes his head, smiles in the darkness, and strides on.

An hour of steady walking brings him down into the wooded valley of the Fowey. At Treverbyn Bridge he stops in the shadows of the trees that overhang the river and looks back the way he came. He is sure that none saw him leave Penpillick but since last night and Maisie's story he knows he is of interest to men who wish him less than well. But he is not afraid now, even smiles at the remembered knocking of his knees that night a week past when he saw the figure in the shaft. He may be still a boy but now he is a miner. He grips the satchel, vowing that he will defend his father's book with his very life. Hearing nothing but the chuckle of the river, he sits upon the parapet of the bridge and takes his flask from the satchel and drinks. As he puts it back he hears the steady clip-clop of a horse coming up the lane from Dobwalls. Who would be travelling on horseback this time of night and on this road? A smuggler perhaps, riding up the valley after business on the coast. He drops over the side of the parapet, crawls beneath the bridge and waits.

As the horse approaches he smells it on the wind and hears the rider's whispered, 'Easy, Nelson, easy boy,' as horse and rider stop above him on the bridge. Thomas holds his breath. The horse whickers and Thomas can hear the creak of leather and the jingle of harness as the rider turns in the saddle. Horse and rider wait. Thomas, crouched beneath the bridge, considers leaping out to scare the horse, to make it bolt. Perhaps the rider would be thrown but more likely not. And what if the rider is armed or rides him down? No, best stay hidden, he cannot tackle man and horse. Well used to crouching in darkened holes he waits, and waits. He listens as the horse's breathing slows, hears it shift its hooves on the cobbled bridge, and again the creak of leather as the rider settles in the saddle. His calves begin to cramp but he dare not move. He scarcely breathes. Still he waits, listening to his heartbeat.

'Walk on,' the rider says, and Thomas breathes once more. Does he know that voice? Not Captain Clymo's. As the horse breaks into a trot, he crawls out and up the bank and peers around the parapet. There, in a gap in the trees and silhouetted against the sky, he sees the rider wears a hat, a bowler hat.

' Mr Scoble,' he whispers. He ducks down again in case the man should turn and look. He stays there until the only sounds are the river and the sighing of the wind. Back on the bridge he considers what to do. He will not go back. St Neot lies not far ahead and there Scoble, if it is indeed he, might well pass the remainder of the night. Or just as likely wait on the road again, for he must know that Thomas is on his way to Bodmin.

'I will avoid the village, if I can,' he tells himself, and sets off along the lane, slower now and cautiously. At Wenmouth Cross a finger post marks St Neot straight ahead so Thomas takes the northern lane. He does not know the land around but assures himself that he will find his way once he is walking west again.

Daybreak finds Tom Pascoe, tired and hungry, walking down the turnpike a mile north of Bodmin Town. Fog fills the valleys as if they were the inlets of a frigid sea. There is no warmth in the sun rising over the moor. The frost-rimed grass and sedges at the roadside glisten reddish in its light. Tired and hungry, he sits on a milestone, eats half the pasty from his satchel and drinks the last of his water. He saw no more of Scoble nor indeed of any other person, though his passage past the villages set dogs barking, and a cock crowed in Cardinham. Now his mind turns to the day ahead. How will he find the Reverend Dippenden? At church of course, it being Sunday. And not at chapel, for the Reverend Dippenden, an educated man, would scorn the Methodism of the miners. The idea of entering St Petroc's church fills Thomas with trepidation. From where he sits he can see the massive tower dominating the town spread out in the valley below him. In fact, Thomas is nervous at the prospect of entering the town at all. He has been to Liskeard which is of a size with Bodmin. But at Bodmin there is a railway and a fearsome gaol with gallows where his grandfather died of shame. And Scoble will be looking for him. But Scoble does not know that Thomas knows he seeks the book. With a shrug he gets to his feet and walks down into the waiting, waking town.

The bells ring out on this cold, crisp Sunday morning. Parishioners in ones and twos and family groups converge on St Petroc's. Thomas stands in the churchyard, his back to the north front of the church, the jumble of slate rooves climbing up to Beacon Hill before him. A coach and four pulls up and the coachman hands down a fine lady wearing a feathered hat and a full black dress edged with lace. She is followed by an equally fine-looking gentleman. Surely they would know the Reverend Dipppenden? But he is far too shy to approach so noble a couple. He watches the townsfolk filing past him into church. Some cast him curious looks. Finally Thomas steps forward to address a very stout and kindly looking gent dressed in a black frock-coat, his face below the top hat framed in bushy grizzled whiskers.

'Excuse me sir, would you know where I might find the Reverend Dippenden?'

The man looks him up and down. 'I would know boy, but what would a young miner want with the Reverend?'

'Miner, sir? How do you know I am a miner?'

'The paleness of your face tells me that you see little sunshine. And

76

the breadth of your shoulders and the muscles in your arm speak of hard labour. What else would you be but a miner?' He taps a forefinger on Thomas's chest. 'Now tell me young man, why do you want to find the Reverend Dippenden?'

'He was a friend to my father, sir, and my father died these six months past and my father wrote me before he died that I must needs talk to Reverend Dippenden. So I have come to Bodmin and it is a long walk from Penpillick, sir.' Thomas is surprised how easily the lie tripped off his tongue but he dares not mention the truth behind his quest.

'Hmm, Wheal Emma eh? That is a longish walk indeed.' The church bells change their peal and the man looks at his watch. 'I must go in. Will you not accompany me to the service?'

'Oh no sir, I may not. Go into the church, I mean. I am a Wesleyan and go to chapel.'

'Well, be back here when the Turret Clock strikes twelve.'

'The Turret Clock?'

'At the bottom of Fore Street, boy. You cannot but hear its clangour – new-fangled thing. Afterwards I will take you to the Reverend. He is a friend of mine. My name is Richard Carew. What is yours?'

'Thomas Pascoe, sir.'

'Right then, Thomas Pascoe, until twelve o'clock then.' He shakes his hand and hurries into the church, and Thomas turns away. And there walking his chestnut stallion slowly down the street is bowler-hatted Scoble.

12

SCOBLE'S MEN

 IT WAS LATE WHEN JETHRO LOAM REACHED THE LODGE and hammered on the door. An outraged porter opened it and held back the pair of barking dogs.

'Who are you and what in God's name do you want? Tis nearly midnight.'

'My name is Jethro Loam. I am a miner and I have urgent business with Mr Scoble.' He held up his makeshift lantern – a candle in a treacle tin pierced with holes.

'What sort of business?'

'Mining business.'

'Come back in the morning. I'll not risk his wrath by waking him at this hour.'

'His wrath will be worse if I wait till morn. The business cannot wait. An' keep they bloody dogs off.' The dogs, disquieted by the stink of sweat and black powder that hung about his body, sniffed at him and snarled, pulling at their leashes.

The porter hauled them back. He had been on the wrong side of William Scoble's temper more than once and knew what power he wielded with the duke. 'I'll let you up, but I ain't going with you, not at this hour. You know where to go?'

'Course I don't. I've not been here before.'

'It's a mile up the drive and then round back of the big house, you'll find his office beside the stables. He lives above it. Ring the bell.'

By the time he stood at Scoble's door Jethro was near exhausted. A day of sinking shaft, the ladder climb, the spying, and then the hurried four-mile walk was more than enough for any man. He rang the bell.

'Loam, what the devil? How dare you come here? Are you drunk, you infernal bugger?' William Scoble in nightgown and slippers held a candle up to Jethro's face.

'I ain't drunk. And when you hears what I got to say you'll be glad

I come. Tis to do with the boy and the book.'

'Who saw you come?' Scoble peered beyond him into the darkness then shut the door.

'Just the porter at the gate.'

Scoble snorted. 'I'll tell him not to talk. Now get inside.' He ushered the miner into his tiny parlour. 'My God, Loam you stink worse than a ferret's arse. Did you not wash today?'

'Didn't have no time when I come up to grass. I were following the boy like you said and he just scampers up them ladderways. And now I run all the way from the village. You got a drink for me, Mr Scoble? I'm as thirsty as a dog.'

'You'll have to make do with water. It's all I have.' This was an utter lie. William Scoble kept a fine cellar but he would not share good ale or grog, much less his claret with his filthy spy. He went to the scullery and returned with a pewter mug of water. 'Now what is it? You have the book?'

Jethro gulped the water down then wiped the drops from his moustache 'No I ain't but I knows where it's goin'.'

'And where's that?'

'Money first.' Loam held up his hand, rubbing grimy thumb on grimy fingers.

'Ah Loam, foul in body, foul in mind. Wait here.'

Loam listened as the stairs creaked to Scoble's footfall and looked around the tiny room. A single armchair stood before the unlit grate, an empty dresser against the wall and Loam himself sat on one of two wooden chairs beneath the window. Lives like a pauper, he thought as Scoble came back into the room, a coin in his open palm.

'Here's a crown for you, if what you say is worth it. Now talk.'

'Right then. After I come up to grass I watched the Pascoe house from my spot down by the river till it were good and dark. Then I parked myself beneath the window lying on the ground again, well hid. At first I couldn't hear a lot, much talking but all too quiet to make out what were said. The Tuttle women were there so prob'ly it were all just neighbour gossip. Then I heard the door go and goodnight said, then the Pascoe boy spoke loud and clear to his mother, "I will leave for Bodmin tonight. I'll take the book. We cannot wait another moment." Those were his very words, I swear. Then he shut the window and I couldn't hear no more.'

'So why come here, you bloody fool? Why not follow the boy and take the book from him?'

'I ain't going to tackle young Pascoe. Since he be down the mine with us he's put on muscle like a bull calf in spring. He can swing a hammer twice as hard as I already. No Mr Scoble, you can get someone else to do your dirty work. An' I ain't following him across the moor at night neither, don't think I am. So if you wants that book you'd best get after him yourself on that great horse o' yourn, and right quick. Like as not he's on his way already which is why I run here. So I'll have that crown Mr Scoble, if you please.' He held out his hand again.

'You're a coward and a damned scoundrel, Jethro Loam.' He slapped the coin in Jethro's palm and Jethro closed his fist.

Jethro stood, stepped to the door as if to leave but turned and said, 'I ain't no coward. No miner is a coward. Best you remember that. An I don't take kindly to bein' swored at, Mr Scoble.'

William Scoble slammed the door behind him, hurried up the stairs and donned his riding clothes. From a dresser drawer he took a slim dagger in a leather sheath and tucked it in his belt beneath his waistcoat. Downstairs again he collected a hunk of bread, a slab of cheese and a bottle of ale from the kitchen and packed them in his saddlebag. He grabbed his hat from its hook behind the door and rammed it on his head. In the stable his horse whickered, unsurprised to be saddled in the night and Scoble stroked his neck before leading him out into the cobbled yard. 'To catch a boy and his book, that's where we're off to this night, Nelson.' He did not mount but led the horse out into the drive and walked a hundred yards before lifting himself up into the saddle.

'We'll not wake the duke now will we, Nelson,' he said, leaning forward. Then he rapped his heels on the horse's flanks and they flew down the drive, scattering gravel and almost riding down Jethro Loam who cursed and waved a fist. At the gate he bellowed for the porter who scuttled out and seeing Scoble, bowed and swung the gate wide open.

'If the duke asks after me tell him I have ridden to the mine and then to Bodmin on mining business. I'll be back tomorrow night. And say nought about that bloody miner.' The porter bowed again, and Scoble was gone.

He found his way by starlight and the map he kept in his head of all the country between Tavistock and Bodmin. Much of what was not Duchy land belonged to the duke and the duke's business often took Scoble out at night. He galloped hard up the road to Penpillick but slowed before he reached the village, not wanting to be seen or heard. There was the unknown watcher to consider, whoever he might be, and whether he was still about. He guessed the boy would skirt the southern edge of Bodmin Moor and drop down into the valley of the River Fowey. He could follow him and accost him on the moor but there the going on horseback was not good. So he turned westward and at a steady canter followed the easy byways through St Cleer and on towards St Neot. He knew the boy must cross the river at Treverbyn Bridge and it is there that he would wait and catch him. And if that failed, a boy, a stranger in Bodmin town, would not be hard to find and Scoble had his contacts there. He smiled, leaned along the horses neck and whispered in its ear. 'Yes, Nelson, we'll catch the lad, oh yes.'

So midnight found him on Treverbyn Bridge, waiting, silent, sensing that the boy was near. He stood in the saddle and peered into the dark woods along the river bank but saw no sign of him. Nor was there any sound of nailed boots coming down the lane but still he waited. He thought he heard a whisper, a sigh of breath and stilled his own, but no, it was just wind in the trees. But he waited on, ear cocked to the chuckle of the river. Finally he turned the horse and trotted on to St Neot and waited yet again. But seeing neither hide nor hair of Thomas Pascoe, he knocked up the keeper of the London Inn, took a room and slept till dawn.

He rose early and now he rides down Bodmin's Priory Road looking all about him, looking at the churchgoers, looking at Bodmin's fine ladies in their Sunday best, looking for a callow miner who has come to the town for reasons he does not understand but soon will. And Scoble knows that Thomas Pascoe will stand out in these crowds just as the red stone tower of St Petroc's stands out against the morning sky. He stops opposite the church and watches the throng. 'He'll not be going in there, Nelson, not a Methodist bugger like him,' he mutters. 'More likely the chapel in Fore Street.' He trots away from the church and up towards the new-built clock tower.

Thomas peers out from behind a great old beech in the churchyard and watches him go. He is safe where he is and here he will stay until Richard Carew finishes his Sunday devotions at St Petroc's. He wanders around the shaded graveyard well hidden from the street and finally sits upon the crumbling wall, head in his hands. What if Scoble sees him in the company of his new-found friend? Thomas will not flee nor can he tell Richard Carew that he is a hunted man. He will brazen it out, dare Scoble to accost him in the street, and if needs be then confide in Mr. Carew. He listens as the turret clock strikes the half hour, wanders among the mossy headstones once again, until finally the church bells ring out above his head, loud and joyful, pealing out the authority of the church across the town. The congregation pours out of the double doors and Richard Carew, clearly well acquainted in Bodmin Town, moves among it, shaking hands or bowing to his betters and chatting to one and all. At last he stands alone talking to the vicar, sees Thomas and nods. He takes his farewell of the vicar and walks slowly across the churchyard.

'How was Chapel then , boy?'

'I did not go sir.' Thomas looks anywhere but at fat Mr Carew.

'Why not?'

'I cannot say sir.'

'Really?' He looks at Thomas, head on one side. 'I'm sure you have good reason. Shall we seek out the Reverend Dippenden then, Thomas Pascoe?'

They are halfway up Fore Street when Thomas spots William

Scoble, slouched in his saddle coming down. He stiffens, thinks of running into a side street but then head up, looks Scoble directly in the eye as he approaches. By his side, Richard Carew senses the change in his demeanour just as Scoble reaches them and reigns in his horse.

'Well, I'll be damned. If it's not young Pascoe. Now what would you be doing in Bodmin on a Sunday morn?'

Thomas, surprised at his own boldness says, 'On my own business, sir. And that is none of yours.'

Scoble straightens in his saddle. 'That's where you're wrong, boy. You are a tenant of the duke, you work in the duke's mine. I am his agent. So your business is my business, and my guess is that our business lies in that satchel you clutch so tightly.'

'I think not, sir. The agent of the duke has no jurisdiction here.' Richard Carew steps forward.

'And who might you be?'

'My name is Richard Carew of Carew, Carew and Trewin and this young man is under my protection. We are on our way to see an old friend of mine, the Reverend Dippenden.' He puts his arm across Thomas's shoulders. Thomas bites his lip.'

'A damned lawyer, by God. The boy's a thief. He fled Penpillick in the middle of the night, with stolen goods, in that satchel.' Scoble leans down from his horse and tries to snatch the bag but Thomas is too quick and steps back. The horse shies and Scoble almost falls 'Steady, Nelson, steady, blast and damn you.' He hauls viciously on the reins.

'The book is mine,' Thomas cries, clutching the satchel to his chest.

'Ahh, so it is the book.' Scoble grins down at him then straightens in the saddle. 'Walk on Nelson, walk on.' As he trots away he turns, 'Good day to you, Mr Carew. And take care Thomas Pascoe, take very good care.'

Thomas and Richard Carew watch Scoble ride off down Fore Street.

'What a disagreeable man. And such language on the Lord's Day,' Richard Carew says.

'It was kind of you to protect me, sir. I swear I stole nothing. The book was my father's and he left it to me. I left the village in the night

84

as I must be back at the mine for first core tomorrow morning.'

'Tell me Thomas, is it about this precious book you wish to consult the Reverend Dippenden?'

'Yes sir.'

'And why would it be of interest to him?'

'I do not know that it would, sir. But my father was a very great miner and he wrote me that the book would make our fortune. It is about Wheal Emma. But we cannot understand it.'

'You can read?'

'Oh, yes, sir. I was at the grammar school in Liskeard before my father died. But he wrote in code and symbols and we don't know what they mean. I thought the Reverend Dippenden might know for he taught my father when he was a boy.'

'Right, then we had best be on our way. It is a tidy walk to Harford House.'

Scoble meanwhile gallops off down the hill. A boy chasing his hoop down the street runs out in front of him. The horse shies and Scoble, almost thrown again, hauls on the reins. 'Whoa, Nelson, whoa you blackguard. Out of my road child,' he yells.

At the White Hart he hands his horse to a stable boy and stomps into the inn. He takes a room for the night and bellows for dinner – veal cutlet with egg sauce, beef stew and potatoes, gooseberry jelly tarts, and two pints of ale, and sits himself at a table by the fire. The bar is empty. His early morning ride has made him hungry and knowing that the book is almost in his grasp further whets his appetite. He is well into his second pint by the time the waitress brings his food. He falls on it as if starving, wolfing it down between swigs of ale. Finally replete, he sits back, wipes his mouth on the back of his hand and calls the waitress over.

'Bring me an envelope.' He takes out the little notebook and a pencil from their customary place in his waistcoat pocket. He writes in the notebook and tears out two pages, reads them and nods to himself. The girl gives him an envelope. He folds the pages and slips them into it and asks the girl who can take his message. She leaves him and some minutes later a ragged child appears.

'Sir?'

Scoble sniffs at the smell of the child's unwashed body.

'You know Bell Street, boy?'

'Yes sir.'

'Go to number 12. Knock on the door and ask for Davy Bates. Have you got that – Davy Bates?'

'I knows 'im, sir.'

'Do you now? So much the better. Give him this note.'

'Yes, Captain.'

'Go now, quick sharp. There's a copper in it for you.'

The child sidles from the room.

'Girl,' Scoble shouts, 'Bring a bottle of your best claret.'

Scoble stands in the doorway of the White Hart, glass of wine in his hand, looking at the sky. The wind has veered southwest and the sun is veiled by streaks of cirrus. Storm coming, he thinks. So much the better. If Bates and Kelso don't get the boy this afternoon they'll ride him down on the moor tonight. Foul weather for a foul deed. If they have to kill him so be it, but Scoble will have that book, God's teeth he will. The bastard boy has brought it to Bodmin, has it with him now, of that he is sure. How sharply his hand went to his satchel when he braced him in Fore Street. If he had not been with that fat filthy lawyer he would have had it off him there and then. But why was he with Carew? Could he have aught to do with Wheal Emma's secrets?

He turns and lifts the latch of the inn door, goes to his place by the fire and pours another glass of claret. Raising it to his nose, he sniffs. It's good, the inn's best, which he can now afford. Not as good as the damned duke's, but once the mine is his he'll lay down a cellar and the duke can go hang himself. His bully boys should find the boy with ease. They're on their way to him right now. They'll have the book within the hour.

Scoble settles in his chair, legs stretched out before the fire and falls asleep. He snores and spittle drools from the corner of his mouth.

13

THE REVEREND DIPPENDEN

 'STAND BY THE LIGHT THERE, BOY. LET ME SEE YOU.' Thomas moves to the window and looks across the room to where the Reverend Dippenden sits. He is very old, the oldest man Thomas has ever seen. Black leather boots with scuffed toes stick out below the woollen blanket on his legs. He wears a black-frock coat buttoned to his clerical collar. The coat, green with age, looks old as he does. White hair curls above his ears and straggles in moth-eaten whiskers down his cheeks. He stares up at Thomas.

'John Pascoe's son. No question, he's the image.' The voice quavers between a whisper and a croak.

'Well, I'm pleased you recognise him, Reverend,' Richard Carew says.

'I'd have known him anywhere. I was fond of your father, boy. How is he?'

'He is dead sir, this six month. Killed down the mine. We do not know why.'

'Ah, sad, sad. But so many miners die. And what is your name?'

'Thomas, sir. I am a tut worker down Wheal Emma now. I am sorry to disturb you, sir.' It seems to Thomas that the Reverend Dippenden is far too old to unravel the mysteries of his book.

'You've not disturbed me. I like company.' He raises a bony hand, reaches out and points with a trembling finger. 'Now tell me Carew, why have you brought him here?'

The very room smells of age, but Richard Carew knows that age has not diminished the old man's wits.

'He has a book his father wrote that is a mystery to him. He thinks you might elucidate it.'

'Aha, a mystery. I like mysteries. You have the book my boy? You have it there?'

Thomas unbuckles the leather satchel and draws out the oilskin parcel. Moving to the table he unwraps the book and lays it down. The

Reverend Dippenden braces himself on the arms of his chair, pushes himself to his feet, the blanket falling to the floor. Richard Carew takes his arm as he totters to the table and sits. He brushes the marbled cover of the book with a trembling hand.

'Sit down boy, sit down beside me. Let us learn together the way I taught your father. Carew, bring that candelabra from the mantelshelf and call Rebecca. Tell her to bring the boy some food. Are you hungry young Pascoe? You must be. Boys are always hungry.'

'Yes sir, thank you sir.' Thomas sits beside the old man, inhaling the smell of musty clothing. He opens the book. 'The first pages, sir, are simple. They speak of you and how you taught my father of rocks and strata and how he should become a "surveyor". But he never did for my grandfather went to the debtors' prison and Father became a miner.'

'Yes, yes indeed. I remember well. But where is your mystery then?'

'Here sir.' Thomas turns the pages. 'Here, look, no words, just lines and numbers, letters and strange symbols that I cannot understand. And here again, page after page. Yet he says this book is for me and our family and it will make our fortune. Men say he was the best tributer at Wheal Emma.'

'Ah, aha, do they indeed?' The old man claps his bony hands and gives a strange croaking laugh. 'Hmm, puzzling, yes, very puzzling. It is indeed some sort of code. Now here's a symbol I recognise. Look Carew, what think you?'

'I'm with Thomas, Reverend. It's all gibberish to me. Looks like a spider fell in an inkpot and skittered across the page.'

There is a knock on the door and a maid comes in carrying a tray which she places on the table. 'Food, sir, as you ordered. Strange time to be eating if you ask me.'

'I didn't ask you Rebecca. But thank you. You may go.' The maid leaves.

'Somewhat forward, my Rebecca, for a daughter of paupers but a good body nonetheless. Fall to young Thomas. Carew, open that desk over there and bring me a sheet of paper and pen and ink. Now let me see . . . ' He slides the candelabra close to the book.

Thomas cuts himself a slice from the loaf on the tray, lays ham upon it and eats. He is indeed very hungry. He watches as the Reverend Dippenden begins to write, copying symbols from the book and stopping every now and then to brush the quill across his lips.

'Aha, now, d'ye see boy? Look at this, Carew – John Pascoe's private code.' Carew leans over his shoulder. 'This, ♀, is the symbol for Venus. Hmm very odd. Was your father interested in the stars and planets boy?'

'Yes, sir. He used to take me up on the moor on clear nights to show me the constellations.'

'Did he indeed. But why would he put all that in a book eh? Besides, unless I am much mistaken,' he turns a page, 'these are not maps of constellations. Now, here's a strange symbol – ◑. Does he mean half moon? No, I think not, for it is repeated time and again and never changes. Ah yes, hmm – **fm**, might that be fathom suggesting we are below the ground? And here we have **43 → E**. Could **E** be east and that would make **N** north? But why the Venus sign?'

His musings subside to a mumble, and then a silence broken only by the scratching of his quill.

Thomas looks up at Richard Carew, who puts a finger to his lips and mouths, 'Patience, patience.'

Finally the Reverend Dippenden sits up, scratches his head and points with shaking finger to the books that line one wall of his parlour.

'Thomas my boy, in the middle of the middle shelf you will find a volume entitled *Alchemical Signs and Symbols*. I think in that we'll find the key we need.'

Thomas gets up and runs his hand along the shelf. 'This one, sir?' He pulls out an ancient musty tome.

'Yes indeed. Bring it here.' The Reverend turns the yellowed pages then runs his finger down a list of symbols. 'Aha, just as I thought, the Venus symbol means "woman" for it represents a mirror. But more importantly for us, it also is the alchemical sign for copper. You see Carew, mirrors were once made of copper and the old alchemists took it as its symbol. So, let us substitute **Cu,** the symbol we use today for copper. And I believe that your clever father, Thomas, used ◑ to signify the main shaft at your mine.'

'So, if I'm not mistaken **160fm ☽ + 43E** ♀ ♀ ♀ **L ==>N**: means from the shaft at 160 fathoms go 43 fathoms to the east and we find a rich copper lode – see, he repeats his copper symbol three times and my guess is that the double arrow shows that the lode plunges to the north. Do the lodes at Wheal Emma trend east to west, young Thomas?'

'Yes sir, they do.'

'Aha, and did your father use a miner's dial?'

'He did sir. We have it still at home.'

'Perfect. The mystery is unravelled.' The old man claps again. His voice has strengthened, lost its quaver.

'And here you see, with two simple lines he joins that observation to another in the crosscut twenty fathoms to the west, and hey presto, he knows he has twenty fathoms of rich lode. Your father was not just a miner, Thomas, he was a geologist, a surveyor and a clever man. These are maps, boy, maps of rocks, and if I'm not mistaken maps of the copper lodes at your mine. He has made geologic maps just as old William Smith taught him all those years ago. Come look, Carew. By heaven, John Pascoe did become a surveyor after all.'

Thomas sits, bread and meat in hand and mouth agape. Dippenden turns another page.

'Perfect, 180 fathoms, the shaft symbol again and **xcut + 12 → N** ♀ ♀ **L ==>N**. He's found the lode on the next level down in the north crosscut, but not so rich now but still plunging to the north. Ha, beautiful, Carew, beautiful, just look. William Smith would have been proud.

Now boy, see what you can do.' Dippenden turns the page, smoothes it down and Thomas leans forward.

'Um, yes, he is back on the 160 fathom level but west this time, eight fathoms from the shaft but here's a different symbol, a circle with a cross through it and nothing else. What does this mean?'

'No lode, boy, no lode. It's gone, crossed out. No point in mining there. But you're doing well. Carry on now.'

'I must leave you to your studies, my dinner calls me,' Carew says.

'I am pleased, young man, that your journey has been worthwhile. Reverend, I bid you farewell.'

'Farewell, Carew, farewell. And I thank you for bringing me this boy and his fascinating book. Now, young Thomas Pascoe, let us carry on.'

Thomas turns the page, muttering to himself. 'Here, we are back on 120 fathom level, very rich again and here's another crosscut with yet more copper. Oh, my father found a very kindly lode, your Reverendship. This is what he meant when he said that this will make our fortune.'

'Carry on, carry on, turn the page, boy. We shall find yet more, I do not doubt. Indeed, I and William Smith taught your father well.'

Boy and aged cleric sit, heads bent in the candlelight, turning the pages, studying and murmuring to each other. They are well into the book when Thomas hears a knocking at the outer door, men's voices and a muttered conversation with the maid. He lifts his head as two men burst into the parlour. Kerchiefs cover half their faces and soft caps are drawn down over their eyes. One grabs and holds Thomas by the arms, the other lunges for the book, knocking the candelabra to the floor.

'How dare you? Get out, you villains,' the Reverend Dippenden cries out in a croaking voice, hands down on the book in a vain attempt to protect it.

'Let go old fool, or you'll get hurt,' the intruder growls as Thomas, twisting free from his assailant, leaps from his chair, spins round and drives his fist into the man's lowered face. The ruffian staggers back, drops the book, and swings a blow at Thomas but, missing, grabs the old man's chair to save his balance. The chair teeters, then topples over, tipping out the Reverend Dippenden whose head strikes the corner of the brass fire surround. He lets out an awful rattling groan, his heels drum on the wooden floor and then he lies still and quiet, blood pooling around his head. There is a silence. They stare aghast.

'By Christ, you've killed him. Let's get out of here,' the other ruffian shouts. They both dash through the door, one bent low, clutching his bleeding face.

With a cry Thomas drops to his knees. 'Reverend Dippenden,

your Reverendship!' He lifts him, cradling his head and shoulders in his arms but the old man's head lolls back and his mouth falls open.

Rebecca shrieks as she comes into the parlour. 'Oh Lord preserve us. The master, the master, is he dead?'

Thomas looks up. 'I don't know, I don't know. Fetch a doctor, quickly.'

'Oh Lord, oh Jesus Lord, I'll be back directly.' She rushes out as Thomas gently lowers the body to the floor. He stands at the table, too stunned to move, staring down at what he knows is now a corpse. His punch drove the intruder backwards, the chair fell over. It's his fault that his father's friend, his teacher, lies dead before his eyes.

Thomas moves slowly, puts the book in his bag and takes up the rest of the bread and meat and puts that in too. He walks out into the dusk, down through the town, up past St Petroc's and out on to the Launceston road. He straps the satchel across his shoulders and begins to run.

He runs up the long turnpike out of the town, his hobnail boots ringing sparks off the stony road. He runs at a steady pace his breathing slipping into the easy rhythm he has found climbing out of Wheal Emma's darkness. He must get home, away from Bodmin, away from Scoble and Scoble's men, away from death.

So Thomas runs on as the sun sets behind him and darkness falls and the wind gets up and the first raindrops patter on his jacket. He runs back the way he came the night before, turns off the turnpike to Cardinham and along the muddy lanes. The book jogs gently at his side and his father's symbols swim before his eyes – copper, shaft and crosscut, arrows this way and that, picking out the wayward lode, showing where the riches are. And he can read it. But for what? The Reverend Dippenden is dead.

At St Neot in pouring rain he rests to catch his breath and eat the Reverend Dippenden's meat and bread. Seized by a fit of coughing he spits black phlegm. He drinks water from his bottle and refills it at the pump beside the inn. He runs on, panting up the long hill, rain and sweat dripping from his nose, then down again to Treverbyn Bridge.

Here he halts. Must he go the way he came, north up through the woods, or straight on and up the hill? It is too dark, too wet and stormy to cross the moor to home and safety; he'll lose the path, he must go by the road, the longer way. Three hours have passed he judges, time enough for Scoble and his men to be on his track but not enough to catch him.

So on he runs, feet blistered now in his miner's boots, pain in his legs and chest, darkness, wind and rain all about him. The road is steep out of the river valley, the slope seems endless, his boots skidding in the mud and on the stones. He stumbles up and up, gasping at the pain. Finally he breasts the hill and the wind off the moor buffets him and he would rest again. But above the pounding of his heart and the hiss of rain, he hears a single shout carried on the gale. It must be them.

Thomas turns, runs on, not looking back, even at the sound of hoof beats still far behind. He is flying, wings to his feet, he will outrun the horses, run and run. But the pounding hooves are right behind him now, he looks back – too late, the horse is on him and he trips, sprawls headlong and knows no more.

'C'mon there, get up, get up,' and the horse breaks into a trot as Mathew Clymo flicks the reins and the rhythmic squealing of the overloaded cart's ungreased axles picks up pace.

He glances back at the two kibbles and winding rope that he bought at a sale of gear from the failed Wheal Betsy mine. They should serve well to increase the hoisting rate at Wheal Emma, unless Wheal Emma too is headed down that sorry path to failure. Then this tedious cart trip to Redruth and back will have been a royal waste of time. At least last night's storm has blown itself out, leaving a bright clear autumn morning and the moor shining from the rain. Away, below and to the south, cloud shadows race across the farmlands and beyond them the sea glints blue. He sniffs to smell it on the wind and flicks the reins again, heading homeward to his mine.

This will be Grace Pascoe's first day in the counthouse. He sees himself sitting on his stool studying the week's production in the ledgers. She'll be bustling round with broom and duster and he'll ask her for a dish of tea just to watch her face. He spent the night at Dobwalls, left in the cool wet dawn but now the sun is high and warms his body. He would be content if not for the thought that lurks maggot-like in his head, emerging in any idle moment night or day – how is it that his mine is losing money? He shrugs and shifts his bottom on the hard wood seat – this week we'll turn it round. His tributers will cut rich ore, good bunches in every end. And Grace Pascoe, how will he court her – with gifts or looks or fancy words? He'll buy her the frocks with frills and ribbons the bal maidens love to wear on high days and holidays. And if she will have him, he'll marry her and she will live with him in the house he has built at the top of the village. It cost twice what he had estimated and he was forced to sell a portion of his Cornish Consol stock to fund it. But if Grace Pascoe comes to live there, that would be bliss.

Stretching and yawning, sitting high on the cart he spies a bundle, something lying in the road ahead. He stands to get a better look. Sits again and picks up the peeler's truncheon he keeps beneath the seat, just in case. As he draws near he sees the miners' boots then recognises who it is – Tom, Thomas Pascoe, Grace's son.

Leaping from the cart he squats beside the body, bends down and puts an ear to the open mouth. The boy is breathing. He takes a flask from his coat pocket and trickles grog between his lips. Tom stirs, his eyelids flutter but he doesn't wake. His face is battered, an eye completely closed, lips pulped, still bleeding. One hand is smashed, the fingers broken and blood still seeps from a deep and swollen cut in his scalp. Mathew slides an arm beneath his shoulders, the other under his legs, and with a grunt lifts the body from the ground. He lays him gently in the cart, fashioning a pillow from folded sacking, then takes off his cloak and covers him. He climbs aboard his cart. 'Walk on,' he calls.

Two hours it takes before the smoking stack of Wheal Emma's engine house hoves into view. From time to time Mathew twists on his seat and studies the prone figure. There's something here he has not understood – first John Pascoe's death, now his son left for dead up on the moor. And Grace, she knows more than she is telling.

'Steady now, steady.' He hauls back on the reins as the horse takes the downhill weight of the heavily loaded cart. As they draw up before the counthouse, as if he were the captain of a ship, Mathew gives a great bellow that can be heard above the clank and hiss of the engine, 'Hey counthouse ahoy.'

The head of Francis Pryor, purser, appears at an open window. 'Francis, quick man, call Grace Pascoe. I have her boy here. I found him on the road. He's injured. And send for the bal surgeon, right this minute.' Pryor's head withdraws and moments later the door flies open and there is Grace, bareheaded, with Jenny Tuttle right behind her.

'Lord help us,' Grace screams, running to the cart, 'Not my Thomas, not Thomas.' She cradles him lifting his head and shoulders. 'My boy, my boy, they've killed my boy.'

'He's breathing, Grace. Here, help me get some brandy in him.' This time the boy stirs and his eyes blink open to see his mother looking down. 'They chased me Ma, from Bodmin. I lost it.'

'Hush now, never mind that.' She turns to Mathew Clymo who stands close by her looking at the boy. 'Can you bring him home in the cart?'

'Best we take him into the dry. We'll clean him up. We've sent for Dr Couch. Come Jenny, help us lift him.'

But Thomas sits up with a groan and says, 'It's alright Capun, I can walk.'

They help him down off the cart and supported by his mother on one side and Mathew Clymo on the other, he staggers into the dry, a new stone-built lean-to hard against the wall of the counthouse. Inside, they lay him on the wooden bench below the rows of hanging day clothes left by the miners now underground. The room is warm, heated by vented steam from the engine house, and smells of men's sweat, damp wool and coal smoke. His mother eases off his boots with a sucking sound. His feet are raw and bleeding and blood drips from his boots as Grace upends them.

'Where has he been? What was he doing on the moor? Who

chased him? What has he lost?' Mathew Clymo asks, leaning over, his body almost touching hers.

She shakes her head and strips the boy to his underwear while Jenny Tuttle brings warm water in a bucket, and a towel. He groans again, eyes closed as his mother sponges down his face and bathes his cuts and the great lump on his head. His nose is broken and his split lips reveal a missing tooth. She lifts his broken hand, gently wipes his broken fingers and he winces at the pain, and finally she sits him up. 'Feet in the bucket Thomas, it will soothe them.' He nods and does as he is told.

'Now tell us what befell you, Tom,' Mathew says.

He looks up at him, then with a sigh he drops his head and props it in his uninjured hand.

'Tom,' Mathew almost shouts. But the boy just shakes his head.

'Leave 'un be, Capun,' Grace says. 'Let 'un rest awhile. You say bal surgeon's on his way. He needs them fingers splinted or he'll not hold steel again. Lie back now Tom.' She eases him back on the bench, lifts his legs and makes a pillow of his sodden jacket. Tom closes his eyes, his injured hand laid across his chest. He is instantly asleep breathing noisily through battered lips.

Mathew Clymo, torn between a desire for knowledge and desire for Grace Pascoe, can only nod. He turns away and leaves the dry.

'My, he's sweet on you alright,' Jenny Tuttle murmurs.

Grace gives her a look and says quietly, 'It'll be his help I'll need, not his lovin'. Tom'll not be workin' for a while.'

'Mine Club'll give you a shillin' a day hurt pay,' Jenny says.

'No it won't. Tom weren't hurt minin', was he. I'll get nothin' there. Besides I already had club money when poor John died. And how will I pay bal surgeon?'

'Capun Clymo'll pay, don't doubt it,' Jenny says. 'But what about that there book? He said it was stole. Who would do that?'

'I dunno, Jenny. So far it just brought us a heap of trouble, so good riddance, I reckon.'

Couch, a serious doctor and bal surgeon to many of the mines in the district charges Mathew a fair five shillings for setting Tom's broken fingers and nose and stitching his head plus twopence more for a flask of laudanum.

'How soon will he work again?' Mathew asks.

'Two weeks perhaps. Boys heal quickly and he's strong. But I listened to his chest. He shows signs of black lung already.'

Mathew shakes his head. 'What can I do? They all get it, if not sooner later.'

'Get better air down there. You know that, Mathew Clymo.'

'I plan to sink a new vent shaft, just as soon as it can be afforded, that is.'

'They say Wheal Emma's the richest mine round here. Is that not so?'

'Of course, of course. But the Trevithick engine cost us a fortune.'

The doctor picks up his bag. 'And the Adventurers will want to see their dividends, no doubt. Well, good day to you, Mathew.'

Mathew sits alone in the counthouse. The Adventurers' dinner is but a week away and what will he tell them? There'll be no hiding the fact from them that the mine is losing money. He shrugs, gets off his stool and stands in the open door looking down the lane to the village. He'll visit Grace tonight – just to see how the boy is doing.

14

THE COUNTHOUSE DINNER

THE BAL MAIDENS LOOK A PICTURE IN THEIR STARCHED white gooks and white walking-out aprons. Some have knotted lace at their throats and all have polished their square-toed boots which have lately become the fashion. They stand now, all fourteen in a row waiting his inspection, all save Grace and Jenny Tuttle who will serve the dinner. He too is dressed for the occasion in top hat, high collar and black bow tie.

For the last week Mathew has had the maidens picking through their piles of broken rock and putting aside the richest ore. Most of it comes from the 140 fathom level where, thank the Lord, Henry Hopeful Down and Caleb Chapman have finally broken through and found the lode again. He admires the neatly stacked piles on the dressing floor and the coloured glint of minerals iridescent in the morning sun: yellow copper pyrites, the purple-blue of peacock ore, and the silver-grey of mundick. This last is arsenical and to be discarded once the Adventurers are gone, but most of them don't know one mineral from another. He hopes to show them that the cost-book numbers are unimportant, a minor hiccup, and that his mine is cutting rich again. And then he'll fill them up with beef and grog and puddings and send them home replete. If not convinced, they'll be dumping Cornish Consols stock as fast as they can get back to London and Liskeard.

He hears the first carriage clattering in the cobbled yard and looks up to see a four-in-hand with four top-hatted gentlemen aboard. With a deep breath he squares his shoulders. Touching his hat to the maidens who bob a curtsey back, he strides across the dressing floor and past the engine house to welcome the guests.

Once in the counthouse Mathew gazes round with pride. The bare oak floors are freshly holy-stoned. The portrait of old William Morris has been dusted and twenty chairs surround a trestle table. The cost books and production ledgers are laid open for examination on the shelf around the wall, and the three clerks sitting on their stools are dressed in newly-pressed black tail-coats. He spent the night before going through the ledgers time and again but still could find no error that would account for Wheal Emma's loss. He wishes the whole accounting business were already over and Grace and Jenny were serving food and drink. The smell of roasting meat and baking pastry fills the room and his mouth waters.

Above the background thump and hiss of Trevithick's engine he hears the sound of hoof beats and jingling harnesses and cries of 'Good Morning, sir' and 'How d'ye do?'. James Sanderson, the broker and now Chairman, and young William Morris come in and shake his hand. Morris has his father's shaggy beard and unruly mop of hair but not his easy manner. He says directly, 'You received my letter about a man machine? I have as yet had no reply.'

'That sir, is because I haven't written one. You will understand today why your suggestion is not practical.'

Morris is about to argue when they are joined by a small man dressed in a frock-coat and yellow waistcoat.

'Mathew, let me introduce you,' Sanderson says. 'This is a friend of mine, James Yelloly Watson, a new shareholder. He has bought your stock on my advice. I hope you have good news for us.'

Yelloly Watson shakes his hand and says, 'So very good to meet you, sir.'

Mathew smiles. 'You will not be disappointed.'

'I am sure I shall not. I am a modest investor but I am greatly interested in your Cornish mining.'

This registers in the back of Mathew's mind, something about a survey of English mines. 'I know your name. Are you not a journalist or from the government perhaps?' he asks.

The little man beams. 'You have heard of me. No, I am not a journalist nor a government man, just a humble writer fascinated by mining. It is my passion. I study it in all its facets and never miss an opportunity to visit another mine.'

Mathew nods and turns towards the door as William Scoble enters, dressed in his usual brown serge suit and bowler hat.

'Morning Scoble,' he says.

'Morning Clymo. I trust things have improved since my last visit.'

Mathew stares at him wondering at the man's arrogance and the glint of satisfaction, even triumph in his eyes. 'You'll know soon enough,' he says.

The room fills slowly, the men are seated, their top hats laid before them on the table. James Sanderson sits at one end, Clymo faces him at the other. Pryor the purser sits next to him. Mathew takes a breath and gets up to speak.

'Gentlemen and fellow Adventurers, good morning and welcome to you one and all. I am pleased to report that this past three months we raised one thousand four hundred and seventy-eight tons of copper ore, which is a mere eight tons short of our record last quarter.' He waits for the round of applause to die down. 'The quantity of copper metal contained amounted to seventy-nine tons.' He pauses again. Sanderson has caught his eye and is frowning. There is a slight shuffling and whispering around the table. Two or three are making notes.

He continues, 'Valued at seven thousand five hundred and eighty-four pounds. The duke's dues on this sum,' here he looks straight at Scoble, 'amount to seven hundred and fifty-eight pounds and eight shillings. Our costs for the three months amount to six thousand two hundred and twenty-four pounds three shillings and seven pence.'

There is a bit of scribbling, mutters then absolute uproar around the table. Sanderson's usually florid face has gone grey and he is on his feet, arms outstretched trying to calm the men around him. 'Gentlemen, gentlemen, let Captain Clymo explain himself.'

'Thank you sir. I regret that on the basis of these results Cornish Consols will pay no dividend this quarter.'

They are on their feet immediately, banging the table, shouting and stamping. 'Shame, shame on you sir.'

'Disgraceful, a knacked bal, by God.'

'Ha, mining's nowt but a knave's game. I should have left my money in Brunel's Great Western.'

'Gentlemen, gentlemen, please. Hear me,' Mathew shouts above the hubbub. 'I do have some good news.'

'Hear him, hear him.'

He waits for them to settle, smiles and speaks. 'Fortunately we have a small cash reserve so I do not need to call on you for further funds, and – ' he pauses for effect, looking around at their expectant faces. 'Two days ago at 160 fathoms we cut it rich, yes, very rich.'

The room erupts again, top hats thrown in the air, more banging of the table this time with cries of 'Huzzah for Captain Clymo and Wheal Emma.'

He catches Sanderson's eye and smiles. 'With this discovery I guarantee next quarter I will announce a record dividend.' They cheer once more and he continues:

'Gentlemen, you may examine the new find at your leisure. We have laid out samples on the dressing floor. But before we go outside and brave the weather, our books are here for your inspection and Mr Pryor and his clerks are at your disposal.' He gestures to the clerks, then bows and says, 'I thank you for your attention.'

Mathew sits amidst applause, and turns to Francis Pryor, 'I thank the Lord that that is over.'

'Sticky going for a moment there. They were ready to string you up.'

Outside a cold November wind whips up gritty dust from the dressing floor. The Adventurers stand in groups around the piles of ore, clutching their hats. Joseph Yelloly Watson squats on the ground picking up specimen after specimen and studying each one with an eyeglass.

'Very nice, Captain Clymo, very nice, very rich, no question. But this is mispickel if I'm not mistaken.' He stands, holding out a glittering grey lump.

'Mundick, we call it. Plenty of it on the attle dump,' Mathew says.

'It has no value?' William Morris asks.

'I believe the French calcine it to make a green pigment,' Yelloly Watson says.

Morris nods. 'Might I have a specimen?'

'Help yourself,' Mathew says.

'Take this.' Yelloly Watson passes him the mineral. 'But take care. It is arsenical and most poisonous.'

'And all this glittering stuff, what is this? It looks more like gold than copper.' Scoble has joined them and kicks at a mound of brassy mineral set to one side.

'Neither gold nor copper I'm afraid. Just iron pyrites, though some call it "fool's gold",' Yelloly Watson says.

'I put that out just for collectors,' Mathew says. 'There are fine crystal specimens that would look well in a cabinet of curiosities. There's no gold in this mine, Mr Scoble.'

'And would you tell me if there were?'

Mathew draws himself up and is about to reply when it starts to rain. James Sanderson puts an arm round his shoulders and draws him away. 'You've the luck of the devil, Mathew. I knew that the first time we met. But to cut it rich again just as the mine starts to lose money, is felicitous to say the least.'

'It is that. We'd have been finished otherwise. What say you we get them inside for dinner?'

Sanderson nods and they move amongst the Adventurers, herding them towards the counthouse door. The room is nicely warm, pervaded by the smell of food. They seat themselves around the trestle table now covered with a rough but snow-white cloth and laid with glasses, silver cutlery and plates. Opened bottles of wine are set at intervals between the places. A great joint of beef and a bowl of punch occupy the centre of the table. To cheers, Jenny Tuttle appears carrying giblet pies, one in each hand. Grace Pascoe follows holding high a platter bearing a roast goose surrounded with apples. Both women are bareheaded, wear their best white aprons and black tight-cut jackets with lace tied at the collar, bright against the black. Mathew tries not to stare at Grace but fails; he cannot keep his eyes away. She is wearing the agate brooch he gave her that night last week.

It was dark when he knocked on her cottage door that evening two days after he had brought Tom home.

'Evening Grace,' he said, ducking through the doorway. He took her hand and kissed it.

She half shied away and said, 'I ain't no lady, Mathew Clymo.'

He smiled. 'To me you are. How does the boy?'

'Mendin' slowly. Upstairs asleep with Emily and James. So speak softly now.'

He liked the closeness that seemed to bring between them. 'I brought you club money to tide you over till he works again.'

'That ain't club money is it?'

He smiled again. 'What matter, Grace. May I sit?'

She gestured to the chair by the fire, took the kettle from the hob and filled it from the pitcher at the sink. He watched her in the feeble rush-light, still possessed by the question he had wanted to ask her in the counthouse all that day. It was on the tip of his tongue, but instead he said, 'Grace, who attacked Thomas and left him for dead?'

She bent to poke the fire and the kettle on the hob began to hiss. 'I don't know. Nor does Thomas. He never saw them, though he thinks they might be William Scoble's men.'

'Scoble's men? Why Scoble?' He leaned towards her across the hearth.

'I suppose I mun tell you. Maybe I should have told you long before.' She took the now boiling kettle to the table, made tea, gave him a cup and sat down with her own.

She looked up at him. 'I lied to you. John left a book. He wrote in it near every day – what he saw in Wheal Emma each core. Said it would make our fortune. But we couldn't understand it, all in code it was. So Thomas took it to Reverend Dippenden in Bodmin who taught my John when he were a lad. Thomas won't tell me what happened there except that the Reverend showed him how to read it. Then two bully boys, Scoble's men he says, tried to steal the book but he fought them off and ran from Bodmin through the night. But the devils must have caught him, left him for dead and now the book is gone.'

He sips his tea. 'Why did you lie to me?'

'I knew not who to trust. And Thomas was set against it. He still don't trust you even though you rescued him. But we knows now that Scoble is a villain.'

'Do you trust me now?' He put his cup and saucer on the hearth, leaned forward and laid his hand upon her arm.

'I do,' she said, but did not look at him. 'You promised to find out who killed John.'

'I've got no further. But now I know he kept a journal and you say that William Scoble sought it, that makes a difference. If they left Thomas for dead perhaps they had a hand in John's murder too. But none but a mining man could have killed him underground.'

She took his hand from her arm and held it. 'What will you do now?'

'Leave my mother alone, Capun, that's what you will do.'

They turned and standing in the shadows on the bottom stair was Thomas, his head and hand still bandaged and dressed in his father's nightgown. Mathew Clymo stood up and said, 'Thomas, I wish your mother and your family nothing but well. If you had trusted me from the first all this might not have happened. You would still have the book. Will you tell me what was in it?'

Thomas sat down, head in his hands and muttered, 'I suppose it does not matter now the book is gone. It was full of maps and drawings of the lodes at Wheal Emma. "Geologic Maps" the Reverend called them, that my father made.'

'Ah, I guessed as much. But what makes you think the ruffians were William Scoble's men.'

'He tried to take the book from me that same morning, in Bodmin High Street.'

'You are sure it was him.'

'We knows him well round here, Capun.'

Mathew looks around the table as he eats, and watches Scoble deep in talk with Francis Pryor as they shovel in their food. Now what would they be talking of so earnestly, he wonders. He has not yet braced Scoble with Thomas Pascoe's accusations. He needs more facts, more certainty, before he dare accuse the agent of the duke of attempted murder. And why would Scoble want John Pascoe's book?

'Gentleman, a toast.' Sanderson is on his feet beside him, glass in hand.

They stand and raise their glasses. 'To Wheal Emma and her gallant captain.' Mathew catches Scoble's eye, stares at him until the man looks down. Yes, he and Scoble will have their talk – but what of Francis Pryor? He knows little of him other than that he was second purser at Dolcoath before he joined Wheal Emma. Perhaps there's more to him than meets the eye, though he's fat enough. He shrugs, refills his glass and eats. When Grace Pascoe clears his plate her arm just brushes his and he looks up. She smiles, looks him in the eye as if to say, 'What now Capun Clymo?' Then Jenny Tuttle lays a bowl of figgy pudding before him and he eats again.

The dinner over, the Adventurers stand around in noisy groups, smoking cigars, chatting, most still drinking punch and some are frankly drunk. He surveys the room with satisfaction. It has gone well, much better than he expected. He sees Joseph Yelloly Watson standing alone and turning the leaves of a ledger left open on the shelf. He walks over to the little man. 'Might I help you Mr Watson?'

'Ah Captain Clymo, could I have a private word?' He looks around, grasps Mathew's elbow and manoeuvres him to the corner closest to the engine house where they will not be overheard. 'Forgive me but I was taking the liberty of studying your production records.'

'Were you indeed? I hope you found them to your satisfaction.'

'Do not take this amiss, Captain, but I believe there is something not quite right.'

'Not quite right? What can you mean, sir? Are you suggesting my clerks have got their sums wrong?'

'Oh no. It all adds up. In fact it all adds up a bit too well. All in a package and tied up with a pretty bow, so to speak.'

'Mr Watson, I know that mining is awash with knaves and villains but indeed I would take it very much amiss were you to imply that there is skulduggery afoot at Wheal Emma.'

'I am afraid I do believe I must risk your wrath and tell you that there is – not the usual sort, quite the reverse, in fact.'

'I am fascinated. Please continue.'

'Well, for the last three months certain figures, the exact same figures, keep re-appearing.'

'You find that strange?'

'Well, yes I do. You see I am collecting data on the quantity of metal in various minerals from different British mines. I have found that in nature the exact same number, and I stress the word exact, is not oft repeated. I do not know why this should be so, but from my observations at other mines it is invariably the case. Now, if you will check your figures you will find that certain quantities of ore, in tons and hundredweights, were raised not once or twice but on many different days. And I found the exact same thing with copper content – numbers re-occurring time and time again. It cannot be so. Nature is a most random thing, I promise you.'

Mathew strokes his chin, then says, 'So, if I understand you Mr Watson, my production figures have been tampered with.'

'I believe so. And not very cleverly. It was careless of whoever did it to repeat himself so often and give his game away.'

'Not so careless as you might think. I have studied these figures time after time and I could find no fault.'

'Ah but Captain Clymo, I suspect you were looking for arithmetical errors – there are none. What these numbers tell us is that somebody is making false entries either to overestimate or underestimate the amount of copper Wheal Emma is producing.'

Mathew is silent for a moment staring down at the little man. Then he grins, grabs his hand and pumps it. 'Mr Watson, you are a genius. I could not understand why my mine was losing money. Each day I visit each producing end, and just by looking I can tell if it is rich or poor – some are up or "kindly", as we miners say, and some are down. But they are never all up or all down together so the total copper brought to grass should stay more or less the same. And it has not. It has gone down. By God, when I catch the infernal villain who did this, I'll string the bugger from the bob plat.'

Yelloly Watson blinks and smiles at the profanity. 'And what would a villain gain from this?'

'Ha sir, I believe you know the answer.'

'I do indeed. The price of Cornish Great Consols has been much in the doldrums these last weeks. Which I confess was to my advantage, for I bought very cheap on Mr Sanderson's advice.'

'And now you'll reap a rich reward, of which, my friend, you deserve every penny.'

'Thank you. You know who did this, and why?'

'I have a very strong suspicion which will be simple to confirm. The ore is weighed and assayed each day as it comes to grass. On tribute day we pay the miners according to the copper they have mined. These figures are entered in the books by the ledger clerks. Now, either we have a conspiracy between the clerks or the person who takes the numbers from the assayer is feeding false numbers to them.'

'The latter seems more likely.'

'Indeed it does. I will say no more, Mr Watson, except that I cannot thank you enough.' He shakes his hand again. 'Now you must excuse me. I have matters to attend to.'

15

ARREST

GRACE, CLEARING PLATES AND GLASSES FROM THE table, watches Mathew stride across the room. How fine he looks dressed as a gentleman in black frock-coat and tie. And how easy he is with these fine London folk. She fingers the agate brooch – his mother's, he said it was.

He had stayed on after Thomas went back to bed. For a while they sat in silence and she was sure he would ask her for her hand, in spite of Thomas's command. And she would have assented, but now she wonders. How would she shift amongst her betters, amongst fine gentlemen like these? Just a bal maiden – always was and always will be.

Yet this is not true. Before John's death she had left it all behind and now again her callused hands are softening; her back and arms no longer ache from hours of breaking rock on the dressing floor. But she is still a servant and no lady. Plates piled high, she goes into the kitchen where Jenny Tuttle sits on a chair, eating beef and bread and drinking.

'Best not let the capun catch you,' Grace says.

'He'll not come in here while there's drinking to be done out there.'

'He ain't a drinking man, Jenny Tuttle and you knows it. It's his business to keep them gents contented.'

'Well they oughta be contented, what with our cookin' an' the mine cuttin' rich again.'

'If it weren't, we'd be in the poorhouse soon enough.'

'Me maybe, but not you. When you goin' to marry him?'

'He ain't asked me. Come on Jenny, leave that grog afore you get too drunk. We need to get the counthouse cleared before the boys come up to grass.'

Jenny slams the beaker down, gets to her feet and says, 'I ain't at all drunk.' She lurches to the door. Grace follows. The counthouse smells of cigars and men and drink and food.

Mathew turns and sees them, and calls across the room. ' I thank you, ladies, for a splendid dinner,' then he follows the last of the Adventurers outside.

'See, he calls us "ladies".' Jenny pats her hair, her blue eyes bright with drink.

'Get on with you. Here take hold.' They grasp the tablecloth with remnants of the feast inside and take it to the kitchen. Once the dishes are done, Grace scrubs the counthouse table while Jenny sweeps the floor.

'He didn't ask you to marry him last evening, then?'

'No, he didn't. I already said.'

A sharp rapping sounds on the counthouse door. Jenny opens it to see a policeman, billy club in hand and about to knock again. He wears a tall silk hat and high-collared black tunic with six brass buttons, the middle one of which is level with Jenny's nose. He looks down. 'I am Constable William Smale. I am looking for Thomas Pascoe.'

'What for?'

'He'll know what for. You been drinking, Missus?'

'So what if I have. Drinkin's no crime. 'Sides, it were our counthouse dinner.' She turns and yells, 'Grace, there's a constable at the door – lookin' for Thomas.'

Grace comes to the door and stands arms folded, staring at the policeman. 'What do you want with Thomas Pascoe?'

'Who are you?'

'I'm his mother, Grace Pascoe.'

'So where is he, Mrs Pascoe?'

Grace sniffs and wipes her nose with the back of her hand. 'I don't know. He went to Bodmin more'n a week ago. He ain't come back.'

'He was at a house in Bodmin on the afternoon of October the twenty-eighth where murder was committed. I have a warrant from the magistrate for his arrest.' Constable Smale takes out a paper from his tunic and shows it to Grace.

She keeps her arms folded, and says, 'No matter what's written there, my Thomas is never no murderer.'

'No he ain't,' Jenny says, 'he's . . .' Grace nudges her and Jenny says, 'I'm goin' indoors. I got work to do.'

But she goes straight through the counthouse into the kitchen and out the back door, behind the dry, and runs down the hill to the village, hair coming unpinned and apron flapping in the wind. At the Pascoe cottage she goes in without a knock, finds Thomas sitting at the table, hand splinted and a bandage round his head. His left eye is still closed, the bruising turned purplish green, but he peers at a book through his bloodshot right eye. The two little ones, Emily and James, sit on the floor in front of the unlit range playing with wooden dolls.

Breathless from her run, Jenny pants the words out, 'Tom, a constable at the counthouse . . . come to arrest you. Says you murdered a man in Bodmin.'

For several seconds Tom sits rigid, staring at her. Then he is on his feet, grabs his mining hat and bag from the peg behind the door, and is out, running up the hill. Before he turns the corner that would bring him in full view of the counthouse, he swings off right to the attle dump. Scrambling across the slope of broken rock and rubble, he ducks down into a gully between the attle dump and the hill. He limps now, his damaged arm hanging free. He works his way behind the engine house where Old Harry sits dozing on his stool.

Thomas creeps out on to the timbered flat atop the shaft and looks around – no one has seen him. He clambers on to the first rungs of the ladderway, gazes down into the darkness of the shaft, then clutching hat and satchel to his chest, he descends the ladder one-handed. Twelve rungs down his boots find footing on the first sollar. Here he stops, and taking tallow and lucifer from the bag he lights the candle and sticks it with dripping wax onto his hat. Easing the hat on to his bandaged head, he moves more quickly, his good hand slipping from rung to rung, down ladder after ladder, the falling water soaking him, the familiar taste of sulphur in his mouth. The core is nearly over. His workmates will be on their way up but he will reach 120 fathoms first, and hide himself in the dark place where his father died and no one works. Down, down, counting as he goes until he hears a shout from below; he almost slides down the last ladder to the sollar where he snuffs his candle out and ducks into the black entrance of the drive.

Feeling his way, back against the wall, good arm outstretched along it, he shuffles his way in utter darkness until he feels the wall bending away and there he squats facing the shaft.

He hears them first – the faint thump of boots on wooden rungs, their deep and steady breathing, a rattling cough and spitting and the occasional muttered 'Move up there, move up, get on, boy.' Then the tunnel mouth is outlined in a faint glow and there is the glimmer of a tallow on a hat with a man's head beneath it, which disappears upwards to be followed by another and another and another. Thomas wishes he were climbing with them, even more so when he sees the bulk of Henry Hopeful Down appear then disappear. He squats there staring, watching them, all eighty-seven of them, on their way to grass as dusk falls over the village. He is alone now, more alone than he has ever been, alone in the dark, listening to the fall of water in the shaft.

He lights his tallow, gets to his feet, and head bent walks into the darkness, remembering every inch of the passages that lead to the rock fall. How long must he hide? Will the constable dare to come down the mine? Surely not; surely he will go away when he finds no sign of him at home. And none will talk – or will they? He has no enemies amongst the miners and their families, the community is close-knit but if they hear he is a murderer – he feels again the crunch of his fist on the ruffian's nose and sees the Reverend Dippenden lying on the hearth. Was that his fault? – he knows so little of the law.

Thomas comes to the first fork and sees the arrow he scratched what seems an age ago. He follows the twists and turns until he reaches his father's mark on the crosscut wall, the circle with the cross below and an arrow – copper, just as in the book, the book now lost to him. Reaching the rock fall and the splintered timbers, he stops for a moment then scrambles up until his hat brushes the back and knocks his light askew. He takes another tallow from his bag, lights it from the other, and with drops of wax lodges it on a ledge in the wall.

Then, starting at the very top of the fall where it abuts the back, he begins one-handed to pull rocks out from the rubble. He throws them down to the floor behind him working with a steady rhythm – pull, lift and throw – pull, lift and throw. He keeps at this until, blocked by a rock too large for him to move one-handed, he sits back wiping sweat from his face. Sliding down the rock fall on his backside, he breaks off a split of timber from the fallen props, climbs back up, levers out the rock and watches as it tumbles down the slope. Dust trickles from a fissure in the roof, but Thomas carries on removing rubble until, to reach more loose rock he must lie on his stomach, his head and shoulders in the cavity he has created.

Finally exhausted, his fingers bleeding and his injured arm aching, he stops face down in the dirt. Wriggling backwards, he takes the tallow from the ledge and lies down with his back against the bottom of the slope. He folds the sodden felt of his hat, makes a pillow on a rock, lays down his head and sleeps.

'Thomas, wake up boy. Wake up.'

He starts awake, sees the face of Captain Clymo bent solicitously towards him. He sits up.

'I knew I'd find you here. Come Thomas, let's go back up. Your mother cries with worry for you.'

'How did you know I was here?'

'The engineman saw you going down.'

'You saw the constable?'

'I did.'

'And he told you?'

'Yes, he said a man was killed in Bodmin and you were there.' He squats beside him his hand upon Tom's shoulder. 'Is that true?'

Thomas nods.

'Then you must face the constable and tell him all.'

'I will not. I cannot.' He shakes his head.

'Thomas, you must. He is waiting in the village. You are trapped.'

'He knows I am here?'

'Yes.'

'Who told him?'

'I did.'

Thomas struggles to his feet. 'Why? Why did you tell him? You want me to go to gaol don't you, so you can be with my mother.' He hears the echo of his shout fade in the darkness of the tunnel – my mother, my mother, my mother . . .

'Thomas, you cannot run away. Whatever happened in Bodmin, you must face the consequences.'

'You cannot force me, Capun Clymo, you are not my father. I will stay here. I will die here where he died.' He sits again, lights the tallow in his hat and puts it on his head.

'That's just fool's talk, boy. Did you kill a man in Bodmin?'

'No.' He looks up at the mine captain. 'But I hit a man and another man died. They'll hang me so I might just as well die here.'

'No you will not, not here in my mine. You will come to grass with me, and let justice be done. Either now or when I return with the constable.'

'I'll not go with you.'

'Then stay. But I'll be back with a crew and if needs be we'll bind you and hoist you out like a bucket of attle.' Captain Clymo turns on his heel and ducking his head strides into the darkness.

Thomas sits for a while, head in his hands, listening to the fading crunch of the captain's boots. Then, getting to his feet, he turns and stands for a while looking up at the hole he has created at the top of the rock fall. He shrugs, picks up his mining bag and walks back down the crosscut towards the shaft. One-handed and one rung at a time, his climb is long and slow and difficult, but finally his head emerges from the shaft and he sees them waiting in the lee of the engine house: his mother, who starts forward, Henry Hopeful Down on one side and the captain on the other, holding her back – and the black-hatted constable who strides forward to face the wet, dejected boy.

'Thomas Pascoe, you are charged with the murder of the Reverend Dippenden at his house in Bodmin on Sunday October the eighth. What do you say?'

'I did not kill him, sir. I did not.'

'You must come with me. I am going to take you before Mr Lethbridge, the magistrate.'

'No, no, you shall not take him.'

He hears his mother's cry, turns towards her and would reach out. But the constable takes him by the arm, leads him to his horse-drawn gig and forces him to climb up.

'Come quietly now, Thomas Pascoe, or 'twill be the worse for you.'

16

THE THIEF

THE FAINT RED GLOW OF A DYING BONFIRE REFLECTS on the sloping ceiling of her attic room. They burned a Guy Fawkes effigy in the town square just after dusk and revellers kept her busy in the bar and parlour of the inn until late. At least she had no time to dwell on thoughts of Thomas Pascoe. She sits now on the edge of her bed, hands folded in her lap, holding back the tears. She wants to cry for him, just as she had wanted to cry when she heard they left him for dead up on the moor. But she didn't cry then nor will she now. Although this is worse – Bodmin Gaol.

Maisie has never seen it, never even been to Bodmin but she has heard – heard of its great stone walls, heard how the condemned are hanged on its gallows while thousands watch and laugh and jeer at the hanged man's horrid death. And Tom Pascoe, whom she would have kissed at his cottage door the last time she saw him, will hang for murder, so they say.

She hears talk of it downstairs in the bar and in the dining parlour. Serving breakfast to three gentleman off the Truro coach this very morning, she listened horror-struck as one unfolded the 'West Briton' at the table and read aloud the headline: 'Dreadful murder in Bodmin Town. Boy strikes Parson down'. Maisie Tuttle could not believe that this was true. None in Penpillick believed it either, or so her mother said. Why would Tom kill the man he went to see about his father's book?

The book, that was the key – surely the same book that William Scoble passed to the whiskered gent at supper. Again she'd tried to eavesdrop on their conversation but the hubbub in the bar was too loud, and a grinning Scoble sat head bent and muttered through his soup. But she could see he was cock-a-hoop. And Josiah Hocking made no secret of his satisfaction. He tapped the book as it lay beside his plate and suddenly above the din of other diners she heard him say, 'Don't worry Scoble, I have a mining friend in London who'll break this code with ease.'

They were drinking still when she left the parlour, a third bottle of claret between them. She knows that later when the man is abed in the room below hers, she'll hear his drunken snoring; she has heard it before. Maisie bites her lip and her pulse races as she thinks of what she plans to do. She unpins her cap, and her hair springs into red curls around her head like a halo in the candlelight. Then, slipping her nightgown over her day clothes, she kneels at the bedside and prays in a whisper only she can hear, her hands tight clasped and resting on the bed.

'Dear Lord help me save Tom from that dreadful place and from the hangman. Make me strong to do what I must. I know it is a sin to steal. So forgive me Lord for this, and all my sins.'

It is a long time before she hears his step on the stairs below, the rise and fall of the door latch and the creak of springs as he sits upon his bed. Her candle has guttered out. She waits alert now in the darkness, sitting up, her back against the bedhead. The springs creak once more, there is silence for a while and then it comes – the heavy snoring of a drunken man.

Maisie slips barefoot from her room, her button boots in one hand and a small carpet bag in the other. She creeps downstairs, treading carefully to miss the step that creaks, and stops outside his door. The snoring is at full pitch now, and she worries it will wake the landlord and his wife whose room lies down the passage, or Scoble in the room next-door. But she puts down her bag and boots and eases up the latch and opens the door, catching her breath at the stink of wine and sweat. Josiah Hocking's snoring is loud enough to rattle windows but nonetheless she gropes her way across the darkened room without a sound.

Hocking's travelling case was on the chest beneath the window when Maisie made up his bed that evening. She feels for the case beneath her outstretched hands and gently tries the lid. It opens but as it does so there is a slither and a thump as something slides against the panelled wall. Holding her breath, she turns back towards the bed where the snoring stops, then starts again to a slightly different rhythm.

She reaches across the suitcase lid and there it is – the book, resting against the wall. Picking it up, she creeps backwards, leaves the room and drops the latch without a sound. She lifts her nightgown over her head, wraps it around the book and puts them both in her carpet bag. Then, still barefoot Maisie Tuttle, a thief in the night, goes down the stairs and out through the kitchen, raiding the larder as she passes for half a veal-and-chicken pie left over by Tom's enemies, as now she knows them to be.

Out in the stable yard coach horses whicker to each other as she passes. She stops only to put on her boots and bonnet. The town is silent, save for the creak of the Fountain Hotel's sign as it swings in the wind. Maisie hurries now but does not run. She must be far from Liskeard by dawn when the hue and cry will start.

A bleary-eyed Josiah Hocking sits down at the breakfast table across from William Scoble. He looks with distaste at Scoble's plate of fried sprats. 'Did you take the book while I was sleeping?' he asks.

'The book? No, I did not.'

'Well, it's no longer in my room.'

Scoble lays down his knife and fork. 'You mean you've lost it?'

'No, I haven't lost it. It was in my room last night. Now it isn't.' He looks up as Mrs Mullins, the landlady of the Fountain Hotel, appears beside his chair.

'What will you have for breakfast, sir? We have kidneys, eggs, ham, kippers and sprats as you see.'

Hocking leans back in his chair and massages his belly. 'No sprats. Just egg and kidneys.'

'No parlour maid this morning, Mrs Mullins?' Scoble says.

'No sir. Maisie's disappeared. It's very strange. She's a good girl but she left in the night with her things. Trouble at home, mebbe. But she shouldn't have run off without a word.'

Hocking is about to speak but Scoble kicks him under the table, then asks, 'And where would her home be?'

'Penpillick, sir. She's a miner's daughter.'

'Is she now? And who would her father be?'

'I don't know, sir but her name is Tuttle, Maisie Tuttle. Why do you ask?'

'As you know, Mrs Mullins, I am the duke's agent and what goes on at that mine is a part of my responsibilities. So I have a natural interest in the people of Penpillick.'

Mrs Mullins nods. 'Well, I'd best be getting on with your breakfast, sir,' she says and leaves them.

'By God sir, you kicked me. How dare you?'

'I'm sorry, but you were about to tell her the girl has stolen the book.'

'Of course I was. We should send for the police.'

Scoble leans across the table and murmurs, 'No police, Mr Hocking, no police.'

'Why ever not?'

'Keep your damn voice down. We cannot accuse the girl of theft for the book is clearly Thomas Pascoe's – it bears his father's name. But never fear, I'll find the girl and get it back. That book's the key to the riches of the mine and one man has died for it already.'

'What? What man died?'

'The murder in Bodmin. There was a fight over the book.'

Hocking does not reply but looks around the parlour, then out of the window.

Turning back to Scoble he says in a low voice, 'I want no more of this Mr Scoble. A little share speculating is one thing but I do not wish to be involved in dirty deeds. Besides, Cornish Consols will soar once gossip from the counthouse dinner gets about the City. I'll not be able to talk it down again. The stock will reach thirty pounds I warrant, and I bought for you at eighteen. You should be content with that.'

'I'm not at all content, Mr Hocking. As I recall, it was our intent to gain control of Wheal Emma. We're within an ace of that.'

'We hold fifteen per cent between us and we'll need twenty. I'm afraid my pockets are not quite deep enough and I doubt yours are. As I said, I want no more of it.'

'But if it got about in London that you had bribed the Purser to cook the books?' Scoble spears the last two sprats on his plate and eats them.

'Do not attempt to blackmail me, William Scoble. Remember you gave me your authority to buy and sell on your behalf. What would your precious duke say if he were to discover his agent was queering Cornish Consols stock?'

'Let us not quarrel. I will get the book back and send it to you. Once we know its contents we can decide what we must do.'

Josiah Hocking shrugs. 'As you will, but I leave for Plymouth on the morning coach.'

Scoble rises from his chair, wiping his mouth with a napkin. 'I am leaving now. The girl will be on the road to Penpillick on foot. I'll catch her soon enough.'

'Then good day to you sir, and take care. Ah, Mrs Mullins, thank you.' The landlady places a large plate bearing two fried eggs and six fat fried kidneys leaking blood before him. He bends over the food and begins to eat.

'Good day to you, Mr Hocking. Mrs Mullins, have the boy saddle my horse and bring it to the front. I will be off directly.'

It is a cold, clear morning as William Scoble rides out of Liskeard. Nelson's hooves clatter on the cobbles and his breath steams in the frosty air. When they reach the packed earth of the lane to Pensilva, Scoble leans forward out of the saddle and slaps the horse's neck. 'We'll ride that bitch of a girl down boy, ride her down.'

The horse breaks into a canter, then a full gallop. Horse and rider fly down the lane, and Scoble expects every minute to see the slight figure of the girl in front of him. Surely she will be around the next bend – over that hedge – beyond this straight. But the lane remains empty, not a soul to be seen; after two miles Scoble eases back on the reins. 'Easy, Nelson, easy now,' and the horse slows to a trot, almost blown, its breath coming in great plumes, its withers sweat-darkened.

'For sure we'll find her at Penpillick,' Scoble mutters to himself but knows that wresting the book from her there will be less than easy.

Maisie sitting beside Bill Burrows on his cart, wraps her shawl tight around her and draws her skirt down to cover the tops of her boots. She knows the old hawker is watching her from the corner of his eye. He picked her up just as the rising sun was faintly warm on her shoulders and the roadside grass sparkled as the frost began to melt. She heard the slow clop of the carthorse and the creak of wheels in the otherwise silent valley long before, but she did not look round, just bent her head and hurried on. But as he drew level she could not help but look up at him.

'Good morning, maid, 'tis early to be out,' he called then stared at her.

'Good morning, sir,' she replied, and ducked her head sensing the warmth rising to her cheeks.

'I know you, don't I? You're from Penpillick. What you be doing so early and far from home? Whoa there.' Horse and cart stopped.

'I'm on my way to Bodmin, Mr Burrows.' She remembers him from the summer Saturday when he spread his wares on the green at the bottom of the village. She had wanted to buy ribbons for her hat but had no money. He comes to the village in the early spring and again in high summer and the bal maidens flock around his cart like anxious geese, spending their meagre earnings on ribbons and bonnets and, for those that can afford it, an ell of cloth for a bright new frock. But that summer Maisie could only look on with envy, for she was yet to start at the Fountain Hotel and had no money of her own.

'That's a tidy step. Climb up, maid, and ride with me.'

He leaned down with outstretched hand. She put one booted foot on the side of the cart and her cold hand in his and stepped up. And now she sits beside him on a bale of cloth on the road to Bodmin, with her bag on her knees. Pots, pans, household goods and farm tools clink and rattle in the well of the cart behind her. His clothes smell of wood smoke and she guesses he spent the night beside the road.

'So what takes you to Bodmin Town?'

Maisie purses her lips. She dare not reply that it is Tom Pascoe whom she is going to see. The hawker knows everything about everybody and has surely heard that Tom is accused of murder. So she tells the first lie that comes into her head. 'I'm to fetch my auntie from the poorhouse, take her home to live with us.'

'Are you now?' The hawker gives her a sideways glance.

Sensing his disbelieving eyes upon her, she stares at the road ahead. It is a foolish lie. She does have an auntie, her mother's only sister but she lives in Looe, married to a fisherman. They ride on, and the steady clop of the horse's hooves, the sun on her back and the soft jingle of the harness lull her into a doze.

'Wake up, maid. There lies Bodmin.' Maisie wakes with a start, jerking her head off his shoulder, and there indeed is the town spread out below them.

'Poorhouse lies t'other side of Beacon Hill but there's the gaol.' He points to where a great grey stone building looms over the town. 'They tell me the Pascoe boy from Penpillick is locked up in there for murder. He wouldn't be a friend of yours now, would he?'

Maisie stares at her boots, saying nothing but the blush on her cheeks tells the hawker all he needs to know. 'So,' he says, 'you're sweet on him. I guessed as much.'

Maisie nods, then speaks in a near whisper, not looking up. 'He never did it, sir, not Tom Pascoe. I knowed him since we was little. He never hurt a fly. I have to help him.'

The hawker, one hand on the reins strokes his chin. 'Listen maid, you want to see that boy of yours, you find the warder, John Verran. He's a straight man. Tell him Bill Burrows sent you. He'll remember me and he'll help you if he can. Come now, I'll drop you in the town for I'll ride straight through. Them shopkeepers have no time for Bill Burrows – not like country folk.'

He clicks to the horse, 'Walk on now,' and the cart rolls slowly into Bodmin Town. They stop again at the top of Crockwell Street and there he lets her down, handing her her bag. 'Down there, maid, and turn to your left you'll see the prison on the hill. Good luck now.'

'Thank you Mr Burrows, sir.'

Maisie plods to the end of the cobbled street, footsore after her night walk, then sees the clustered buildings of the gaol looming above her on the hillside. She stops to stare, then carries on until she stands before great double doors set in an unbroken wall. She is not alone. An old woman sitting on a three-legged stool by a brazier is selling hot pasties. The smell of meat and onions remind her that she has not eaten. Two roughly dressed men lounge against the wall and stare openly at her. She is at a loss what to do next.

A shadow falls across her and a quiet voice asks, 'Well now, Maisie, what you doin' here, maid?'

17

BODMIN GAOL

HE STANDS BACK AGAINST THE CELL DOOR LOOKING up at the barred window high in the opposite wall. He cannot see the sun or the sky, just the light penetrating the gloom of his cell. He lays a hand on the wall, runs his fingers over the rock – purple killas quarried close to granite, he knows it just by feel. He listens to the drip of water in the stone corridor; he is beneath the ground and almost comfortable; this dank dark place itself holds no fears for him. Given a hammer, a length of steel and powder, he'd tunnel out. But that would solve nothing. They think, they say, he murdered the Reverend Dippenden.

Brought to his hearing at Bodmin's Shire Hall, Thomas Pascoe stood handcuffed in the dock below Mr Lethbridge and two more justices of the peace. Head down, he glanced around the courthouse, intimidated by the finest building he had ever seen: wood panelled with fine wood benches, the magistrates above him gazing out over their domain. The public balcony was full and from the body of the courthouse wigged lawyers looked up at him or consulted amongst themselves.

'On Sunday afternoon, October twenty-eighth, were you at the house of Reverend Dippenden?' Mr Lethbridge asked.

'Yes sir.'

'Why were you there?'

'The Reverend was my father's friend. I took him my father's book to help me understand it.'

'Were you alone?'

'No sir, I was with Mr Carew but he left for his dinner.'

'So you were alone.'

'Yes sir, but then two men came in. They tried to steal my book.'

'Who were these men?'

'I do not know. They had covered up their faces.'

'Then what happened?'

Thomas bowed his head. He could not answer.

'Answer, boy!'

Without looking up he said, 'I hit one man, he fell back and knocked the Reverend off his chair. The Reverend struck his head when he fell…and died.' The last words were just a whisper. He looked up, tears trickling down his cheeks, and watched the magistrates confer then stare at him.

'Call Rebecca Grose.'

He watched her mount the witness stand across the court. She did not look at him. She was dressed in black but for a white mob cap fringed with lace. What will she say, he wondered. She swore on the bible as requested by the clerk and began her evidence.

'You were housemaid for the Reverend Dippenden?' Mr Lethbridge asked.

'No, your Worship. I were cook.'

'Housemaid or cook, just tell us what happened that afternoon – in your own words, now.'

'It was afternoon your Honours. The prisoner there come in with Mr Carew but Mr Carew left soon after. Then he was alone with the dear Reverend, God rest his soul. I took him bread and meat which he stole when he ran away. And he stole the Reverend's book.'

'She lies, sir. That is untrue.'

'Silence, Thomas Pascoe, silence. Were they alone?'

'Yes, your Worship.'

'Did anyone else enter the room?'

'No, your Worship.'

Thomas drew breath, stared at her and clenched his fists.

'You are sure?'

'Yes, your Worship.'

'Then what happened?'

'I heard a cry, so I went into the room and saw the Reverend lying on the floor and that boy standing there with blood on his hands.'

That was just yesterday and, as he recalls horror of it, his fists clench again but this time of their own accord. He feels once more the dreadful sinking in his stomach, sits down on the wooden cot, head in his hands. Why did she lie, what harm had he ever done to her? The magistrate has committed him to the next assize in three weeks' time, where they will surely find him guilty and he will hang. He feels tears welling behind his eyelids and shakes his head. There must be a way. He is not guilty, not of murder; it was an accident, he cannot hang.

But who will vouch for him? His mother? Of course she would, but she has no weight with these fine people. Capun Clymo? Yes – he will swallow his pride and call on him for help, for all that he cannot bear the capun's feelings for his mother. Surely the magistrate would take his word. And what of Richard Carew? He could tell them that the book was his and the maid was lying. But he was not in the court yesterday and as a lawyer, surely he would have heard what they were saying in the town – that he, Thomas Pascoe, murdered the Reverend Dippenden. Thomas groans aloud.

'Silence in the cells.' the warder's cry echoes in the stonework.

'What ails you, boy? What you in for?' The whispered voice comes from the shadows of the corridor. 'I'se your neighbour. Saw them bring 'ee down. What you done, boy?'

'I'm up for murder but it was an accident, I swear,' he whispers back.

'They all say that but tis no defence. You mun' get some one to talk up for 'ee. Don't you know no gentlemen?'

'I do but how should I get a message to them?'

'Can you write?'

'I can.'

'Then ask for pen and paper and send your letter to Governor Everest. He's a fair man. He let me off the treadwheel when I took sick. Hush now, here comes warder back again.'

The sound of hobnailed boots on granite floors rattles down the corridor. Thomas bangs on his door and peers out through the grille. 'Warder, sir, I will write a letter please.'

The footsteps stop outside his cell, a moustachioed face peers in

127

and Thomas steps back. 'You need the governor's permission, boy. I will ask for you but cease your chatter with your sheep-stealing neighbour. He's lucky not to hang. Ain't that right you blackguard, Sloat?'

'If you says so Mr Verran, if you says so.'

''Tis croust time now besides. Ain't that what you miners call it?'

'Yes sir.' Thomas hears the rattle of a tin pail and the clatter of plates. His door is opened by the warder. An aproned crone hands him a bowl of gruel, a slab of bread. He sits and realises he is hungry. The cell door slams, bolts are shot across top and bottom. He spoons in the slop and wipes clean the bowl with bread and chews upon the rest. It tastes of stale and musty flour but he doesn't care. He has some hope now, something he can do.

He begins the letter in his head – 'Dear Captain Clymo . . .'

18

HENRY HOPEFUL DOWN

 HE IS NOT SURPRISED TO SEE YOUNG MAISIE AT THE gates of Bodmin Gaol. Not that it's common knowledge in Penpillick that she is sweet on the boy, but Henry has a more than casual interest in anything to do with Thomas Pascoe. He wishes now that John Pascoe hadn't spoken as he did that summer evening five months ago.

But they'd been friends since starting down Wheal Emma on the selfsame day. At first six months they were a pare, a team, tributers who bid on pitches, the best of which they often won – although just how John knew how much to bid Henry didn't understand. When Henry caught the smallpox and was all but given up for dead, John Pascoe still shared a portion of his tribute money with him though Jethro Loam became his partner. But after two months, revolted by his drinking, John broke the partnership with Jethro; from then on John Pascoe bid and worked his pitches all alone. And when to everyone's surprise Henry Hopeful Down recovered, badly scarred of course, yet fit and strong, he thought to work with John again.

John Pascoe said, 'I'm sorry Henry, but I'm used to being solitary now, won't have it any other way.' So Henry took to tutwork, not having any feel for the hidden ways of copper lodes himself.

But they stayed good friends and on that summer's eve, watching the water tumbling beneath the bridge, John Pascoe said, 'Should aught happen to me, Henry, would you keep an eye on that boy o' mine?' And Henry promised that of course he would but what did John think might happen to him?

'Down there alone, you never know.'

Henry said, 'So take me as your partner, if just for safety's sake.'

'If I was to have a partner, Henry, be certain you'd be that man. Perhaps I will one day, but not just yet.'

Later, standing at John Pascoe's grave, he recalled his promise and, looking across at Grace and her children, felt it weigh heavy on him. Those first weeks when Thomas started down the bal, Henry looked out for him, taught him what he could – though he was no skilled prospector for copper ore. He watched him, too; had happened to be abroad that night when he saw the boy go down the shaft alone; he'd followed him unseen but waited on the 120 fathom sollar, supposing he sought the place of his father's death to grieve. He waited until he saw Tom's light return then climbed quickly up to grass, not wanting to face the boy and have him think he cared too much.

Henry had watched from the shadows of the engine house then followed Thomas home, but stopped short, glimpsing the figure of Jethro Loam lurking beneath the lighted cottage window. He stayed hidden across the street until he saw Loam slink away. He was tired by then, went back to his own cottage where he lived alone, and next day worked in his garden digging potatoes and storing them in straw beneath his bed. From that time on he tried to watch both Jethro Loam and Thomas Pascoe; but many nights after a full day core down the mine, the climb to grass and doing for himself at home, exhaustion took him.

Standing before the gates of the gaol now, he wishes that he had followed Thomas here to Bodmin that Sunday. But the first he knew that Tom had left Penpillick was when he heard that Capun Clymo had found him injured up on the moor. He visited him next evening, sat by his bed as the boy muttered in his sleep – but Henry felt quite useless, felt he'd failed his promise to his father.

Henry was deep underground, shaft sinking with Tuttle, Loam and Jakeh James, when Thomas fled to the fatal crosscut. Later he watched, helpless, as the constable arrested him. But that evening, sitting with Grace Pascoe as she wept, Henry vowed to do all he could to help – yet not knowing what that might be.

Next day he cornered Jethro Loam alone at croust time, grabbed him by the throat and held him up against the face. Loam's hat and tallow fell to the floor, his reddened drinker's face illuminated by Henry's light.

'Tell me Loam, what happened to the boy in Bodmin?' he said through gritted teeth.

'Let me down you filthy oaf. How would I know? I been here all the time. You knows it. We work together and you been following me enough.'

He squeezed the skinny neck. 'You tell me what you know. I seen you following the boy.'

'I'll tell 'ee but let me down,' wheezed Loam.

Henry lowered him and Loam squatted in the darkness, gasped and rubbed his throat. 'He's got a book. There's men in Bodmin wants it. That's all I know.'

'And what of William Scoble? You went to him the night that Thomas went to Bodmin.'

'I did not. I were poachin' on the duke's estate. You want to know more, go to Bodmin your own damn self.'

Henry left him then but followed his advice not knowing what else to do. Even this he could ill afford – he'd lose many days of tutwork and there'd be little money at this month's end. He'd have to eat potatoes.

So, after walking all night, here he is towering over Maisie Tuttle and staring up at the stone walls of Bodmin Gaol. He looks around. It is a bleak and ragtag group that hangs about the prison. An old woman is seated on a stool before a brazier. She calls out now and then 'Hot pasties, tuppence each, hot pasties.' Two ruffians lounge against the wall; a few women, poorly dressed, gossip by the postern gate; three urchins throw stones at the flock of rooks that hop and peck in the rubbish that lies in drifts beneath the wall. At each thrown stone the rooks fly up, circle cawing, swooping and turning in the updraft from the wind against the wall then land again to resume their hunt for something edible.

Henry wishes he were back in Penpillick. The day is already clouded over and the wind carries spits of rain. Maisie, clutching her bag in both hands, looks up at Henry Hopeful Down from beneath her bonnet. 'I come to help Thomas,' she says.

'As did I – but I know not how. Tis a terrible lookin' place. Don't like to think on young Tom bein' in there. Will they let us in to see 'un, maybe?

131

'I come partway from Liskeard on Bill Burrow's cart. He told me to find a warder called John Verran. He would help me, so he said.'

'But how do we find him if we can't get in?'

'Why not ask her? She must know who comes and goes.' Maisie gestures towards the pasty seller.

Henry walks over. 'Mornin' missus. There is a boy, a prisoner here. The maid's his sweetheart. How would a body get to see him?'

She looks up at him then across at Maisie. 'You two breakfasted?' He shakes his head.

'Buy two pasties and I'll tell 'ee. Four pence that'll be.' She holds out a grimy hand.

Henry fumbles in his pocket and passes her the coins. She unwraps a cloth in her basket, takes out two pasties, hands them to him and says, 'Ye cain't see nobody in there,' she lowers her voice. 'But there's a turnkey who'll mebbe take a letter.'

'Would that be John Verran?'

She looks up at him and cackles. 'So you knows already. Give us tuppence, I'll give your letter to him.'

'We ain't writ it yet.'

'Well, come back at dusk when the turnkeys change. You can give it to him yerself when he comes out – if he likes the look of 'ee, that is.'

'How will we know him?'

'He's a big fella, almost as big as you. You cain't miss 'un.' She laughs again.

'Thank you missus, and here's your tuppence.' He gives her two more pennies.

'Make sure you tell John Verran a sad old story. He may be big but he's soft at heart, that one.'

Henry smiles and goes back to Maisie. 'She says John Verran will take a letter in.' He hands her a pasty. 'Hope you're hungry, maid, I am. Tis the smell o' taters and onions.'

'I ain't eat proper since yesterday but I'd as lief not eat here.' She stares at the two louts who lounge against the wall. They have watched the whole exchange and mutter to one another. She turns away and says. 'Mebbe we should find some lodging in the town where I can write the letter.'

Henry nods. 'Come on then, maid.' He takes her by the elbow. As they walk back towards the town, Henry glances back at the gaol. One of the ruffians is squatting in front of the pasty seller talking to her.

They find room in separate dormitories at a common lodging house on the Lostwithiel road. At a shilling a night it is as much as either can afford. Maisie finds a place at the table in the noisy day room. She wrinkles her nose at the stink of unwashed bodies, dirty feet and cheap perfume. Men in battered working clothes and women, some in rags and some in tattered finery, sit on benches or stand around in groups. She takes out the pencil and paper which cost her sixpence in the town, and begins to write.

A black-haired, painted bawd stands at her shoulder and yells across the room, 'Look here girls, this maid can write. To yer lover is it, dearie?'

Maisie bends her head and covers the paper with her arm, too shy to speak.

'Leave her be, she's but a child,' a woman calls. She is dressed in mob cap and a ragged cloak, with a baby at her breast.

'Old enough to work the street. How about it, dearie?' the painted woman says.

A sullen line of men seated on a bench against the wall look up at this. One says, 'She is that.'

'Touch her and I'll break your neck.' Henry Hopeful Down shouts as he ducks through the doorway and pushes through the crowd. 'She's my friend.'

'And who might you be, big fellow?' asks the bawd.

'I'm a miner from Penpillick and Maisie's a miner's daughter. So leave us be.'

The woman shrugs, sits on the bench beside the men and whispers in one's ear. He looks at Maisie and shakes his head. Maisie bends to her writing still covering it with one arm.

Henry lowers himself on to the bench beside her. 'What you saying to him, Maisie?' he whispers.

'That I am here with you in Bodmin,' she whispers back then looks up at him. 'That I have his book.'

'His book? Jethro Loam said summat about a book. Why is it so damned important?'

Maisie looks around the room and mutters, 'I don't know. His father wrote it about Wheal Emma. It were stolen here in Bodmin then Mr Scoble had it at the Fountain. So I . . . I took it back and ran away, came here. I thought to give it back to Tom but if I can't see him I can't. I dursen't send it to him in the gaol.'

Henry scratches his head. 'No, you mun' do that. But ask him what we can do. Best you take the letter to the warden by yourself. More like to touch his heart, you alone.'

She bends to her writing again. Henry gazes round the room. He's been in a place like this before in Plymouth – part lodging, part a bawdy house. But those times he visited with purpose. He eyes the black-haired bawd then shrugs. Not this time – he has this pretty maid to care for.

'Come with me to the gaol at least,' she whispers, as she folds the letter and puts it in an envelope. 'I'm frightened to go alone.'

'I will, but I'll leave you by the gate till Mr Verran comes. I'll watch you, don't you worry. Are you ready now?'

She nods, takes up her carpet bag from beneath the bench and follows in Henry's wake across the room.

Outside, it's almost dusk and raining hard. Heads bent they hurry down the road to town then out again towards the gaol. Twice Henry looks back, feeling that they are followed. At the open space before the prison walls he turns full around and stares back but sees no one.

'I'll wait over by the walls,' he says. 'You wait by the gate. The pasty woman said John Verran's near as big as me, so you'll know him.'

She holds out her bag and says, 'Here, take this. Look after it. The book's inside.'

Henry takes the bag. 'Good luck, Maisie.' He wanders off towards the wall, suddenly aware how odd he now appears carrying a woman's floral-patterned carpet bag. The rain has reduced to a thin drizzle blowing in the wind. He squats with his back against the wall and the bag between his knees wondering at its weight. Barely aware of what he is doing he unbuttons the clasp, opens up the bag and looks inside. He sees the leather spine of the book. He lifts it out and turns it in his hands. But Henry cannot read so he puts it back unopened, closes up the bag and tucking it beneath his knees leans back and closes his eyes. Tiredness catches up with him, his head droops, he dozes.

Maisie eyes the little group of women before the postern gate, some with food and others empty handed. Three wardens wearing blue serge and caps are waiting to go in. There is a commotion and the women surge forward as the postern gate swings open and three more warders come out. They ignore the women, pause briefly to chat to their colleagues then stride away from the prison towards the town. The women plead with the warders going in, one holds out a cloth-wrapped parcel, another a ragged blanket, but they are ignored again and the postern gate clangs shut. Maisie looks across to where Henry Hopeful Down sleeps against the wall, hesitates then hurries after the departing turnkeys. The tallest of the three, who must be John Verran, turns down a side street and Maisie has to fairly run to catch him just as he reaches the door of his terraced cottage.

'Sir, sir, may I speak with you?' she calls to his back.

He stops, turns around and stares down at her. 'Hello pretty miss.'

Maisie looks up from beneath her bonnet and says, 'Are you Mr John Verran, sir?'

'I am. And who are you?'

'Sir, Mr Burrows said you'd help me. I am a friend of Thomas Pascoe from Penpillick. They says he's in your gaol.'

'Not my gaol, my dear. Thomas Pascoe? Now – what would you be wanting with a murderer?'

Maisie flushes and looks down at her boots. 'He ain't no murderer, sir.'

'That's as maybe. He'll be up before judge and jury week after next and they'll decide. I suppose you'll be wanting me to take a letter to him.'

'Yes, I do. How did you know?'

135

'You're not the first and I don't suppose you'll be the last.' He sighs. 'You know it's against the prison rules?'

'No sir, I don't know nothing about prison. But Mr Burrows said you're a kindly man, and I must help my Thomas.'

'And will your letter help him?'

'Yes – I don't know. There is a book – and evil goings on and bad men who wish him ill. I do not understand, sir, but if he knows that I am here in Bodmin, he will tell me what to do.' She takes the letter from her bodice and holds it up. 'Please sir.' There are tears in her eyes.

John Verran slips the letter into the inside pocket of his jacket. 'He'll have it tomorrow morn, my dear, so no need to cry. You'd best be on your way now. Tis almost dark and young maids should best not be out alone at night in Bodmin Town.'

'Thank you Mr Verran sir, thank you.' Maisie turns and hurries back towards the gaol.

'Ugly bugger's asleep. Let's take him now. The bloody book we stole is in the bag.'

The ruffians keeping watch over the comings and goings at the gaol are Scoble's men, They have spent their day lurking in the alleyways of Bodmin, following Maisie and Henry Hopeful Down. They watched as Henry took the book from Maisie's bag and nodded to each other. Now, their eyes fixed on the dozing figure against the wall, they edge closer.

But Henry is not asleep. Like many of his fellow miners he has learned to catnap, apparently asleep yet still aware, meanwhile sloughing off the tiredness brought on by night work. He watches their approach through half-closed lids. They dart towards him but Henry's on his feet, back to the wall, fists up and the bag behind him. 'Come on then, boys, who's first?'

They stop, look up at him, then at one another, shrug and saunter off.

'Come near me or the girl again, I'll break your necks,' Henry shouts to their retreating backs. He shakes his head. These men are part of something he doesn't understand.

If only he could only read the book perhaps he might. He takes it out again but this time opens it. Even he can see that they are not ordinary words that fill the pages. He sighs and puts it back, and looking up sees Maisie walking towards him.

'Did the warden take the letter?' he asks.

'Yes. He said Thomas will have it in the morning.'

'That's good. At least he'll know he ain't alone.'

19

LETTERS

 THOMAS WAKES TO THE SOUND OF CLANKING PAILS and the thud of his neighbour's door closing. Grey dawn light seeps through the grille high above him and he sits up and places his bare feet on the floor. He scratches the welts and lumps on his skin where lice and bedbugs have fed on him in the night. Yet in spite of this, in spite of everything, he slept well. He draws breath, taking in the familiar dankness of life beneath the ground and the faint wheaty odour of hot breakfast gruel that penetrates even here. The top and bottom bolts of his cell door are shot free and there stands Warder Verran, the crone beside him bailing his breakfast slop into a tin bowl.

'Morning, boy. Seems you have a friend outside the walls, your sweetheart maybe, a pretty red-haired lass?'

'Maisie Tuttle here, in Bodmin?' Tom jumps to his feet.

'She didn't tell me no name but she give me a letter – here.' Warder Verran holds out a small wooden tray on which is a sheet of paper, a quill, a tiny pot of ink and a letter. 'The Governor's feeling generous too so you may write. But take care of what you say, for he will read your letter afore it can be sent.'

'Be sure I will, sir. Thank you sir, I thank you with all my heart.'

He takes the tray and lays it on his cot then takes the bowl of gruel in both hands and sits and eats as the cell door is closed and locked. He eyes the letter on the tray, wondering at the presence of Maisie Tuttle outside the walls. He remembers the look she gave him that evening before he set out for Bodmin. He is cheered now by the thought of her so close and, with an unfamiliar sense of longing, picks up her letter. It has been opened and read, perhaps by Governor Everest, but he does not care. He takes out the single sheet with shaking fingers. The writing is the childish scrawl that he and Maisie first learned at the dame school when they were together there as children.

Dear Tomas,

I am here in Bodmin. I have come to bring to you your book which Mr Scoble did give to a gent in the Fountain Hotel. I took it when the gent was asleeping. I know I did wrong to steel but I did it for you as I knows that this book is dere to you and I herd that it was stol from you on the road. Pleese if you can write me sayin what I must do. I will wait outside the prison every day with Mr Henry Hopefull Down who looks out for me most careful.

    Your lovin frend,

    Maisie Tuttle.

Suddenly he sobs. Tears stream down his cheeks and on to the letter, blurring the ink then dripping into the remnants of his breakfast gruel. He feels the weight of Bodmin gaol bearing down on him as if it were the weight of the law. He remembers the dread he felt when first he saw the great stone walls, how he would have turned and run if Constable Smale had not gripped his arms as the gate swung open and thrust him through.

Now Maisie Tuttle and friendly Henry Hopeful Down wait outside the walls in hope. He will get word to them with messages for his mother and a plea to Capun Clymo to speak for him at the assize. Thomas will beg his help, and hide his feelings against the man who would supplant his father. He lays the letter beside him on his cot, wipes his eyes and puts his tin bowl on the floor. He takes the tray upon his knee and begins to write, slowly at first, raising the quill off the paper, dipping it in the ink – something he has not done for a long time now, but has not forgotten. He remembers his father's neat hand, the symbols in the book and the sound of the quill scratching on the paper as his father wrote and sketched each evening.

He writes:

My Dear Maisie,

How happy I am that you have come. It is a great comfort to know that you and Mr Down are out there beyond these stone walls which imprison me. But I think it best that you return to Penpilick as fast as you can and do not dally in Bodmin for you have that thing which is precious to me. Keep it very safe and hidden for it was for this thing that I am now here charged with murder . . .

He stops writing, brushing the feather across his lips as he thinks.

He would write more about the Book but the Governor will read these words. They say he is a good man but Thomas does not know how the law works, who is against him and who might be for him, if there are indeed such persons. He continues:

Please give this letter to Captain Clymo as I have written to him also as you will see over this page. And give my affectionate love to my dear Mother and also my greetings and thanks to Mr Down.

    Maisie you are a comfort to me.

He signs his name, wishing he dare say more, wanting say he loves her – for surely that is what this longing is – his need to see her, her face framed in red curls tilted up at his. He takes a deep breath, gets off the cot and paces round his cell. Is fifteen old enough? If he is old enough to hang then he must be old enough to love. Perhaps this same longing is what Captain Clymo feels for his mother. He shakes his head at the very thought but sits again, takes up the tray and turns the page and slowly, hesitantly, begins to write again:

Dear Captain Clymo,

I have been charged with the murder of the Reverend Dippenden and will be tried at the assize here in Bodmin on the 19th of November. As I told you in the mine on the day that they arrested me I am innocent. The Reverend's maidservant has borne false witness against me. I do not know why. I beg your help to clear my name. If you could find a certain Mr Carew who is a lawyer here in Bodmin he may also vouch for me as it was he who took me to the Reverend's house that Sunday afternoon. He too knows of my father's book. I beg you Captain Clymo to help me . . .

He stops writing, quill poised and gazes round his cell. Then with a deep sigh dips the quill in the ink and continues:

. . . for the sake of my dear Mother.

Your humble servant

Thomas Pascoe (miner)

20

THE LAWYER

HE SITS IN THE CHAIR BY THE RANGE IN THE candlelight watching her bathing Emily and little James. Soon they will be his stepchildren. He will take them on his knee, tell them bedtime stories and when they are asleep he'll be alone with Grace. He watches as she dries their sturdy little bodies, slips nightgowns on them, then shoos them up the stairs.

'I'll come up my babes, come up when you're abed.' She feels his gaze, looks round at him and wipes her brow with the back of her hand then smiles. A surge of happiness, love and simple lust makes him catch his breath and he feels a grin stretch almost from ear to ear. He would fain take her now but he respects her word. 'I'll not marry you nor lie with you till I get my Thomas back,' she said when he proposed.

So tonight he must ride. It is three days since Maisie Tuttle brought the letter from Bodmin Gaol. He now believes the boy is innocent, just as Grace has so passionately declared. And it was Scoble's men who half killed Thomas and stole the book that Grace has shown him and now lies on the table. He has studied it page by neatly written page, but though he knows it for what it is, a record of John Pascoe's observations in his mine – he can make little sense of it. They are cutting rich but he cannot be sure how long the new lode will hold. Now, if he understood the book which doubtless guided that subtle miner's eye – ahh then, perhaps he could be confident in the continued richness of his mine.

He has yet to challenge Scoble – even though he now knows it was the agent who put Pryor up to falsifying the mine accounts and nearly did for Cornish Consols. No, he will keep his powder dry; Scoble's time will come when Mathew lays proof before the duke.

Tonight he has more urgent business. He must find this lawyer Carew. Yesterday he sought him in Bodmin but returned in haste hearing that the man had gone to London the day after the Reverend Dippenden's untimely death. Tonight, now, as soon as he can tear himself away from this sweet domestic scene he will ride to Tavistock and then across the moor to Moretonhamstead and thence down to Exeter. In the morning he will take the train to London. There he'll seek out Richard Carew and bring him back to bear witness for Thomas Pascoe at the assize. He will bear witness too, and perhaps the combination of their pleading will save Thomas from the hangman. He will move heaven and earth to help prove the boy is innocent – for only then will Grace Pascoe marry him. He sighs and gets to his feet.

'Grace, I must leave. I must ride to Exeter tonight to catch the *Flying Dutchman* which will have me in London tomorrow night. We have but a week before the trial.'

She listens to the hoof beats fading in the distance, sits in the chair still warm from him and knows she has chosen rightly. Besides, what else could she have done? She has no one else to turn to. Mathew Clymo is a man of substance, accepted amongst the gentry even though he was once a miner. His word at the assize will carry weight and this is what fills her mind – her son, her Thomas, alone in Bodmin gaol, that place of doom where he will hang unless fine folk speak up for him.

She and John Pascoe had such hopes for him. They said he was quick at school – it came easily to him the writing, reading, reckoning. How proud she was. How proud his father was. 'He's a scholar now, Grace, who knows what he might become – an engineer like Master Trevithick or even a Gentleman.'

Tears fill her eyes. She lets them flow now that she is alone but weeps silently, staring into the embers in the grate. She could not bear to lose him, not so soon, not ever. She sees again the broken body of his father, feels again that heartbreak that rests so heavily at the bottom of her soul. Then she cannot help but see her Thomas, twisting, kicking at the end of the hangman's rope. She has never seen a hanging but she has heard tell. She wraps her arms about herself as her body heaves with almost noiseless sobs so deep she feels her heart must stop. With a juddering sigh she brings her crying to an end. It does not help, it will not free Thomas from the gaol. Only Mathew Clymo can help with that and she must wait for his return.

She must have faith in him, she tells herself. He loves her with a passion. She sees it in his eyes and she could love him too she thinks, given time. And once his words, his help, his influence have bought freedom for her son, Grace will marry him as she has promised. He held her as she wept the day that Thomas was arrested, then walked her to her cottage door.

'Marry me,' he said, 'and I can help you.' She stared at him through tears coursing down her face, then shook her head and shut the door.

But next day in the counthouse she made her promise to him. And she will keep it even though she knows her son resents him so and will not accept him as a father. But it is to Mathew Clymo that he too has turned for help, his pride forgotten – so perhaps he will grow to like the man whom she will marry. She shrugs, gets up from the chair and climbs the stairs to her sleeping children.

Monday morning and a well breakfasted and much refreshed. Mathew Clymo stands outside the Great Western Royal Hotel. He is conspicuous amongst the crowd of top-hatted and frock-coated men waiting for hansom cabs to take them to their business in the city, dressed as he is in the riding coat and boots he wore for the ride to Exeter on Sunday night. He stretches to ease his back which still aches from six hours of a bone shaking, high speed train ride. 'Sixty five miles an hour!' a fellow passenger bellowed in his ear as the *Flying Dutchman* roared and rattled its way to Paddington. He draws breath, his nostrils flaring at the stink of coal smoke that, mingling with the morning's mist, turns the Praed Street traffic almost ghostly. Finally his turn comes and a street urchin shouts 'This way, sir, this way, this one's yours,' and guides him to a cab. He gives the boy a penny as he climbs up into the cab.

'Where to, mister?' the cabbie calls.

'Lambeth Palace.' They told him in Bodmin that Richard Carew was gone to London on some legal matter for the church – so that's where he might find him or at least start looking. They swing out into the traffic and at a smart trot head off through Bayswater and down beside

Hyde Park. They cross the river at Vauxhall then follow the river up to Lambeth Palace. The cabbie pulls up at the gatehouse where Mathew asks after Richard Carew.

'Be a Cornish gent like you then, would 'e?' the porter replies.

Mathew nods, 'That's him. Is he still here?'

'Fraid he's gorn, sir, yesterday.'

'Back to Cornwall?'

'I wouldn't know sir, but I can ask if you can wait.' The porter disappears inside the palace and Mathew waits beside the cab. He takes his watch from his waistcoat pocket and checks the time – near mid-morning already. He needs to find his man today if they are to start their journey back tomorrow. It is half an hour before the porter reappears. 'Sorry I was so long but they was all at prayer. Clerk to the Archbishop says your Mr Carew has business at the Inns of Court today.'

'And where might they be?'

'Across the river, sir, Temple Lane.'

So Mathew climbs back into the cab and with a jingle of harness they clatter across the cobbles away from the river. He wonders where he is being taken until they swing north into Blackfriars Road and cross the bridge. He gazes out at the river, amazed at the sight of a paddle steamer thrashing its way upstream, shouldering aside the barges their sails slack in the still and smoky morning. The cab turns on to the Embankment then into Temple Lane and stops. The cabbie raps on the roof.

'Which Inn will it be sir?'

'I have no idea,' Mathew calls.

'Best alight then, sir. It'll be around here somewhere. That'll be two shilling sir, and another shilling for the wait.'

Mathew fishes in his pocket for coins and passes them up to the cabbie. Looking around he finds himself in a small square surrounding a lawned garden. A wigged and gowned lawyer is seated on a bench, leafing through sheafs of papers. On the bench next to him sits another reading a newspaper. Mathew approaches him and says, 'Excuse me, sir, I am looking for a certain Mr Carew from Bodmin. All I know is that he is at the Inns of Court this morning probably on church business.

Have you any idea where I might look?'

The lawyer looks up. 'Church business? Then you'll want Thavie's Inn. That's at Holborn Circus. You might find him there.'

'Is that far? I am a stranger in town.'

'It's just a short walk from here.'

'Could you point me the way?'

'I can do better. I can show you the way.'

'That is most kind of you, sir. I really must find this Mr Carew as soon as possible. A boy's life is at stake.'

'Is it indeed, I say.' The lawyer rises from his bench folding his newspaper . 'Look, I will accompany you if you'll do me the honour of taking a coffee with me on the way. There is a splendid coffeehouse in Fetter Lane where we lawyers are wont to gather.'

'I am sorry but I have no time for coffee. Now, which way?'

'I will go with you just the same. Let me fetch my hat and coat from chambers. This way.' He catches Mathew by the arm and steers him across the square to the door of a four storey house facing on to the lawns. 'Bear with me just a moment if you please.'

The lawyer is in and out of the building before Mathew has time to remonstrate. 'Right you are, off we go, my good sir. My name is Benjamin Lurie, Member of the Bar at your service.' He holds out his hand.

'Mathew Clymo. I am pleased to make your acquaintance.' Mathew shakes his hand and they hurry across the square. Reaching Fleet Street they are held up by the constant flow of traffic – people, carts, hansom cabs, folk on horseback, fine carriages, and scuttling amongst them all, a pair of urchins collecting horse droppings in a sack. At a brief gap in the traffic they dash across the road and Lurie guides Mathew into Fetter Lane. 'Here is the coffee house of which I spoke. Are you sure you will not join me?'

'Mr Lurie, I must find Mr Carew. Please take me to this Tavy's inn or whatever you called it. Perhaps I will join you after I have found my man.'

'Of course, of course. Off we go.' They hurry up Fetter Lane, turn right into a narrow street where Benjamin Lurie stops before a large black-painted door which bears a brass plate *Thavies Chambers*. 'Here

147

we are. Good luck! If your business takes less than an hour, you will find me still at the coffeehouse.'

'Thank you, yes, I will join you if I can.' Mathew shakes his hand then turns and raps on the door with the brass doorknocker. He waits, watching the lawyer stroll back down the street once more engrossed in his newspaper.

The door opens and a dowdily dressed clerk peers out. 'May I help you?'

'Yes, I hope so. I am looking for Mr Richard Carew. I was informed he might be here on church business.'

'Mr Carew from Bodmin? You were informed correctly, sir. He is indeed here but he is occupied at this moment. Would you care to come in and wait?' He ushers Mathew into a broad hallway and indicates a seat beneath a hissing gaslight. 'Your name sir, that I might announce you?'

'I am Mathew Clymo but Mr Carew does not know me. Please tell him that my business concerns a boy, Thomas Pascoe, and the murder of the Reverend Dippenden in Bodmin.'

'Murder, oh my goodness. Yes, yes, I will tell him of your arrival this instant.' The clerk disappears up a flight of stairs. Mathew checks his pocket watch and sighs – almost midday and he has yet to convince the lawyer to return with him to Bodmin. He sniffs the unaccustomed smell of coal gas which mingles with a pervasive mustiness. He hears a door slam, loud voices, then a very fat man in breeches, white stockings and a frock coat appears at the top of the stairs. He grasps the banister and hurries down one step at a time.

'My friend the Reverend murdered,' he exclaims, 'That cannot be. Who are you, sir, to come with such dreadful news?' He reaches the hallway and stands in front of Mathew.

'Mathew Clymo, Captain at the Wheal Emma mine, at your service, sir.' Mathew makes a slight bow 'You are Mr Richard Carew of Bodmin?'

Carew nods.

'You have not heard the news then?'

'No, indeed I have not. I have been closeted with these church people since I arrived in London. But I am deeply shocked. You must tell me all.'

Mathew looks around the hall and at the clerk who has joined them at the bottom of the stairs. 'If you have finished your business here perhaps we could find somewhere else more private.'

'Yes, yes of course. I will make my farewells upstairs and be with you directly.'

The two Cornishmen make an odd pair as they make their way to Fetter Lane, one tall, bareheaded and wearing a red kerchief at his neck, the other top-hatted, be-whiskered and struggling to keep pace with his companion's stride. 'Would you take coffee while we talk?' Mathew asks.

Carew nods. 'Is Reverend Dippenden actually murdered?'

'I am afraid so. Here, read this. This is as much as I know.' He takes Tom Pascoe's letter from an inside pocket and hands it to his companion. Carew scans it quickly as he walks.

'Upon my word, this is a dreadful tale. I remember the boy perfectly and I will vouch for him of course. I am no mean judge of character and I am certain he could not do a deed like this. But he needs a criminal barrister to plead for him. I am not called to the bar. I just look after the Church's estate in Cornwall.'

Mathew stops outside the coffeehouse. 'I have an idea,' he says.

Once inside he spots Benjamin Lurie at a table, drinking coffee and chatting to another bewigged lawyer. He bends down to speak quietly to Carew. 'The gentleman seated over there,' he points discreetly, 'he brought me to Thavies Inn. He is a barrister. Perhaps he can help us.'

'Indeed. And if not, we are in just the place to find exactly what we need. I'd say most in here are of my profession.'

'Ha,' Benjamin Lurie says as they join him at his table, 'You are welcome sirs. Please take a seat. More coffee here.' he shouts to a passing waiter. 'And you must be Mr Richard Carew?' He reaches across and shakes Carew's hand. 'Benjamin Lurie, Member of the Bar at your service.'

'Delighted to meet you, sir? Forgive me for my directness, but would you be a criminal barrister by any chance?'

'Afraid not sir, maritime law is my patch. But you gentlemen are

Cornish by your accents. If it would not be indiscreet, might I know what crime brings two Cornishmen to London?'

'Murder, sir,' Mathew says. 'A good friend of Mr Carew was killed two weeks ago in Bodmin Town and one of my miners, a boy, is locked in Bodmin Gaol accused of the crime. He did not do it – of that we are both agreed. Is that not so, Mr Carew?'

'Indeed. It was I who took the boy to meet my friend, the Reverend Dippenden. I cannot conceive that the boy would kill him. He sought the Reverend's help. Besides, there is no motive. So we seek a barrister to defend him at has trial next week.'

'Extraordinary. Next week you say. But you are in luck. You see the gent over there reading by the window. That's James Barrington-Purdue and he's one of the best criminal barristers in town. Won't come cheap mind you. Come, I'll introduce you.' He gets up and leads them across the room. 'Barrington, might I introduce two Cornish gents in need of help?'

'What, hey? Cornishmen by God. Of course, splendid. Take a seat, gentlemen. Thank you Benjamin, well done. Amazing coincidence. Here I am reading up on one of your Cornish mines and up walk two Cornishmen. God moves in mysterious ways eh?'

Scarcely drawing breath he continues, 'My problem is that I think I may have made a fool's investment in one of your mines. It came highly recommended by one Josiah Hocking whom a colleague of mine successfully defended in a fraud case. Honest as the day is long, my colleague said and I believed him, more fool me – invested the better part of a hundred pounds, and no sooner had I done so than the share price halved. Put the tip some colleagues' way too and they're most unhappy with me, as you can imagine. Now I read that the mine is on the up – at least, so says a report in the Mining Journal here.' He taps the opened paper on the table. 'So my dilemma is – do I and my friends sell and cut our losses and have nothing more to do with these damned scoundrels, or do we buy more and hope to make it up?'

Mathew smiles. 'Scoundrels you say. Tell me, in which mine did you invest?'

'Cornish Consols sir, Wheal Emma I believe the mine is called. I have my doubts of its very existence in spite of what is written here.'

Richard Carew, hand before his mouth, coughs and looks across the table at Mathew who nods and smiles.

Carew says, 'Mr Purdue, I can assure you as one man of the law to another, that the mine does indeed exist. It is well known in Cornwall and thereabouts. As to its worth, well, no man is better placed to inform you than Mr Mathew Clymo here. He is Captain at Wheal Emma.'

'Good Lord, is this true, sir? If so I do beg your pardon. Oh my what a happy, no I mean an unhappy coincidence. I did not mean to offend, but I was afraid I had invested in another South Sea bubble.'

'I take no offence, sir. The price of Cornish Consols has been manipulated of late. I have not had time to get to the bottom of the matter but at least one of those responsible is already dealt with. And there is other skulduggery about. May I see what your journal has to report?'

Barrington-Purdue turns the paper back two pages, then flattens it on the table before passing it to Mathew. 'Here it is, Wheal Emma, two full pages by a Mr Yelloly Watson. Is that not a peculiar name?'

'Aye, it is somewhat. I met the gentleman himself at our last counthouse dinner. He told me he was not a journalist but I do believe he was honest on all other counts.' Mathew is silent as he reads.

'Mr Barrington-Purdue,' Carew says, ' We have a most serious matter we would discuss with you but let us wait until Mathew finishes his reading.'

'Perfect, perfect. Meanwhile, this is fine coffee is it not? Java's best they say.'

'I am afraid I am not a connoisseur of coffee. It's not much drunk in Cornwall.'

'He has it mostly right,' Mathew taps the newspaper, 'although I would not agree that our new strike is as good as our first. But then he is a shareholder too and it's in his interest to see the price increase.'

'Oh dear, is there nobody one can trust? What should I do – sell or buy?'

'My advice to you, Mr Purdue, is to do neither. The collapse of

Cornish Consols was engineered. Now that is resolved our shares are on the up and you will at least recover your investment. Also, I have great hopes of a certain document that has come my way that may guide us to new discoveries. But that is all in the future. Meanwhile, we have a most serious matter to lay before you. We need your help. Here, read this.' Mathew hands over Thomas Pascoe's now much thumbed letter.

Barrington-Purdue nods as he reads. 'Hmm, yes, I see, I see. A nasty business. And you want me to defend the boy?'

'We do indeed. Of course, both I and Captain Clymo will speak up for him but that will not be enough to counter the maid's false witness.'

'Correct. But we have little time and I will need to talk to the boy before Monday. Unfortunately I must be at the Bar all day tomorrow. The earliest I could leave for Bodmin would be Wednesday. That gives us four days before the trial. How long will it take me to get to Bodmin?'

'Two days, sir – six hours by train to Exeter then a short day's coach ride to Bodmin. We could be at the gaol on Friday.'

'Perfect, Mr Carew,' Mathew says. 'What say you Mr Purdue? Will you help us?'

'I will, if you'll pay my fees.'

'I will do better than that. What say you to more Cornish Consols shares?'

Barrington-Purdue laughs and holds out his hand. 'A deal Captain Clymo. I look forward to meeting you at Bodmin Gaol on Friday.'

21

SCOBLE RIDES AGAIN

 'BLOODY CLYMO MAY THINK HE'S WON AGAIN BUT HE ain't. Nor will he'. William Scoble turns up the collar of his riding coat and rides head down into the wind. He takes a deep breath and lets his hatred of the captain of Wheal Emma dominate his thoughts. He cannot forget how Clymo humiliated him before the duke the day the miners mobbed the gates for better housing, and he was sent like an errand boy to quell the riot. And that's all he is to them now, the miners of Penpillick – errand boy for the duke. While Clymo exalts himself as Captain. And those damned counthouse dinners where Clymo preens and struts and looks down his nose at him. He shakes his head and drops of water fly from the brim of his hat.

From Penpillick to Bolventor is a morning's ride across Bodmin Moor, longer if he had gone by road. But the moor holds no fears for him or his horse – even on a day like this, when a bitter northwest wind drags sleet and rain across the bogs of Witheybrook. The horse picks his way between tufts of bog cotton and rills of sodden peat. 'Know it Nelson, don't we boy, we know it.'

He has duke's business in Bolventor, with rents to collect from recalcitrant tenants, and he'll have a quiet word with the innkeeper on his own behalf. Scoble feels for the dagger that he always wears beneath his riding coat. Thinking of tenants puts him in mind of those useless Tuttles. He would have them out, evict them if he could. That would sort Maisie Tuttle, the thieving little bitch, and her lying mother. By the time he reached Penpillick that morning with no sight of her he was spitting fury, but managed to hold his temper when he strode into the cottage only to find it empty. He rode up to the counthouse, and asked her mother where her daughter was.

'Liskeard, at the Fountain Hotel of course,' Jenny Tuttle said, standing at the counthouse door. 'Where else would she be?'

'You've not seen her then?'

She shook her head. 'Don't 'spect her till last Saturday of the month. What would you want with our Maisie, then?'

He looked down at her, lips pursed, and turned his horse away. It was only as he rode out of the village towards the duke's estate that it dawned on him. The girl must have gone to Bodmin with the bloody book. Jethro Loam had told him she was sweet on the Pascoe boy – but he'd given that no mind.

The horse slithers on the wet and stony track that takes them down to the lane below Dozmary. 'Easy boy, easy now. Just a mile or so and we'll be in the dry.' As they ride up the lane to Bolventor the sleet has turned to steady rain and the wind has strengthened.

Yes, the loss of the book was a blow. He sent a message to Davy Bates in Bodmin to look out for the girl outside the gaol, and take the book back if the chance arose. But it didn't. She was with that poxy oaf Henry Hopeful Down – and God knows where the book is now. 'Probably with bloody Clymo.' He shouts the name into the teeth of the wind. And Clymo knows that he Scoble has been manipulating Cornish Consols share price. Once faced with talking or losing his reputation, his livelihood and his job, the purser, Pryor, told his master he'd been paid by Scoble. Yet Clymo has made no accusation, and why would that be? Instead, he's gone to London in a blazing hurry, or so Jethro Loam has said.

The business is a mess, no doubt. The bungled theft at the blasted parson's house in Bodmin, and then the wild pursuit across the moor. He thought that Bates had killed the boy – but that too was bungled. At least the boy's in prison and tomorrow they'll find him guilty. He's made sure of that. They've paid off the maid who lost her place but still has mouths to feed. Besides, it took no more than a look from Bates for her to know that if she blabbed in court her children would be motherless. So Thomas Pascoe will hang and the truth about old Dippenden's death will die with him.

And Scoble has his Cornish Consols shares. He would rub his hands if they weren't fast on the sodden reins. Hocking has been shrewd. After the counthouse dinner the share price rose, but slowly with frequent falls as investors cashed their profit. Hocking and his friends bought at every chance, and now between them they near control the mine – just a little more is needed, just a little more. But he and Hocking are clear out of cash and his friends have lost heart; the price is now beyond their reach. But just five hundred pounds will do it, Hocking says. He's paid back the duke and dare not steal from him again. Clymo is bound to tell the duke that he bribed the purser to cook the books – which he will just deny. But mud will stick and doubtless the duke will take a closer interest in the management of his estate. So he must find the funds from another source, and that lies just up the lane.

William Scoble, with eyes and ears across the county and a fondness for night riding has known for years that the gentlemen of the night who work both coasts use Bolventor as a base. So far, he has turned a blind eye when they cross the duke's lands. But they know he knows. And now the time has come to use that knowledge and charge his toll. He smiles a thin smile and pats his horses neck. 'Yes Nelson, my beauty, they'll see it my way. Five hundred pounds is nothing to them – less than a dozen barrels of brandy and a chest of tea.' And with that money control of Cornish Consols will be his.

What a pleasure it will be to watch Mathew Clymo's face when he dismisses him from his captaincy. 'Clymo – get off my lease,' he shouts into the wind. 'Get off my lease you bloody bastard. God damn you, Clymo.'

22

THE TRIAL

HE STANDS IN THE DOCK, HANDS RESTING ON THE oaken rail before him. The court smells of bleach and the damp which rises from the cells below. His heart beats with a fast but steady rhythm just as if he were climbing up to grass. He lifts his head and looks across at the jury. These men have just taken their seats and stare at him. Thomas does not meet their collective gaze but looks down into the body of the court, then up to the public gallery. There are shouts and murmuring as the crowd pushes through the double doors, jostling for seats. A young woman dressed in frilled bonnet and ribbons as if for a country fair, points at him. Then he sees his mother and Maisie Tuttle and behind them the bulk of Henry Hopeful Down, and the tears start from his eyes.

'All rise.'

He watches now as the judge in red robes and a long grey wig with pointed ends walks in, head bent, and takes his place on the bench. It's not a bench, more like a throne he thinks, though he has never seen a throne. It was Mr Barrington-Purdue that called it a bench. And there he is too, just below him to his right, a handsome man in a neat white wig tasselled at the back and a black gown. And beside him is Mr Richard Carew and behind him Capun Clymo who catches his eye and almost winks. He breathes deep and blinks away the tears. His heart calms and hope replaces near despair. These three men are his salvation.

On Saturday Mr Purdue came to his cell saying he would defend him, and so must question him. They spent two hours together, Thomas sitting on his cot and the lawyer sitting on a wooden chair brought by Warder Verran. Thomas told him all he could remember. But on Sunday evening the lawyer came again saying, 'You will not be allowed to testify in your own defence so I must do it for you. I have been to Harford House and made an examination of the parlour. Now I need you to tell me your story once more, for I must have the facts at my fingertips when you stand in the dock tomorrow. Miss nothing out, not the tiniest detail, for the case is strong against you.'

Once more Thomas cast his mind back to that cold night three weeks ago when he left Penpillick and came to Bodmin Town. In his mind's eye he traced his steps across the moor, recalled the rider on the bridge, his meeting Mr Carew on Sunday morning – which seemed so lucky at the time. He told of William Scoble accosting them in the street, and finally the fateful details of that afternoon in the Reverend Dippenden's front parlour.

'So you took the book and some food from off the table, and then you ran away?'

'Yes, sir, I ran away.'

'With blood on your hands.'

'Yes sir. I held the Reverend's head in my hands.'

The lawyer stared at him unblinking. 'Why did you run?'

'I did not know what else to do. I thought I was to blame. I hit the man, he knocked over Reverend Dippenden, Reverend Dippenden was dead.'

'Hmm, that might be manslaughter – but if what you say is true, you are not a murderer.'

'It is true, sir, every word.'

'And the candelabra?'

'Sir?'

'The prosecution believe the Reverend was killed by a blow from the candelabra, which was lying on the floor when the doctor arrived.'

Thomas bent his head. 'Yes, I remember – the candelabra was on the table while we studied the book. It must have fallen to the floor when those men attacked me.'

'Are you sure?'

'No sir. But I am sure that the Reverend died when he fell and hit his head on the fire surround. I did not hit him. I could not hit him.'

'At your arraignment, the maid, Rebecca Grose, said you were alone in the room and that you killed the Reverend. She made no mention of other men.'

'I was alone when she came in. But the two men had already run from the house. She must have seen them go. Besides, she let them in.'

'So she was lying.'

'Yes sir.'

'You are sure? Remember you will be under oath?'

'I am absolutely sure. I do not lie, sir. I am a Methodist.'

'Then tell me all you can about this lying maid, for she is the key to the evidence against you.'

'I only saw her twice. She brought us bread and ham and said it was a strange time to be eating. The Reverend said she was forward for someone from a pauper's family. Then after the accident, she came in and screamed when she saw the Reverend on the floor. I told her to call a doctor and she ran out. Then I didn't see her again until she spoke against me at the court. She lied, sir. She lied.'

'Yes, but why?' The lawyer paused then asked, 'What was she wearing?'

'Wearing, sir?'

'Yes, what clothing, that afternoon?'

Thomas thought for a moment, 'A maid's uniform, I think. Yes, black dress, white pinafore and white cap.'

'You are sure?'

'Yes sir. I remember it clearly.'

'And shoes or boots?'

'Small black buttoned boots, sir.'

'Is there anything else you can remember about her?'

'She wore a fabric belt about her waist – dark red I think it was, with a buckle and keys hanging from it. That is all I can think of.'

'Good.' The lawyer pursed his lips. 'I will give this much thought. Mr Carew will speak to your character, as will Captain Clymo. I warn you now that the prosecutor, Sir Alexander Cockburn, is formidable in court. He will push you to your very limit. But do not let him break you. He will try to catch you out but if you tell the truth and only the truth it will be your word against the maid's. So bear up, boy. Tomorrow we have a heavy task before us.'

The morning sun streams in the eastern window as he stands alone before them all. With his hand upon the Holy Bible he has sworn that he will tell the truth. The charge of murder has been read against him, and he has pleaded 'not guilty' in the loud clear voice he used to declaim poetry at school. Now the prosecutor is describing to the court how he killed the Reverend Dippenden, broke his skull and left him dead upon the floor. His eyes are hard and unforgiving as he stares at Thomas, and his voice rings out across the court. The tale he tells is so convincing that Thomas can almost see it for himself. He shakes his head. No – it was not like that, no, not at all. He looks up to the gallery and sees his mother, her hand covering her mouth. He breathes deep, and would shut his eyes against the accusing stares as the prosecutor tells his tale, but knows that he must not.

'A murderer stands before you gentlemen of the jury, a cold-blooded murderer and a coward. Do not think that this is mere supposition. We have a witness who saw him with blood still on his hands, who saw him in the room with the deceased, who saw him run away. But first I will call the doctor, who will describe to us the dreadful injuries that the Reverend Dippenden suffered at the hands of this evil boy.' Sir Alexander Cockburn's voice rings out across the court.

The doctor takes the stand and swears upon the bible.

'Doctor Morrison, would you please tell the court what you found that afternoon when you were called to Harford House.'

'I was called to the Reverend Dipppenden's house that Sunday by a boy sent by the maid Rebecca Grose. When I arrived, it was she who opened the door to me and showed me through to the parlour. There I found the Reverend lying on the floor in front of the hearth in a pool of his own blood. I examined him and ascertained that he was dead, although the body was still warm. There was a deep wound in his skull above his left ear which was undoubtedly the cause of death. There was a candelabra beside his head with blood on it.'

'Do you believe that the candelabra was the murder weapon?'

'In the absence of any other evidence, I do.'

'Thank you doctor.'

Barrington-Purdue rises to his feet. 'Doctor Morrison, the body was lying in front of the hearth was it not?'

'Yes.'

'Did you notice if the hearth had a brass fire surround?'

'Yes, I think it did.'

'Do you remember if the corners of the fire surround were square or rounded? I ask you to think carefully now.'

The doctor pauses for several moments. Thomas holds his breath.

'I think they were square.'

'Is it possible that the injury to the deceased could have been caused by his head striking the corner of the fire surround.'

'Yes, I suppose it is possible.'

'Thank you Doctor.'

As the doctor steps down from the witness box, there is a murmur from the gallery and Thomas breathes again – at last a point in his favour.

Sir Alexander Cockburn gets to his feet. 'Please call Captain Mathew Clymo.'

Mathew, sitting beside Barrington-Purdue looks up in surprise, then mutters to the lawyer who nods. He takes the stand.

'Captain Clymo, you know the defendant well do you not?'

'I do. I have known him since he was a child.'

'And you will speak as to his character for the defence.'

Mathew looks across at Barrington-Purdue who grimaces, then nods again. 'I will.'

'Before you do that I would like you to answer some questions pertaining to the events occurring on the day of the defendant's arrest. Do you remember that day clearly.'

Thomas's heart sinks.

'I do. It was the day of our counthouse dinner,' Mathew says.

'Indeed. When Constable Smale came to Penpillick to arrest the defendant, where was he?'

'I do not know.'

'Hmm. But you know where he went, do you not?'

'I do.'

'Please tell the court where that was.'

Mathew licks his lips and looks up at the gallery. 'He went down the mine to the 120 fathom level where his father was killed.'

'Did he go down to work?'

'No.'

'Why did he go down, Captain Clymo?'

Mathew looks down at the floor then again up to the gallery.

'Answer the question please.'

'I suppose he was hiding.'

'He was hiding.'

'Yes.'

'Hiding from whom?'

'The constable.'

'Captain Clymo, do you think hiding from a constable down a dark hole in the ground is the act of an innocent man?'

'I do not know. I am not a judge.'

'No indeed. Yet you will speak in defence as to the defendant's good character.'

'I will.'

'Thank you Captain. That is all.'

As he steps down Mathew catches Thomas eye and gives the slightest shake of his head. Thomas leans on the bar trying to restrain the tears. He can hear his mother's quiet sobbing from the gallery.

They call Rebecca Grose. There is a stir and mutter in the court as she takes the witness stand across from Thomas. She is dressed in black from head to toe, and does not look at him as she too swears to tell the truth. The prosecutor's voice takes on a kindly tone, the voice of a gentleman talking to a child. 'Tell us in your own words what happened to your master that dreadful afternoon three weeks ago.'

She speaks, head up, her gaze shifting around the court and from time to time catching the prosecutor' eye, who nods. She does not look at Thomas. He watches her, listening to every word as she repeats the tale she told before. Until finally she points at him and says, 'He were standing there with the candlestick in his hand and there were blood on it.'

162

Once again he cannot help his outrage and shouts out 'She lies, she lies again,' and turns to Barrington-Purdue, who shakes his head as the judge bangs his gavel and calls for silence. Thomas does not hear what else she says for his head is swimming and the prison breakfast gruel rises in his gorge. But he grips the rail, his knuckles white and bows his head. Finally he regains his self control and looks up to see his lawyer standing looking at Rebecca Grose.

'Mrs Grose,' he says, 'I want to take you back a little further on that afternoon.'

'Yes, sir?'

'Yes, starting the moments before Mr Carew and the defendant here came knocking at the door. What were you doing?'

'I were in the kitchen sir, ironing linen.'

'Then you let the gentlemen in.'

'Yes, sir. I knows Mr Carew well. He comes often. He's a gentleman but the other ain't.'

'Then what did you do?'

'I went back to finish me ironing.'

'Then what happened?'

'Mr Carew called for food and I put up some bread and ham and took it to them in the parlour.'

'What were they doing?'

'They was readin' a book. Then Mr Carew left.'

'Then what did you do?'

'I went back to the kitchen.'

'And then?'

'I made some tea.'

'For whom?'

'For meself, of course.'

'What were you wearing?'

'Sir?'

'Your dress, what were you wearing?'

'What I always wear, me maid's dress.'

'With a white pinafore.'

'Yes.'

'And a maid's cap?'

'Yes, of course. Everybody knows maids wear a cap.' There are titters from the gallery as she looks around the court smirking.

'And a belt?'

'Yes.'

Sir Alexander Cockburn gets to his feet. 'Objection, your Grace. This has nothing to do with the case. My learned friend is badgering the witness.'

'Yes. Where do you hope to go with this line of questioning, Mr Purdue?' the judge asks.

'I believe this will become apparent shortly, your Grace, if I may continue.'

The judge nods.

'So you were wearing your maid's uniform with a dark red belt and a buckle?'

'Yes.'

'And black boots.' The questions come quickly and the maid barely has time to answer before Barrington-Purdue poses the next.

'Yes.'

'Black boots with black buttons.'

'Yes.'

'And you were sitting in the kitchen?'

'Yes.'

'Drinking tea?'

'Yes.'

'And a man barged in without knocking.'

'Two men. It were two men . . .' Rebecca Grose puts her hands to her mouth as the court erupts.

The judge bangs his gavel. 'Silence in court, silence in court.'

Thomas stares wide-eyed and open-mouthed at a smiling Barrington-Purdue. A great load seems to lift from his shoulders as he turns his gaze to Rebecca Grose. She is looking up at the gallery where there is a commotion at the door as somebody pushes their way out.

The hubbub subsides, and Barrington-Purdue asks very quietly, 'Two men you were saying Mrs Grose – two men broke in?'

'I . . . I don't remember. I . . . I don't know.'

'I remind you Mrs Grose, that you are under oath. You know that the punishment for perjury is prison?'

'No, sir, no, not prison. My children, my poor children. They made me do it. They said they'd kill me if I blabbed.' She begins to cry and looks again up to the gallery. 'They'd leave my poor babes motherless.'

'And who are "they" Mrs Grose?'.

'The two men, sir. They went in to the parlour. Then I heard shouting and banging then they ran out again.' She is crying freely now, leaning on the edge of the witness box, her head in her hands.

'Compose yourself Mrs Grose, compose yourself,' the judge says. 'Would you like to tell us what truly happened that afternoon?'

'Yes, your Grace,' she whispers.

23

CHRISTMAS

'SO, THOMAS, YOU HAVE YOUR FREEDOM, YOU HAVE your father's book. What now?'

'I am a miner, Capun, and I am happy working back down Wheal Emma. But not on tutwork, I'd be a tributer if I may.'

'You may indeed, young as you are, but really there is no need. You're spitting black already, and now the purser's gone I could use a boy in the counthouse who reads and knows his numbers.'

'Thank you, Capun. But I owe you too much already, not least my life. And I would not be seen taking further favour from my stepfather.' That this sounds churlish Thomas well knows, but he cannot bring himself to see this man as father. At their wedding his heart lurched when his mother said 'I do' – and he looked away when they kissed each other.

He looks around at the few possessions his mother has brought to the Clymo house upon the hill. Set apart from the village and built of stone, it is no mansion but nonetheless is grand by Penpillick standards. He will not live here, in spite of her entreaties. 'I will not leave our cottage, Mother. Nor can I forget my father for it was there that I knew him best.' But he helped them move, bringing the younger children who now play upon the staircase while his mother prepares their Christmas dinner in the kitchen.

'You're stubborn, boy,' Mathew says, 'but that's a good thing in a miner. And what of the book, Thomas? This book that has cost one life already and nearly cost you yours? Shall we sit together and work out what it means – what your father knew?'

'It is all I have left of him, Capun. I will keep it if I may. Besides, if the Reverend Dippenden did not understand it, how will we?' The lie slips easily to his tongue: the book is one thing Capun Clymo may not take, for his father left it to him and him alone. He sees himself at night in the cottage, poring over page by page and noting down the meanings just as he was shown.

'As you wish Thomas, as you wish.' In fact the urgency to possess and understand the book has gone from Mathew's mind. His mine is once again in profit and Grace is at his side; his life is near complete. He smiles. It is true that Barrington-Purdue's fees came as a shock and cost him more of Cornish Consols stock than he imagined. And of course a great injustice has been avoided, for indeed this boy was innocent.

'Is there nothing I might do for you seeing that you will not even live with us at home?'

'Yes Capun, there is. Would you teach me how to use my father's miner's dial?'

'Why? Would you be a surveyor or a captain?'

Thomas smiles. 'Maybe, one day. Who knows?'

'Yes Thomas Pascoe, I will teach you. Now let us join your mother and the children and celebrate our first Christmas as a family.'

Mathew Clymo leans back replete and surveys the remains of their meal. 'Grace dear, that was a Christmas dinner fit for a prince. What do you say Thomas? Is not your mother the finest cook this side of the Tamar?'

'Yes, sir.'

Mathew pours himself another glass of wine. He does his best to treat this boy as if he were his son but it does not come easily. Nor does Thomas make it any easier. He is polite, too polite perhaps; there is respect and clearly gratitude for all that he has done for him. But here he sits on Mathew's right, upright and unsmiling, as if he were in chapel listening to a sermon. Emily and little James sit to his left and Grace, God bless her, sits at the other end of the table. He catches her gaze and raising his glass, says, 'God Bless us all.'

'God bless us.' She smiles at him, sips her wine then says, 'Children, you may go play.'

As they scramble from the table, Thomas says, 'Excuse me too, Mother, Capun'.

Mathew nods and Thomas follows the children from the room. They hear the front door close and Mathew looks at Grace, an eyebrow raised.

'He'll come round in time,' she says.

'I think not.'

Grace Clymo sighs. In her heart she knows that he is right. Her son is still obsessed with his father's death, while she must accept her husband's view that it was an accident, no more. He kept his side of the bargain, saved her son from the Bodmin gallows and she has kept hers. They married quietly in the chapel and she is content to be his wife, though John Pascoe still haunts her dreams.

She looks around the room – the sturdy furnishings, the clock upon the mantelpiece, the dresser and the best china now on the table, the fine bay window which looks south across Penpillick Valley towards the sea. As Jenny Tuttle said, 'You ain't no bal maiden now my love. You'm the mistress o' Wheal Emma.' But oftentimes at night she lies awake beside her snoring mine captain, thinking of her first husband and missing the coziness of her miner's cottage.

24

TRIBUTE

IT IS PURE JOY TO SWING THE HAMMER OPPOSITE Henry Hopeful Down and they catch each others' eye and grin while Jethro Loam, gripping the steel, looks from one to the other wondering at the joke and feeling the shock of the hammer blows ringing through his fingers. The three have formed a working pare and now are tributers.

Three weeks ago on January's setting day, Tom bid and won this pitch on the back of the 160 fathom level and now they are cutting rich. The rumour underground is that the son has inherited his father's touch but Thomas knows just what he is at. Through nightly study of his father's book he has begun to understand the disposition of the copper lodes, where to find the richer parts and where the ore is weak.

The fact that he is now Captain Clymo's stepson has earned him both envy and respect, so when Jethro Loam knocked at the cottage door one snowy eve and said, 'Let me in young Pascoe. I would tell 'ee things you ought to know,' he drew him in. They sat across the fire, both silent for a while.

Then Jethro Loam said, 'It were Mr Scoble that set you up in Bodmin. He's desperate for that book of your'n.' He paused. 'But you knows that.'

'I do. So why tell me now, Jethro? You didn't speak for me in court.'

Jethro stroked his moustache and was silent, staring into the fire. 'Well?'

'I would have but I was afeared of Scoble then. Now I wish I had. You may not know this but when your father come here from Dolcoath in '45 I worked with him and Henry Hopeful Down. We was partners, the best pare on the mine we was. Come monthly setting day we was paid the most and we won the best pitches. Your father had a nose for copper like no other. I had more money than I could spend, having no family of me own. So for company I'd be at the inn most evenin's.

But then the drink got hold of me so bad that mornings I weren't no good to no man, least of all your father. He said he'd have no truck with drink nor drinkers and wouldn't work with me no more. So I was on me own on tutwork, which hardly pays enough to keep a man in bread.'

Thomas nodded. Jethro's drinking was common knowledge in Penpillick.

Jethro bent towards the fire and his voice dropped almost to a mutter. 'So when Mr Scoble said he'd pay me to spy on you and Capun Clymo – I needed money, see, for the drink. So I took money off him and followed you some. But Scoble, he's a bad 'un. Curses me like I'm a dog an' I won't have that no more.'

He paused again then looked up at Thomas. 'And besides I've given up the drink. Temperance lady found me lyin' in me own vomit in a Liskeard gutter on Christmas morn. Took me to the chapel, washed me, give me tea. I found the Lord and I ain't touched a drop for three weeks now.'

Thomas nodded. 'I saw you at chapel Sunday last and I wondered at it. But why did Scoble want to spy on me and Capun Clymo?'

'You for that there book I reckon. Capun Clymo I don't know. Anyways I never found out nothing 'bout the capun, 'cept that he went to Lunnon in a hurry after you was took in Bodmin. Look, Master Thomas, I done you wrong but I won't have no truck with killing and Scoble's mixed up in that for sure. He followed you the night you went to Bodmin.' He pauses then looks up at Thomas. 'It was I who told him you was gone – an' it's bin on me mind ever since – what I were cause of.'

'I saw him on Treverbyn Bridge and then again in Bodmin. He tried to take the book from me.'

Jethro nodded. 'He's a dangerous man an' no mistake. And he's agent for the duke.' He gazed again into the fire, then said, 'I know I owes you summat serious and I would pay my debts. What if I were on your side?'

'On my side? How do you mean?'

'Well what say you we makes a pare, work together like, just as I did with your poor dad? You knows I work hard when I ain't been

172

drinkin'. And I'll pretend to Scoble that I'm spyin' still for him but I'll be tellin' you exackly what he's after.'

Thomas smiled. 'You're a devious sort, Jethro Loam. I'll think on it.'

'Say yes. You won't regret it.'

And Thomas thought long and hard. He could have told it all to Capun Clymo. But even after all the man has done for him, he still looks away when his stepfather takes his mother's hand. So he sought out Henry Hopeful Down instead and Henry put an arm around his shoulders and said, 'Listen boy, if I were you I wouldn't trust that bugger as far as I could see him at two hundred fathom without a tallow. He's a drunk and drunks got one aim in life an' that's to drink.'.

'He's says he's given it up, Henry, and I believe him. I need him to keep a watch on Scoble.'

Henry scratched his head then said, 'If it's what you want Thomas, that's right with me. I s'pose Jethro were a handy cove to have around before he took to drink. Good timberman he was too. So let the three of us make a pare and I'll be there to keep an eye on him. We'll keep the scoundrel close.'

So here they are, one hundred and sixty fathoms below the ground, breathing the stink of burnt powder and each other's sweat and driving steel into copper ore that glints yellow in the gloom of candlelight.

'Take a breather, boy,' Henry says and they stand, hands resting on their hammer handles.

Jethro Loam spans the protruding end of steel with thumb and middle finger. 'Three more inches then we'll charge her. She's a right kindly lode, ain't she. Carries on like this we'll be some richer come settin' day.'

'Long as you don't go spending it on cider,' Henry says.

'Look, see how she runs in the back above us.' Thomas traces a finger along the roof. 'Killas this side and a tongue of granite in the wall. This is the leader lode, she'll carry on all right, maybe even richer.'

'Your father used to talk like that but I never paid him no mind. Now I wish I had.'

'Come on, let's to it boys,' Henry says and the stope rings again to the sound of steel on steel.

By croust time the face is drilled and charged and the three sit on broken rocks, unwrap pasties and eat. The only sounds are their companionable munching and the steady drip of water from the roof. His pasty finished Thomas wipes his mouth then picks up the iron tamping bar. 'This was my father's,' he says turning it in his hands, 'See how it's copper tipped. I read his letter again last night. I had forgot – some days before he died a person changed it for an untipped bar which could have blinded him or worse when he fired the charge. But he noticed and did not use it.'

Jethro Loam looks away and picks with a filthy fingernail at meat stuck in his teeth.

'It were you weren't it Jethro?' Henry says.

'It were,' Jethro mutters. 'I were in a jealous rage that I was so poor an' once we'd worked together. I wished to hurt him, no more than that. And now I'm really sorry for what I done. I am ashamed, Thomas, and I thank the Lord that no harm come to him because of it.'

'So it wasn't you who caved the 120 fathom end that killed him?'

'Thomas Pascoe, I swears to you on the body of Lord Jesus Christ that I never did nor could I ever do a thing like that.'

'Drunk or no?' bellows Henry Hopeful Down, on his feet and shaking Jethro like a rat.

'Set me down, set me down you. . . you . . .great lummox,' Jethro yells.

'Put him down, Henry, I believe him. But Jethro, you know as much as any man about what goes on down here. Who do you think might have done it?'

'I don't know Master Thomas, I ain't got no idea. An' for me the biggest mystery is why would someone do it anyways? No miner gained by John Pascoe's death. Fact is he made Wheal Emma richer which were a benefit to us all. Perhaps it were just an accident like the capun says.'

Thomas sat for a while in silence. Then he said, 'One night last year I went down to see what I might find. I found nothing. Any secret must be hidden in the rock fall. I thought maybe if I cleared it to the face I might discover who or what had killed my father. I tried again that day I hid from the constable. But I could not do it all alone.' He looks at his two companions.

'I followed you that night,' Henry says. 'Kept you safe. 'Twere a brave but foolish thing to do for a boy not yet a miner.'

Thomas nods. 'But now I am a miner.'

Jethro says, 'You is. And now you wants us to help you clear the fall.'

'I do.'

'We'd have to ask the capun,' Henry says.

'Not if we work at night. I don't want him to know.'

'Why not? He's your father now and 'twas he who saved you from the hangman.'

'He's my stepfather, Henry. I owe him my life and for that I am already too much in his debt. So if I ask him, it'll be yet another favour I'll owe him. Besides this time he'll say no.'

Thomas sighs. He hates to lie but it is his father's book that has brought him to just this point. Now he reads it fluently and when he thinks on what he may have discovered it almost takes his breath away. That is, if he has interpreted the signs aright and his father's observations were correct. Yes, Capun Clymo saved his life but took his mother in exchange.

For now he'll keep this thing just to himself although he's more than half a mind to tell it all to Maisie Tuttle, who's now his sweetheart. He walked out with her on Saturday and they stood on the bridge above the stream where once they played as children. She barely spoke, just looked up at him from beneath her bonnet, and he would have tipped it back and kissed her but she dropped her eyes. He'll walk out with her to chapel come Sunday – perhaps he'll kiss her after.

He says, 'So will you help me clear the 120 fathom end and perhaps discover why my father died?'

'I'll help you Thomas. What says you, Jethro Loam?'

' O' course I'll help you. Your Pa was good to me till I got the drink. I reckons I owe him that much at least. And I owes you even more for takin' me on after what I done for that bugger Scoble.'

'You just keep an eye on him for us now and all is forgiven. Come on – let's fire the charge and get back up to grass.'

The blast of the explosion roils behind them sucking the breath from their lungs as they trot half crouched along the drive to 160 fathom station. Thomas smiles to himself as he remembers that first day down Wheal Emma, his fear, his awkwardness, the crushing weight of rock above him. He has no fears now, and runs his hand along the rock wall – rocks that are his friends now; he knows their different colours, textures, feel and even the different smells when steel strikes sparks from pyrites, blende or mundic.

And he will learn to use the miner's dial, no longer guessing roughly where he is by mapping in his mind the twist and turns of tunnels, the clambering up and down of ladderways, the scrambling through the stopes, the dead ends leading nowhere. With his father's dial as guide and the help of these his friends, perhaps he will unravel the truth hidden in the last pages of his father's journal.

25

SCOBLE'S DAY

HE SITS AT HIS DESK, ESTATE PAPERS IN NEAT PILES BEFORE him. He has dealt with all these and now contemplates the letter. Postmarked Holborn, it can only be from Josiah Hocking. His meeting with the gentlemen of the night at Bolventor inn bore fruit, and the week after Christmas he sent Hocking a bankers draft for five hundred pounds. This must be the reply. Was it enough?

There is the slightest tremor in Scoble's hand as he takes up the letter and slits it open with the ivory paper knife he purloined from the desk of Viscount Abercorn. He reads:

Dear sir,

It is with considerable satisfaction that I write to inform you that between us, (us being yourself, myself, my good friends Messrs. Barnet and Bolitho) we now hold a controlling interest of fifty four percent in Cornish Consols. I most strongly recommend that you do not inform Captain Clymo of this (his?) situation until the next counthouse dinner at which I and my aforementioned associates will be pleased to be present. We should meet the day before to plan our Strategy.

I remain yours truly, Josiah Hocking

'Got you,' Scoble shouts and bangs his desk with his fist. 'Got you Clymo, you bastard. Now you'll pay.'

He leans back with folded arms and a tight-lipped smile. He will not have to wait long – the next account day is shortly due. He leafs through his diary, yes, here it is – *counthouse Dinner, Monday February 6th* – just twelve days away. Success, finally.

How close he came to disaster. He will not forget the Grose woman's collapse in the witness box. He was seated at the back of the court and felt a dreadful urge to run as the truth came out. He had put

Davy Bates in the public gallery where Rebecca Grose could see him and think on what would happen if she did not do as she was told. But Clymo's fancy London lawyer bamboozled her into a confession, damn his eyes. At least Bates had the brains to quit the court that moment and together with his fellow thug flee the country, just as Scoble had arranged should things not go their way. That had cost him a pretty penny – horses that night across the moor and on to Bideford, where they took ship to Swansea then hired on as crew on a copper barque bound for Australia.

Then damn Clymo accused him in front of the duke of bribing the purser to cook the books. Scoble sucks in breath between his teeth at the very memory. As they closed the books on a review of royalties paid to him that year the duke said, 'Most satisfactory Captain Clymo, most satisfactory. I thank you.'

But Clymo did not rise to leave and Scoble guessed at what was coming.

'Is there something else, Captain?'

'Yes your Grace,' and here he looked directly at Scoble. 'I regret to inform you that Mr Scoble bribed my purser to cook the cost books and drive down the price of Cornish Consols.'

Scoble straightened in his chair, stared back at Clymo and said, 'That is a foul lie, Captain Clymo. The purser may have made false entries in your books but that has nothing to do with me.'

The duke looked from one to the other. 'This is a serious accusation, Captain. What evidence do you have?'

'I could not understand why the mine appeared to make no profit in October and November. I had an expert check the books. He discovered a number of false entries understating the copper brought to grass. I asked the purser, William Pryor, how this could be. After some prevarication, he told me he was paid by Mr Scoble to falsify the records.'

'Is that true, Mr Scoble?'

'Certainly not your Lordship. I've already said that whatever the purser did has nothing to do with me. Besides, who would believe the word of a man who confessed to making false book entries? He's a damned liar as well as a fraudster. He must have done it for his own ends. And I hear he's fled the county.'

'Yes, at your instigation I'll be bound,' Clymo said.

'You're a liar too, Clymo.'

Clymo leaped to his feet and leaned across the table as if to grab Scoble by the throat, 'You infernal bugger, don't you call me a liar.'

'Gentlemen, gentlemen, I'll not have this. Be seated Captain Clymo and I'll thank you to mind your language.' Clymo sat down fuming and glaring across the table.

The duke continued, 'It seems to me, gentlemen, that without the presence of the purser the veracity or otherwise of Captain Clymo's accusation cannot be determined. This being the case I suggest both of you return to your respective duties.'

As they rose to leave the duke said, 'Mr Scoble, I will have a word.' Once they were alone he said, 'Mr Scoble, Captain Clymo has always seemed to me to be an honourable man. Why would he make such a serious accusation against you?'

'He has never liked me, your Lordship, and he particularly hates the fact that it is my duty to examine the mine books and ensure that your interests are properly addressed. These Cornish mine captains think they are a law unto themselves and will answer to none but their Adventurers. And none of them like paying royalties to the rightful owner of the riches that they mine.'

'Perhaps you have a point. But tread carefully Mr Scoble. Captain Clymo is not a good man to cross. You may go.'

'Ha, now we'll see now who can be crossed and who can not,' Scoble says to himself. He reads Hocking's letter once again, folds it in half and slips it into the inside pocket of his jacket. "Strategy" Hocking says: Scoble needs no strategy, he knows full well what he will do once the mine is under his command. First and foremost he'll dismiss so-called Captain Clymo. And what a pleasure that will be – vengeance sweet as honey on his tongue; he can taste it now. He'll need a replacement but that should be no problem – he's heard that the night captain from

Dolcoath is looking for a post. Then he'll wrest the Journal from the Pascoe boy. But how to do that without arousing suspicion that it was he and his bully-boys that attacked him on the moor?

He is sure the boy did not see him that night for if he had, he would have surely made some accusation. But the boy is bolder now. Walking out with the Tuttle bitch on Sunday last, he met Scoble's stare as he rode his horse up through Penpillick.

He should arrange an accident in the mine. With the boy dead, his cottage would be empty and the book would be his for the taking. Scoble is sure it holds the key to the riches of Wheal Emma. Loam came to see him a week since and told him that Pascoe's pare was cutting rich. 'Richest I ever seen since I tributed with his father,' he said. It was good to have Loam close to the boy but the man was weak with no stomach for violence. Could Scoble do it for himself?

As owner, he will have every right to spend all the time he wishes down in the mine. But he knows too little of the ways of working underground – even the words they use are awkward to his tongue, 'Stope, attle, killas,' he says aloud. But that can soon be rectified: he will learn. His new mine captain will teach him. They say Kit Robin, night captain at Dolcoath, is like to get the sack for some tom-foolery with the bal maids. He'll ride to Cambourne on the morrow, stay the night and offer him the job.

But he must take his time, go carefully and let the boy keep mining copper so that more wealth will come to him as owner.

'No,' Scoble mutters to himself, 'Let's not kill the golden goose just yet. I will be friendly to him – and with that bastard Clymo gone, he'll look to me. ' But once he has understood the ways and means of working in the mine he can impose his will just as he pleases. Then things will be different, indeed they will.

26

A MINER'S DIAL

HE LIFTS IT FROM ITS WOODEN CASE AND IT LIES heavy on his outstretched hand. The brass casing glints in the candlelight.

'Right – set her nicely on the tripod now and you can dial this old drive,' Mathew Clymo says. 'It'll be good practice for you. The lode made more twists and turns here than a bent broker. Dial this and you'll dial anything.'

It is Sunday afternoon and they are alone on the 40 fathom level. Thomas has forgone walking out with Maisie Tuttle to learn how to use his father's instrument while his stepfather has given up his Sunday afternoon with Grace beside the fire, to teach him.

Thomas screws the base of the dial to its place atop the tripod which Mathew has already set level. 'Now remember what we did up top. I will go to the first bend and you will fix my candlelight between the sights then read off the azimuth and write her down. Then bring the dial to where I'm at, counting your paces as you go. Then we'll do the same again.'

'Yes Capun.'

'Thomas, could you not call me "father" now?'

'I'm sorry Capun, but my true father lives on in my mind, especially when I am down here. I hear his voice, and even think I see his face though he brought me down but once. And you are captain of Wheal Emma. What would my mates think if they hear me call you "father"?'

'So be it Thomas.' Mathew sighs and walks away down the drive until his tallow is but a glimmer. He turns and shouts, 'Right, boy. I'm at the turn. Take your sighting now.' His voice echoes and re-echoes in the darkness.

Thomas flips up the sighting arms, bends down, and squinting through the brass slit turns the dial until the distant glimmer is aligned. He reads the azimuth and writes it down then carries the whole apparatus to where Mathew waits. They repeat this process through the twists and turns until they reach the tunnel's blind end.

'Good work, boy. You have it now? Plot them angles and your pacing and you'll have a map of where we've been today. Do the same on your new pitch, and you'll save me the work of dialling another end.'

'Thank you Capun. I will show you the map when I have it drawn.'

Mathew claps him on the shoulder. 'You're your father's son, that's for certain.'

They climb to grass, Thomas carrying the boxed dial and tripod over one shoulder and even so reaching surface well before his stepfather. He sits waiting on the attle dump, chilled by the north-east wind that raises grit and dust from the dressing floor and moans in the headgear above him. But he notices none of this.

In his mind he is still underground, not on the 40 fathom level, but deeper where his father died. He puzzles now. Search as he might, there is no page in his father's book that exactly maps the workings on the 120 fathom level, only the symbols whose meaning – if he has rightly understood them – gives him such an inward glow he could almost laugh out loud. Instead he mutters to himself, 'It can only be that he did not dial it. I will do so myself and draw the map as he would have done, once we have it cleared.'

Mathew Clymo's head appears at the mouth of the shaft. They walk side by side to the dry, Thomas almost as tall as his stepfather and already broader in the shoulders.

'Boy, you'll be the death o' me scampering up them ladders like that.' Mathew coughs and spits. 'Will you come up to the house now? Join me and your mother for our Sunday tea?'

'Thank you Capun', but I'll be off home now.' He puts his boots and hat and tallows beneath his peg upon the wall and turns toward the door. 'And thank you kindly, Capun', for the lesson. I have it now, in here. He taps his head. 'I'll dial my pitch tomorrow.'

'I can't get near that boy of yours, Grace, no matter what I do.' They've had both tea and supper and Mathew sits before the fire with his stockinged feet stretched out.

'He'll come round. Just give him time.' Grace sits opposite darning children's socks.

'That's what you said before but he's still cold as ice with me. Lord – I saved him from the hangman, gave him his own pitch and now I teach him like he was my own son, but he still won't call me "father". And he can't stay alone in that house forever. It belongs to the duke. Sooner or later that bugger Scoble will be on my arse. There's plenty of miners' families still wanting. He'll have to come and live with us, grieving for his dad or no.'

'He won that pitch fair and square, Mathew Clymo, and you knows it. An' he's making you richer every day, just like my poor John. 'Sides, I've news for you might take your mind off Thomas.' She drops her darning in her lap and smiles across at him. 'I've not had my visitor this month.'

'What? What visitor?'

'My monthlies, you stupid man. I'm carrying your child.'

'No! Oh my beautiful love, so soon?' He crosses to her, takes her face in his hands and kisses the top of her head. 'A son, my own son. What shall we call him?'

'Him? What if it's a girl?'

'Yes of course – I don't know. My mind was filled with Thomas. I'm sorry. I love you so much, Grace Clymo.' He pulls her to her feet, and with his arms around her buries his face in her hair. 'Oh Lord, my life is perfect. My mine, my wife, my family. I am the happiest of men. I love you Grace Clymo. I'd bed you now and make another.'

'Silly man.'

27

THE ADVENTURERS

THE STEADY BACKGROUND THUMP AND HISS OF THE beam engine goes unnoticed by the gossiping city men. They are all here, the shareholders. Some Mathew knows. James Sanderson, his original backer, is in the chair. Yelloly Watson is chatting avidly to Barrington-Purdue, and there are others he recalls from previous counthouse dinners. But many he does not know, for the shares have changed hands many times as the price has risen, fallen and risen again. It stands now at sixty-two pounds. And there of course is Scoble representing the duke, and in deep conversation with a bewhiskered, top-hatted fat man whom Mathew has never seen before.

They have finished examining the cost books and they are happy men. In the three months since the last accounting two thousand eight hundred tons of copper ore have been brought to grass at Cornish Great Consols. The company has made a profit of twelve thousand five hundred and twenty-two pounds; this quarter it will pay a dividend of twelve pounds per share. And for Mathew Clymo, Captain of the Wheal Emma mine, this will put three thousand six hundred pounds in his account at Bolitho's Bank in Truro.

'Well gentlemen, I suggest we clear the decks for dinner, unless of course there is any other business,' Sanderson says.

The fat man next to Scoble gets to his feet. 'Gentlemen, I am Josiah Hocking at your service.' He looks around the table. 'Mr Chairman, I have some business I wish to bring to the attention of the meeting.'

'He's a broker,' Sanderson mutters to Mathew sitting beside him, then says, 'Certainly Mr Hocking, feel free to speak.'

Hocking covers a cough with his hand then speaks. 'Gentlemen, I have been asked to speak on behalf a number of the shareholders here present.'

One of the Adventurers nods and another two sitting opposite Hocking appear to be studying the table. Scoble looks up and stares at Mathew.

'You will of course recall that for nearly four months last year this mine was in the red and many of us lost considerable sums of money. I put it to you that these losses were the result of gross negligence on the part of Captain Clymo who failed to adequately supervise the purser in the management of the mine accounts. He has also permitted the said purser to abscond.'

'For shame.' 'Disgraceful.' 'Sit down Hocking, you blackguard.'

Half the shareholders are on their feet shouting. Mathew sits rigid as Sanderson waits for the hubbub to subside. 'Gentlemen, gentlemen, please. What is your point, Mr Hocking? Wheal Emma is now back in profit and has just paid a record dividend. All thanks to Captain Clymo and his gallant miners.'

'That's as may be, but we cannot afford to allow such a situation to arise in the future. Consequently I wish to propose that Captain Clymo be relieved of his duties forthwith, and a new mine captain be appointed to manage Wheal Emma.'

There is renewed shouting while several men are banging on the table. Mathew Clymo has gone as pale as one of his own miners, and once again Scoble catches his eye. This time there is the beginnings of a smile on his lips.

'This is Scoble's doing,' Mathew turns to Sanderson. 'Look at his face. Can he do it?'

'I am obliged to put it to the vote.'

'Surely we have enough stock between us to vote down this motion?'

Sanderson extracts the share ledger from beneath the pile of papers in front of him and opens it. He runs a finger down the list of names and looks from man to man around the table.

'I am not sure. I have a proxy for young William Morris. Hocking and Scoble have four hundred between them.'

'What? Why didn't you tell me Scoble has bought stock?'

'I'm sorry but it slipped my mind. Besides, I thought it of little account. I assumed he must be proxy for the duke.'

They are still muttering to each other when a red-faced Hocking shouts over the noise in the room, 'A vote Mr Chairman, I demand a vote.'

'I cannot refuse him, Mathew.' Sanderson gets to his feet.

'Gentlemen, Mr Hocking has tabled a motion that we replace Captain Clymo. I cannot agree with this. Captain Clymo discovered this mine and has served us well. If the motion is passed I shall resign the chair. Now, all those in favour please raise your hands.'

Five hands go up – those of Hocking, Scoble and three other shareholders whom Mathew does not know. Sanderson sits down and makes ticks against the names in the ledger, then says, 'All those against.' Hands go up, Sanderson makes more notes, his lips moving as he counts.

The meeting falls silent. Mathew feels a tightness in his chest. Scoble is staring at him, eyes wide and grinning. Sanderson gets to his feet again.

'Gentlemen, the motion is carried by one hundred votes.' There is an eruption of boos and cheers.

'God rot his soul,' Mathew murmurs through gritted teeth. 'He's stole my mine. I'll stuff his mouth with a month-old turd. No, I'll kill him.'

'No you won't, Mathew,' Sanderson says sitting down. 'You're still a rich man.'

As the hubbub dies down he announces, 'Gentlemen, I think this is a most unfortunate decision and as a measure of my support for Captain Clymo I hereby tender my own resignation. Now – I suggest we move to dinner but I for one shall have but a poor appetite.' Conversation erupts again, amidst the scraping of chairs as the Adventurers get to their feet and mill around.

Little Yelloly Watson looks up at Josiah Hocking. 'Sir, I am but a modest shareholder and clearly my votes counted for little but I have a deep interest in mining affairs. Might I ask you a question?'

'Feel free, dear sir, feel free. What would you ask?'

'I assume have a replacement in mind for Captain Clymo?'

'We do indeed. Yes, we do.'

'And who might that be, if I am not being indiscreet?'

'Not at all, not at all. Mr Scoble here has offered the post to Captain

Kit Robin of Dolcoath and Captain Robin has already accepted. Is that not so, Mr Scoble?'

Scoble can't restrain a smirk. 'Captain Robin is on his way from Dolcoath this very instant.'

'Ah – is he indeed? I am acquainted with Captain Robin. I had the pleasure of meeting him on my last visit to Dolcoath. Thank you, my good sirs.' He gives a slight bow and skirts around the table until he is at Mathew Clymo's side. 'They've given the job to Kit Robin,' he says.

'That philandering wastrel. The bugger's good for nothing but bothering the bal maidens.' He glowers around the room. 'But thank you Mr Watson for your support. Will you join us at dinner?'

The taste of Jenny Tuttle's roast beef in Mathew's mouth is like dust off the dressing floor; he takes swig after swig of red wine to wash it down.

'Easy, Mathew,' John Sanderson says. 'Don't let 'em see how this has hurt you. We'll fix Hocking and his pals. Soon as I am back in the City I'll be selling all my stock. Yours too if you wish. Then I'll sell them short. We'll see how they like a dose of their own medicine. What say you, Mr Watson?'

'I say I'll not hold shares in a mine run by Kit Robin. And I shall put it around amongst my acquaintance that Wheal Emma's on the road to ruin.'

'Good man.'

Mathew Clymo puts his knife and fork down and wipes his mouth. 'It was my mine, my damned mine – and the blackguards have stolen it.'

He gets to his feet, jams his hat on his head and looks once around the table. 'You'll find me at home,' he mutters. He leaves the room without a backward glance.

'Clymo will find himself another mine, you mark my words,' John Sanderson says, 'and I'll back him when he does.'

'And so will I,' replies Yelloly Watson. 'So will I.'

28

MATHEW AND GRACE

 'FOR GOODNESS SAKE, MATHEW, YOU CAN'T SIT HERE all day brooding. Get out and do something. Get up on the moor, clear your head o' last night's brandy fumes.'

It is mid-morning and Mathew Clymo still sits in his armchair beside the fire. He is dressed as if for work, as he has dressed every working day since the counthouse dinner a week ago. But he goes nowhere.

At times he dozes, having slept so little the night before, lying awake and dwelling on his loss. He wants to be underground, making his way alone along the drives and crosscuts and up and down the ladderways, exchanging greetings with the miners – his miners: checking their workplace, their safety, and sharing their good fortune when the copper minerals glitter in the face, and their disappointment when the lode is lost or the ground is poor. He misses the stink of the mine on his clothing and in his hair. He misses the stinging relief of the scalding shower in the dry after he is come to grass.

But all this has been taken away by Scoble's guile. He wakes in the morning after fitful sleep with aching teeth, and Grace tells him he has been grinding them all night.

'No bloody wonder Grace. I am in bloody mourning. I made that mine, I loved it and it's gone. I don't care for all the money I have made by selling Cornish Consols. I may have a fortune at Bolitho's but what good is that? Scoble, the scabrous vagabond stole not just my mine. He's stolen my bloody life.'

She kneels at his side, takes his hands in hers. 'Mathew, am I not your life too? Me and the child I bear?'

'Of course, my lover.' He leans forward and kisses her on the forehead. 'I am sorry and you are right, I must do something. I'll go out, right now, up on the moor. Pack me a croust the way you used to, and I'll walk all day.'

She takes his oilskin satchel from a peg in the hallway where it has hung since the day of the counthouse dinner. In the kitchen she cuts two slices of bread from the loaf she baked the day before. Between the bread she puts slabs of cheese and sliced onion, wraps this in a linen cloth which suddenly reminds her of John Pascoe's shroud. She sighs. She made croust just this way for John when it wasn't a day for pasties.

Mathew says she must get a cook but she will not put on airs and graces just because he has money in the bank; although until last week, Jenny Tuttle took time from duties in the counthouse to help her clean this house. Grace puts the food and a bottle of ale in the satchel and calls out, 'Tis ready my lover,' then Mathew comes into the kitchen and takes her in his arms and kisses her and slings the satchel across his chest just as if he were on his way down the mine. She hears the front door slam, sighs and puts a kettle on the range; she opens the fire door, rakes the coals and adds a log. Then Grace sits at the scrubbed table and wonders at the turn her life has taken.

Here she is, a bal maiden, wife of the richest man in Penpillick, and in half of Cornwall for all she knows; mistress of the big house, and her children in the Dame school learning their letters. And of course there's Thomas. She sighs again, gets up as the kettle boils and makes herself a pot of tea. Thomas: still mining though he need not, were he not so proud and could accept his stepfather's generosity. But he will not and though the ache has faded somewhat, still she worries every day until she knows that he is safe. And she is partly relieved that Mathew sulks at home instead of roaming in the darkness down below. So strange a thing that is – where she has never been and never will; and stranger still when she feels the dull thump of blasting deep beneath her feet marking each core's end.

Perhaps she should suggest they leave Penpillick now that he is no longer owner. But where would they go? A fine house in Liskeard, or even Plymouth? She would be lonely, but she is lonely here. She misses Jenny Tuttle, and some days even misses the dressing floor and the swing of her hammer. She rolls her shoulders and feels the muscles built from years of breaking rock. The day stretches before her. She'll clean the house and fetch the children, make their tea and then his dinner. Later, they'll sit again before the fire and perhaps he will have decided on their future. She pours herself another dish of tea.

'God damn you Scoble, God damn you. I will have you, yes I will.'

He shouts and shouts and his words are carried with the snowflakes on the wind. As if in reply a curlew rises almost at his feet, calls its plaintive cry and wheels away. His boots crunch on icy puddles and frozen mud as he strides out across the moor in the face of a bitter north-west gale. But he cares nothing for wind nor weather or this bleak and dreary moor, is barely conscious of where he walks. His mind is set on vengeance.

He clenches his fists as thoughts of violence rise like bile within him. That would be easy, too easy – his hands around Scoble's skinny neck, squeezing, squeezing and watching the man's eyes fill with the fear of death. But no, that way leads only to the hangman's rope. It is Scoble who belongs in Bodmin Gaol, not him and certainly not Tom Pascoe.

Then he remembers: of course, that was what he was going to do before the counthouse dinner coup – lay Scoble's part in Thomas Pascoe's case before the duke. He will gather all the evidence, for Scoble's motives are now plain for all to see – he has long been plotting to steal the mine and Pascoe's book was part of that. There's not just the fact that Scoble manipulated Consols' stock, or even that he had him voted out of office; but the part he played in Thomas Pascoe's imprisonment and trial – that was clearly criminal. Mathew has no doubt that Scoble stole John Pascoe's journal. He could call on Maisie Tuttle if need be for Thomas has told him how she stole it back. He smiles – a clever girl is Maisie Tuttle.

The book – so much has hinged upon it. Grace lied to him. She had the book that first time he called at the cottage after John Pascoe died. But he forgives her the lie, for what right did he have on that summer evening to take it from her. Besides, it is of no use to him now: Thomas is clearly guided by it and follows Wheal Emma's lodes as if seeing clear through solid rock. So if Scoble had the book, then those that stole it were in his pay. They caused the Reverend Dippenden's demise then attacked the boy that selfsame night; he'll call on Robert Carew as a witness. Yes – he will scupper Scoble's boat, get the man arrested and locked in Bodmin Gaol where he belongs. But then? Scoble's cronies would still control Wheal Emma. He must turn his back on that, forget his mine. 'But I am a miner, I know nothing else,' he mutters.

With that thought Mathew stands still and looks around. The snow has stopped and the clouds lift off the tor ahead. He is high on Caradon Hill, has walked in a great five-mile loop and now is hungry. A winter sun is breaking through as he strides across the springy ground to the shelter of the rocks. He sits, takes out his croust and as he eats he gazes east – clear across the vale of hedge-squared fields, past Callington and Tavistock, until his eye rises to the dark bulk of Dartmoor.

There, that is where he'll prospect, beyond the Tamar. They've been mining tin around the margins of the moor for centuries and where there's tin there's copper. He has found one mine; he can find another. He will start tomorrow. Cooking Scoble's goose can wait.

29

HARD TIMES

IT IS SPRING IN PENPILLICK AND WARM IN THE VALLEY.
A cuckoo calls and calls again and another responds from clear
across the woods.

'My Pa's so sick and we'll have no place to live next week,' Maisie
Tuttle says. They are leaning on the bridge staring at the stream below,
watching strands of weed waving in the current. 'Mr Scoble will throw
us out as Pa can't work no more. He sits by the fire all day coughin'
and spittin'. He can't hardly breathe. But Mr Scoble says 'cos' Pa ain't
no more a miner we've no right to the cottage.'

Thomas takes her hand which rests upon the parapet. 'I'm sorry
about your father, Maisie. Seems some miners get the black lung, some
don't. I been spitting black a while now but that's all. But isn't your Ma
still working for Wheal Emma at the counthouse?'

'Not from Monday she ain't. She'll be back on the dressing floor
breakin' rock. Mr Scoble says there ain't no need for women in the
counthouse, and bal maidens ain't got no right to a miner's cottage 'cos
they ain't miners. What'll we do, Thomas?'

'Tell your Ma you can all come and live with me. I've room enough.
Be company too.'

'You think Mr Scoble will allow that?'

'I don't know. I thought he'd tell Capun Kit to stop me bidding last
setting day but I won the pitch I wanted. He's been nice as pie to me
since Capun Clymo left.' He was silent a while, gazing down at the water.
'Maybe he's still after the book. But if he is he hasn't asked me for it.'

'He don't need the book no more 'cos he's got you. Long as you
go on findin' copper for him, he'll keep you on.'

'You may be right. We're getting good copper on our pitch but
the ground is failing on the south lode where all the other pitches are.
And Capun Kit, he don't know one pitch from another and has no
idea who should be working where and when. Caleb Chapman and

193

Jakeh James are drivin' a winze to catch the leader lode on the 220, but they've barely gone a fathom down in two week. And I'm not sure the lode will be there at all when they do get down. With the cut in pay for tutwork they're not exactly trying hard. Could be months before they reach it. And if they lose the lode he'll want my book, be sure of that.'

'Will you give it to him?'

'No, never. It was my father's.' They fall silent, still gazing at the stream below. Then without looking up but still holding her hand Thomas says, 'Maisie, there is something in the book I have to tell you. I have not told anyone, not even my mother.'

'Well, tell me then. Don't keep me hanging.'

'Swear you'll not breathe a word of what I tell you now.'

'Thomas, I swear, though there ain't no need. You knows you can trust me.'

'In the letter he wrote before he was killed my father said the book would make our fortune. Once I learned to read it, I thought he meant that it would help me be a miner just as good as he was.'

Maisie nods. 'Well, that's no secret. Whole of Penpillick knows that.'

'Yes – but there's something else. On the last two pages he wrote about the crosscut he was working on where he was killed. He used a symbol I've not found elsewhere in the book. For copper he always used this mark – with his fingernail Thomas scratches a circle with a cross beneath in the lichen on the parapet. 'Where he found good copper he repeated the symbol two or sometimes three times. But here he marked the copper symbol followed by this.' Then he scratches a number eight lying on its side. 'You know what that is?'

Maisie tilts her head. 'Number eight?'

'Yes, that's what I thought at first. But he repeats it three times and underlines it.' He scratches two more symbols. 'It's nowhere else in the book. I pondered long and hard on it. Nowhere does he write numbers lying on their side like that. So I thought it must have some meaning and searched in the mathematical books I have not looked in since I left my school. I found it. Guess what it means.'

'Thomas Pascoe, I ain't got no idea. I weren't never good at numbers.'

'It means "infinity".'

'An' what's that?'

'A number bigger than any you can imagine. Don't you see Maisie – he's saying that he has found a huge amount of copper, more than he ever saw anywhere before.'

'And then the roof collapsed and he was kilt.'

'Exactly. That's the mystery. Maybe somebody spied on him and saw the copper then killed him for it. But that makes no sense, as whoever it was would have cleared the end to mine my father's pitch. So Henry, Jethro Loam and I are clearing it in secret on the night core. I want to find out if the copper is really there and maybe how and why the back caved in on him.'

'You're working on the day core and then on nights?'

'No, not every night, we can only manage two or three a week. Even so, we should break through the rock fall soon.'

'And then?'

'If the copper is really there, we'll mine it. Take it to grass on the day core. Pretend it's from our pitch on the north lode. Capun Kit will never know and Scoble knows nothing about mining.'

'You'll be making Mr Scoble even richer now, Capun Clymo's lost the mine.'

'I don't care about that. I need to make enough money to . . .' He pauses and takes a folded newspaper sheet from inside his jacket.

'To what, Thomas Pascoe?'

'Marry you and take you to Australia.' He says this in the rush of a single breath, then putting his arm around her, adds, 'Look Maisie, look here.'

He unfolds the newspaper on the parapet and reads: " Wanted, Experienced Miners at the Burra Burra Copper Mine, South Australia." Capun Clymo told me the pay out there is twice what we get here. With what I know about rocks and minerals I could earn a fortune. We'd be rich. And they say the sun shines out there all the time and I wouldn't get no black lung.'

'Did you say "marry me"? Are you proposin' to me?'

'I am, I am, Maisie. Will you marry me?'

'Course I will, and I'll even go to Australia with you.'

He turns her to him, tilts up her bonnet, kisses her. She leans back against the parapet and puts her hands on his shoulders and pulls her to him. 'Thomas Pascoe – I been waiting for you to do that since you come out of Bodmin Gaol.'

'And I've been waiting to do it.' He kisses her again. 'But let's keep it secret for now. Until we have the money for Australia.'

'And how long might that be?'

'I don't know, Maisie. I don't even know how much the passage costs. But I shall find out.'

She smiles at him then says, 'But if we go, what'll I do about Ma and Pa?'

'My mother has a baby on the way – Capun Clymo's. I reckon she'll need a maid. Would your Ma be housemaid?'

'Anythin's better than breakin' rock. I'll ask her.' The late afternoon sun glints through the trees beside the stream. The cuckoos have stopped their calling and the wood is silent. Then a thrush starts up in the alders, tries a phrase, repeats it, stops as if considering before singing anew. 'I got to get back,' Maisie says, 'I must be at the Fountain come evenin' time.'

As they stroll hand-in-hand up through the village, they hear hoof beats on the cobbles behind them and Thomas turns.

William Scoble reins in his horse beside him. 'Good evening Thomas Pascoe.'

'Good evening Mr Scoble, sir.' Thomas touches his forelock.

'How goes it on the north lode, boy? Your pitch is all that you expected?'

'It is, sir. We're mining good copper though 'tis mixed with a bit of mundic.'

Scoble stares down at him. 'Tell me boy, how is it that every pitch you chose on setting day is always good?'

'Just luck, sir and maybe what my father taught me.'

'Indeed.' He leans down and pats the horse's neck. ' Tsk, tsk, Nelson.'

They watch him ride up towards the cottages, pause outside the Tuttles' then ride on. 'He didn't say nowt to me,' Maisie says. 'No good evenin, nothin'. Like I wasn't here.'

'You stole my book from under his nose. He'll not have forgotten that.'

'"Mundic", Nelson – "mundic"? What in God's name is that?' Scoble mutters. How hard it is to be civil to the Pascoe boy but it has to be. Together with that Hopeful Down oaf and that filthy Jethro Loam, his pare make more between them than four other pares combined. And the more they make the more he gets. And it's not from what Pascoe's father taught him, it's that damned book. But Loam says he doesn't take it underground but notes what he sees on slates and takes them home with him.

Scoble has been down the mine himself three times now with Captain Kit, who gets them lost as often as not, and he finds himself close to panic. To his chagrin he has discovered that he doesn't like it beneath the ground – the darkness, the stink of sulphur, human shit and rotting wood; the sound of ever running water, the sense that the roof might fall in on him at any time. Most of all he hates the timbered tunnels where, looking up, he can see the broken rubble above his head where water seeps or dust and dirt trickle soundlessly in the candlelight. And a dozen times he has cracked his skull on unseen balks of timber holding up the roof. Then last time he was down they blasted in a nearby end, scaring him so much he almost wet himself. No, underground is not for him – but he must go down there if he is to understand the workings of what now belongs to him.

Kit Robin teaches him a little every day – the words the miners use: the lode, the stope, the crosscut, winze and drive. It seems so simple to dig a hole and bring up riches, but more than half the time these clannish miners dig and blast and drill and bring up nothing, yet must be paid. He can see it in their covert looks that they despise him and laugh behind his back; he hears their muttered Capun Clymo this and Capun Clymo that. God damn Capun Clymo. And week by week the price of copper falls and the price of Cornish Consuls with it. But he's still making money, oh yes – for he pays them less than Clymo did, and in spite of all their griping they still climb down those slimy ladders into the darkness every day.

Then there is the letter from William Morris saying he will pay well for arsenic to colour wallpaper, of all things. Kit Robin says there is a great mound of the stuff behind the attle dump but it would need burning – calcining is the word he used – before it could be sold and that would mean investing money. His comfort is he's so much richer than he's ever been now he's left the duke's employ. And how good it is not to have to bow and scrape to his bloody lordship who was less than pleased when he gave short notice.

But goddam Clymo still lives in the big house at the top of the village, and that's a thorn in his flesh. The house should be his but Clymo built it with his own money, not Wheal Emma's . What's more, the rumours have it that he's found copper in bloody Devon of all places. He passed him on horseback on the Callington road a week back. Neither greeted the other, but from the corner of his eye it seemed to Scoble that Clymo smiled. And what would he have to smile about, he wonders.

30

DISCOVERY

SWEAT RUNNELS THE GRIME ON THEIR FACES, SOAKS their woollen shirts and trickles down their arms and legs. It is well past midnight, but to the three miners the passing of time is marked only by their increased exhaustion and the lighting of one tallow from the guttering remnants of another. The air is foul in the dead end on the 120 fathom level. The tendons of Jethro Loam's skinny arms stand out like whipcord as he swings his mallet, driving wedges between the timber props and lagging boards that support the crumbling tunnel roof. 'She's in there now boys, safe and snug.'

'Let's to it Thomas – see what's hiding behind this pile o' duds. We'm almost there, I reckon.' Henry Hopeful Down and Thomas Pascoe scramble up the sloping pile of rubble and using picks and bars and bare hands start slinging rocks down to the tunnel floor. Jethro Loam shovels rock into a barrow and trundles off down the crosscut to dump the load down a mined-out stope.

This is the tenth night in a month that they have managed to sneak underground unobserved to work at clearing the rock fall.

'It's in the book,' Thomas has told them. 'The secret to my father's death lies at the face. I am sure of it.'

'I don't know what that could be, Thomas, but I'll help you,' Henry said, and Jethro Loam nodded his agreement.

But it is desperate work and they have been at it for weeks. They can only manage a couple of hours each night. They start dog tired from a day underground and the climb to grass, only to descend again when all is quiet and old Harry dozes by his brazier. There are timbers and boards to lug in secret from the working areas of the mine to support the roof before they can begin to clear the rubble. But foot by painful foot, they have progressed and perhaps it will be tonight when they break through.

Thomas is lying on his belly now, pushing rocks and rubble behind him with both hands and boots as if he were swimming in the darkness. His back grazes the tunnel roof, and the stink of his own body is in his nostrils as he burrows like a rat a-top the rubble pile. He has taken the tallow from his hat and only the faint glimmer from Henry's candle on the slope below illuminates the rock that blocks his way. He drives his pick between rock and roof and levers downwards. There is the sudden crack of breaking rock and a massive weight across his shoulders pins him down. He tries to wriggle backwards but he cannot move. 'Henry, Henry, I'm stuck, stuck fast,' he gasps.

'Easy boy, easy now.'

Thomas feels Henry grasp his ankles and pull, but rocks dig into his chest as he is jammed more tightly between the rock pile and the slab of roof he has dislodged. He senses the great weight above him – one hundred and twenty fathoms of rock and earth between him and moonlight. His breathing quickens and he squirms in panic. His bowel loosens and he wants to scream. But above his panting and the thudding of his heart, Henry's voice comes again.

'Easy, easy. Calm down now. Up here Jethro, we needs a hand.'

Jethro Loam scrabbles up the rock pile. 'We mun get a wedge under that there slab,' Jethro says and slides back down again. He takes a balk of pine and with expert axe blows splits it lengthways, trims it and climbs back up to Henry.

'Quick, quick. I can scarcely breathe,' Thomas whimpers. He feels the wedge being driven in beside him and cries out as a splinter penetrates his thigh. The pressure on his back eases a fraction and Henry pulls him backwards only to jam him once again.

'He mun go forward, Henry, so's I can drive another timber under,' Jethro says.

'Henry I can't, I dursen't.'

'Yes you can. Go forward, boy. Come on now, do it.'

Thomas slows his breathing and using his pick clears just enough space before him to wriggle a head length forward. He breathes easier now but knows he is still trapped, flat on his belly with his head sideways in the tiny gap he has created. The panic starts to rise again.

Is this where he will die – on the selfsame pile of broken rubble that killed his father? How foolish he has been to dream of promised wealth when all it brings is death in the dark places of Wheal Emma. And what grief his dying will bring to Maisie and his mother.

He feels the tears start and unable to brush them away is suddenly ashamed. He steels himself and in utter darkness stretches out his hand, feels space amongst the rubble and hammers sideways with his pick. Blow after feeble blow he strikes until the pick whistles through thin air and he hears the rattle of falling rock and senses space opening up before him.

'I'm through, Henry, I'm through,' he yells. At the same time he hears the thump of mallet on timber, the creak of lifting rock and they haul him back by the ankles. His chest and back scrape on jagged points of rock, he cries out in pain, burying his face in his arms. Then he is free and lies gasping halfway down the rock pile, like a fish landed on a riverbank. 'I was through Henry, I got through.'

'That's as maybe but you ain't going in there again. Not 'til we got her safe an' sound. If Jethro here weren't so handy with timber an' axe we would've lost you. And what would I say then to your poor Ma and Capun Clymo?'

He rolls gently over on to his back, looks up at the big man's pockmarked face shadowed in the candlelight. 'You're right Henry. Shall we leave it now, go back up to grass? Save it for another night?'

'I reckon so, boy. That sit right with you, Jethro Loam?'

'It do. We don't want no more scares like that, and I needs more timber if we're to make her safe.'

Two nights pass before the three stand once again looking up at the very narrow gap they left between the rubble and the roof.

'No, Thomas Pascoe, you ain't going in there again till she's all shored up and safe.'

Thomas nods and he and Henry set to, holding up the props which Jethro Loam secures with driven wedges. Once the tunnel's back is safe they start again with clearing; hour by hour the space above them widens. After an age of steady labour they take a break and sit down in a row on an as yet unused balk of timber. They drink and eat.

'Scoble knows,' Jethro Loam says.

'Knows what?' Henry asks.

'That we work nights clearing this here end.'

Thomas nods, 'You told him?'

'I did. I said as how you was trying to find out who killed your father.'

'Why'd you tell him that then?' Henry asks.

'So's he trusts me. An' he does.' Jethro sniggers. 'Told me he don't care what we do long as we keep diggin' out copper on day core. Don't even care for your book now. Knows it's what guides us. Anyways, I reckon he's afeared of comin' down here.'

'So much the better,' Thomas says. 'Shall we get to it? Just another hour now?'

Wearily they get to their feet and taking up picks and shovels and steel bars attack the rock fall yet again.

'Know something, young Thomas,' Henry Hopeful Down says, 'you weren't never nearly through t'other night.' He is halfway up the pile of rock looking at the roof. 'Back's lifted up here. Tis a good three foot higher. That were the space you found.'

Jethro scrambles up beside them. 'You're right. Now why would that be? T'ain't bad ground.' He runs his fingers along the roof of the tunnel. 'Hey, this here's been drilled and blasted. Look there's the steel marks but there ain't no vein to follow upwards – so why?'

Thomas holds a candle close to the grooves his father must have drilled. 'I think I know.' he says, 'But I ain't going to say till I'm sure and I won't be sure till I see the face.'

'You'm full of mystery, boy. Is that just to keep us working?'

'No, Henry. If I say what I think before I know it to be true, maybe I'll be wrong.' He crawls forward on his belly. 'I reckon I could get through now.' He holds up his tallow. 'Henry, look. I can see something in there. I'm going in.'

'No you ain't. Come on down. You gave us scare enough last time. Patience now. Just two more props and an' a couple o' they boards an' we'll be safe as houses.'

Finally they stand beneath their timbering, looking over the remnants of the rubble.

'Well, Thomas. Ain't you going in?'

Thomas is silent, remembering his father's broken body and the narrowness of his own escape the night before. His breathing quickens as on hands and knees he crawls through the gap between rock and roof. Then the rock pile slopes away from him and he half slides, half tumbles to the floor losing his hat and tallow. Now the only light is the glimmer of candles from the other side. He gropes on the floor, finds the tallow, sits up and taking a lucifer from the pocket in his shirt, strikes it on the sole of his boot and lights the candle. He holds it aloft, stands and holds it higher still.

'Lord Jesus Christ,' he whispers. He takes three steps forward and is at the face running his fingers over a great mass of metal ore glittering blue and yellow in the wavering candlelight. 'Henry, Jethro, come, come quick,' he shouts, 'You've never seen the like. I've never seen the like. No one's ever seen the like. A new lode. The whole face is copper. Oh my word!'

The light increases as first Henry then Jethro Loam come and stand beside him.

'Look, just look,' Tom says, 'Peacock ore – and here, here look – pure copper.' His dirty forefinger traces out a foot-wide vein across the face.

'Well, bugger me,' Henry says. 'This mun be the richest lode in the whole 'o Cornwall. 'An' it belongs to that Scoble, damn his eyes. But you won't be telling him that – will you Jethro Loam?'

'Never will I breathe a word. I'll keep it dead secret till setting day. We can't mine it till then an' we don't want no one else biddin' against us. Long as we can mine it. Oh I'm going to be so rich.' Jethro Loam does a little jig in the candle light.

'Calm down boy, calm down. Looks like you been at that bloody cider again.'

Thomas is quiet as all three of them hold their candles high to the face.

'Lord, Lord,' Henry whispers.

'Looks like gold, dunnit.' Jethro says.

'I don't know. I've never seen gold in the ground,' Thomas says running his hand across the face again. 'But you're right Jethro, we'll have to show this to Capun Kit before setting day. He'll not sett it to us lest he sees it. I'll bring him down a day before and that's two weeks away. We'll tell no one else and not come here again till then. Agreed?'

Both men nod.

'You mun give it a name, Thomas. What shall we call 'un?'

'How about the Pascoe Lode, after my father?'

'Perfect, boy, perfect. Let's get us back up to grass now.'

As they climb ladder after ladder up to the surface Thomas's mind is in a whirl. He hasn't told them all he knows – and if he did, could he trust them? Henry Hopeful Down for sure, but Jethro? And is either of them wise enough to tell him how he should proceed? He doubts it. No, there is only one man he can turn to now and that is Mathew Clymo. He must swallow all that pride and tell all to his stepfather. But first he must make one more night-time visit to his father's end, to the Pascoe Lode, for that is how he thinks of it. Not tomorrow, he'll be too tired – but perhaps on Sunday night.

31

REVELATIONS

MONDAY EVENING HE STRIDES UP THROUGH PENPILLICK fresh bathed and dressed in shirtsleeves and best flannel trousers, with a red scarf at his neck. His boots strike sparks off the cobbled roadway. He nods to the miners gathered at the door of the Bedford Arms.

'A drink young Pascoe, join your mates fer a drink.'

He shakes his head.

'Too big for your boots,' a miner says, but Thomas just smiles at him. Over his shoulder he carries his satchel which swings heavily against his hip. A blackbird scolds its evening complaint from the hedge that marks the end of the row of cottages. At the top of the village he opens the gate leading to Mathew Clymo's fine stone house, and knocks upon the door.

'You need not knock, my son,' his mother says, opening to him. 'This would be your home if it weren't for your stubborn pride.'

He kisses her on the cheek. 'No matter, Mother. Is the capun home? I needs talk to him and to you too.'

'Me too? It must be serious. He is in the parlour. You go in, I'll bring us a dish of tea.' She bustles to the kitchen while he walks down the dim corridor and knocks at the open parlour door. The room is filled with flickering firelight and smells of wood smoke. Mathew Clymo sits dozing by the fire with his feet up, exhausted after the long ride back from Dartmoor. He has been fossicking for weeks along its northern slopes where there is rumour of copper shows, but he has found nothing worthwhile yet.

'Capun?'

He wakes with a start, sees Thomas and stretches and yawns. 'Evening, young Thomas. Are you come to eat with us?'

'Well not really, Capun, though Mother's fixing tea. I have something I would show you both.'

'Something in your famous book no doubt,' Mathew says with a nod towards the satchel.

'Yes, but not just that.'

Grace comes in with a tray with tea, cups and cake which she puts upon the table. 'Stir yourself, Mathew, my lover. Thomas is here to talk to us.'

They sit at the table and Thomas takes out the book, wrapped as always in its oilskin cover, and lays it beside his cup of tea, but he does not open it. Instead, he takes a gulp of tea then delves deeper into his satchel, and draws out one after the other, three fist-sized stones and lays them on the table. They gleam and glisten in the firelight.

Mathew leans across the table, his mouth agape then closes it and whistles. He picks up one of the rocks and holds it up to the light from the window. 'Now where's this from, boy? Look Grace – your son has found us peacock ore. "bornite" some call it. I only seen it once or twice before in the early days at Wheal Emma. 'Twas your John that found it. Near the richest copper stone there is. Where's it from now, boy? Is there more of this? Speak up.'

But Thomas does not answer. He unwraps the book and opens it at the last page but one and lays it on the table. Then he speaks. 'I did not find it. My father did. See here.' He places his forefinger beneath a line of symbols, thus: $♀ \mathbf{x} \infty\infty\infty$.

Mathew shakes his head. 'Come on boy, tell us what it means, in plain English now.'

'It means a richer lode than my father had ever seen – copper times infinity.'

'Infinity is it? I'll be damned.'

'But where Thomas? Tell us where this comes from,' his mother cries.

'At the 120 fathom end where he died.'

'But that's completely blocked, caved in.'

'We have cleared it to the end and the whole face is in this stuff.' He holds up another glittering piece of ore. 'Near pure copper, is it not, Capun?'

'It is indeed. But "we", who in God's name is "we"?' Mathew is gripping the edge of the table.

'My pare – Henry Hopeful Down and Jethro Loam and me. We've worked at night for weeks and weeks.'

'Lord Christ! You've made that vagabond Scoble richer than Croesus.'

Thomas chuckles 'No we ain't. I dialled it last night. We're beyond Wheal Emma's sett. That's what my father knew. He even wrote it down. See here.' He turns the page and points to a thick line, with two thicker lines inked twice over crossing it. The words **W. E. Sett** are on one side, and on the other, **D. Bed**.

Mathew puts a finger beneath the letters and mutters, 'W.E. – Wheal Emma. D.Bed. – Duke of Bedford.' By God, a complete new lode beneath the duke's land. And richer than anything we've ever seen.'

'Exactly.'

'So my poor John found the wealth he promised us,' Grace whispers. 'And then he died. Why, why did the roof cave in on him? Who done it?'

Thomas reaches across the table and takes his mother's hands in both of his. 'I'm so sorry, Mother. No one done it. It was an accident. He drilled and blasted down the back to hide what he had found. He did not get out in time. Perhaps he stumbled and fell; perhaps the fuse burned too fast. He was on his own as always, so we'll never know.'

Grace is silent looking from one to the other, the tears welling in her eyes. Then she almost whispers, 'An accident, just as you always said, Mathew.' She heaves a great sigh and wipes her cheeks.

Mathew sits with his elbows on the table, chin in his hands staring at the open book. Then he leans back and says, 'Aye it was, my love.' Then he turns to Thomas, 'But tell me Thomas, why bring this to me? I am neither owner nor even captain of Wheal Emma.'

'Because I do not know what I should do and I know you will advise me wisely.' He hesitates, then, head down, he says, 'And you are my father and you saved me from the gallows.'

Mathew gets up from his chair, and Grace looks up too and sees tears in his eyes. He stands behind the boy and grips him by the shoulders. 'And you are my son. We shall drink to that, shall we not? And not with tea.'

He strides across to the dresser and takes a bottle from the cupboard and three glasses from the shelf. He pours three small tots of brandy, sits again and raises his glass. 'Thomas Pascoe, here's to you and your new lode.'

'And to you, Capun Clymo.' Thomas swigs the brandy down and coughs and splutters.

Mathew shakes his head and laughs. 'So you'd still rather call me Capun, then?'

'I would. It is how I think of you in my head. You are the Captain. Is he not, Mother?'

Grace smiles. 'He is indeed, and I am but a bal maiden and you are a but a bal boy.'

'Some bal boy.' Mathew bangs his glass down and pours himself another tot. 'Now listen hard. We must be very careful. We can breathe a word to no one of this discovery. Your work mates, will they talk?'

'No Capun. They are sworn to silence. We agreed we'll bid the end on setting day. Besides, I have not told them it lies outside Wheal Emma.'

Mathew smiles and turns to Grace. 'He's smart, this son of ours. Thomas, this very night you will take me down and we will dial the end together. We must be sure that this new lode indeed lies outside Wheal Emma's sett. Once that is done – tomorrow even – I will send a letter to the duke telling him you have found a new lode under his lands. Then we will meet with him and obtain a lease to mine it. With that in hand, I will write my friends in the City and we will find Adventurers to invest in your mine. You will be rich, Thomas, very rich.'

Thomas looks at his mother. 'It is what my father promised in his letter. Do you not remember, Mother? He wrote that the Book would bring us riches and it has.'

'I would sooner have him alive.'

'It was an accident, Grace. At least we now know that for sure.'

'Yes but I shall always mourn him.' She rises from her chair and stands behind her husband and her son. 'But I have you both. Now eat that cake while I put the little ones to bed.'

'What of Mr Scoble, Capun?' Thomas asks, his mouth full of cake.

'Once you have the lease, Scoble can go hang, damn his eyes.'

32

A NEW LEASE

FROM THE CORNER OF HIS EYE MATHEW STUDIES THE boy in the gig beside him. He sits bolt upright, holding the unfamiliar reins exactly as Mathew showed him when they set out from Penpillick. In truth, Thomas Pascoe is more man than boy – broad shoulders, and those sturdy thighs from climbing up and down the ladderways. He has the mine pallor of course, which in the bright sun makes his skin appear translucent. The cut on his chin suggests he's started to use his father's razor, and violet shadows beneath his eyes tell of the nights spent working underground.

It is three days since they dialled the 120 fathom level from the shaft station to the end. There is no doubt, they checked it twice: the richest copper face he could have dreamed of lies outside Wheal Emma. To be precise, five yards east of the line Clymo drew for the duke those years ago. The wheels of the gig crunch on the gravelled driveway as Endsleigh House comes into view.

'That is the biggest house I have ever seen,' Thomas says.

'Aye and it's not the duke's only house. I heard tell the family seat in Wiltshire is twice as big if not bigger.'

'And we bring him yet more wealth.' Thomas pats the satchel of samples on the seat between them.

'Aye, which is why he'll give us a lease over the Pascoe Lode.'

'So he'll get richer still, while the men of Penpillick work themselves to an early death.'

Mathew turns to look at the boy. 'And where does that idea come from, Thomas?'

'I've been reading a book by Mr Henry Hunt. The preacher gave it to me Sunday. Mr Hunt says children should never have to work nor should any man work more than ten hours a day.'

'Well, if you want to be rich boy, best keep them ideas to yourself. And when we talk to his Lordship, don't forget to address him as "Your Grace".'

'Yes Capun.'

Mathew sighs. The boy is right of course – children should not have to work. And he should have made more improvements at Wheal Emma – sunk another ventilation shaft at least. But the mine is no longer his and Scoble has reduced the rates for tutwork, which makes the miners' lives yet harder. Well, if the duke does grant the boy a lease, he'll go to Sanderson for capital and they will start a new mine. He will apply all he has learned yet could not afford – the latest Trevithick engine, proper ventilation to clear the face of powder smoke, and a man engine to reduce the drudgery of ladderways.

'Which way should I go? Round to the stables as the porter said?'

'No Thomas, we ain't servants nor tradesman. We're Cornish miners. Pull up at the foot of them steps and I'll knock on the front door.'

A footman opens to them. 'Yes?'

'Captain Clymo and Master Thomas Pascoe to see his Lordship.'

The footman closes the door in their faces. They wait some minutes until the door opens again and the butler says, 'This way please.'

They follow him into the Great Hall, where Thomas gapes first at the curving stairway then up to the frescoed ceiling. The butler leads them through a library to a door on which he knocks.

'Enter.'

'The miners to see you, my Lord.'

'Ah Clymo, good to see you.' The Duke of Bedford looks up from the large ledger opened on his desk. 'And this will be young Thomas Pascoe eh?'

'Yes your Grace.'

The duke stares at Thomas. 'Are you not the lad who was accused of murder?'

Thomas is at a loss. He has not expected this. He does not answer.

'He was found not guilty, your Grace.'

'Let the boy speak for himself, Captain. Come on now boy, speak up.'

'I was falsely accused your Grace. The Reverend Dippenden's death was an accident. He fell and hit his head.'

'Ah, but who caused the accident eh? You see Captain, I have been talking to my friend Sir Alexander Cockburn. It was he who prosecuted at the trial, you'll remember. He hates to lose a case at the best of times and this time he was reprimanded by the judge for bringing false witness into the court. He is a vengeful beast and has not let things lie. He has manslaughter in his mind. He gives me to understand that the maid admits that indeed there were two intruders on that unhappy afternoon, and that she heard sounds of an altercation and perhaps a fight. The intruders, whoever they were, have disappeared without trace. This leaves the boy here not just the only witness but the prime suspect. Cockburn has told the magistrate that he must bring further charges.'

'I told the court the truth, your Grace. Two men burst in when the Reverend and I were studying my father's book. They tried to steal it and I hit one of them, and he knocked the Reverend off his chair and the Reverend fell and struck his head.'

'That's as maybe, but you will need to convince a jury. But this is not why you are here, is it Captain? Sit down both of you.' He takes Mathew's letter from a drawer and studies it. 'So you found a new lode, boy, "cut it rich" as you miners say. How did that come about?'

'I did not discover it myself, your Grace. Twas my father found it more than two years ago but the back, the roof, collapsed and killed him. My mates and I cleared the fall and found what he discovered.'

'Your mates?'

'Henry Hopeful Down and Jethro Loam – my pare.'

'Are they not then to be party to this lease which you request from me?'

'Your Grace, I believe that the discovery belongs to Thomas as successor to John Pascoe. Show his Lordship, Thomas.'

Thomas takes his satchel from his shoulder. One he by one takes out the specimens of copper ore and places them on the leather desktop. They give off a metallic whiff of sulphur.

'Hmm, pretty, very pretty indeed. But why should I grant a mining lease to a mere boy who may yet be charged with manslaughter?'

'I have been a miner for almost two years, your Grace. My pare brings more copper to grass at Wheal Emma than any other. And I was not responsible for Reverend Dippenden's death, whatever Mr Cockburn says.'

'Sir Alexander Cockburn.' The duke pauses, lips pursed, then says, 'I take it, Captain Clymo, you will find investors and manage the mine on the boy's behalf.'

'I will, your Grace.'

'You have the map referred to in your letter?'

'I have, your Grace.' Mathew draws a document from his inside jacket pocket, unfolds it on the desk and weighs down the ends with the lumps of copper ore. On it Thomas has drawn the limit of Wheal Emma's sett, and beyond it an outline in careful cross-hatched pencil marked The Pascoe Lode.

The duke studies the map. 'How big is it?'

'We do not know, only that it is wider than the face. But a lode that wide and as rich as this,' he gestures at the samples, 'will undoubtedly have considerable length and depth.'

'Will you mine it from Wheal Emma or despoil my land with yet another of your shafts?'

'That would depend on the current owners of Wheal Emma.'

'And what does Mr Scoble think of this discovery?' Mathew tightens his lips and the duke smiles. 'Ah I see, he does not know.'

'No, your Grace, we believe not.'

'And when he finds out, then what?'

Thomas looks at his stepfather. 'Well,' Mathew says, 'he will not be over pleased – but if Thomas already has a lease there will be nothing he can do.'

The duke smiles. 'I imagine he would be most irate, Captain. Yes most irate – particularly given the bad blood between you. But as it happens I now have my own quarrel with Mr Scoble. Not only did he leave me in the lurch when he acquired Wheal Emma, it seems that while in my employ he used my money for his own ends.' He taps the ledger. 'Mr Vivian, who is my new agent, has been going through the books and found irregularities, hmm yes, irregularities, I say. And Mr Vivian is most thorough and exceedingly well qualified and comes to me with a most excellent reference from the Duchy of Cornwall itself. So I have little doubt of his integrity. What is more, he is greatly experienced in the business of mineral leases, having been responsible for that aspect of the Duchy's business for many years. Unfortunately he is over to Bolventor today otherwise I would have him here to advise me on the wisdom of your proposal.'

The duke pauses and rubs his balding pate. 'Now young Thomas Pascoe, I will not say yea or nay today but once I have discussed the matter with Mr Vivian I will let you know. Is that satisfactory, Captain?'

'Yes your Grace. We thank you.'

'You may leave these pretty stones and this map. I am sure they will be of great interest to Mr Vivian.'

'We will wait to hear then, your Grace. Come Thomas.'

They get to their feet and Thomas makes the slightest of bows and says, 'Good day your Grace and thank you.'

As they drive away Mathew says, 'You did well Thomas. You showed due respect but did not bow and scrape. You are indeed a miner and you make me proud. You would have made your father proud.'

'Thank you Capun. Will the duke grant me a lease do you think?'

Mathew rubs his chin. 'I think he will. He has become rich on the back of Wheal Emma and no man is ever rich enough. And clearly he is at odds with Scoble. But I know of William Vivian by reputation. They say he understands our business like no other and drove many a hard bargain for the Duchy. But even his eyes will pop when he sees that copper.'

They are quiet for a while, each wrapped in thought, lulled by the pony's steady clip-clop and the warmth of the early summer sun. Mathew lets his eyes close and sees again the copper lode gleaming in his candlelight, the boy beside him hacking out the samples with his father's pick. 'The Pascoe Lode' – the boy has named it well. It is like a dream, a dream he will repeat, a dream he need not wake from. He could have stood there for an age, just looking at the face, exulting even, in what the boy has found. He will go down there again, this time

215

alone, on Saturday perhaps. He'll take samples for himself and look again – the richest copper lode in Cornwall, his to mine.

'What if I am charged with manslaughter?'

Mathew jerks awake. 'What?'

'Manslaughter, his Lordship said I am to be charged with manslaughter.'

'Do not worry, Thomas. Six months have passed since you were on trial. The magistrate must have believed your story or you would have been charged by now.'

'It was no story, Capun. I told the truth.'

'Of course you did.'

'I would flee before I'd let them take me back to Bodmin Gaol.'

'I believe you would but there'll be no need. These gentry just like to put a scare in folk. Today is Wednesday. We should hear from the duke by Monday at the latest. Setting day is a week on Friday, is it not?'

'It is. I promised Henry and Jethro Loam we'd show the end to Capun Kit on Thursday so we can bid it.'

'We'll have the lease by then. There'll be no setting of the Pascoe Lode.'

Maisie Tuttle looks a picture, red hair curling beneath the brim of her yellow bonnet, or so thinks Thomas Pascoe, as he walks beside her taking sidelong looks. Up through the village they go, past the clanking, roaring mine, all sulphurous stink from the dressing floors and coal smoke from the engine house. Out on to the moor where the air is clean and a lark rises from almost beneath their feet, rises and rises, hovers then starts to sing. It is Saturday, Maisie's day at home and Thomas has no need to work today. She wears her mother's brocade jacket, and a wide frock hemmed well above her ankles showing her matching yellow stockings. They stop to catch their breath and turn to face the sun and the distant sea.

He looks her full in the face and says, 'You are the prettiest bal maid in the whole of Cornwall.'

'Thomas Pascoe, how dares you? I ain't no bal maid and well you knows it.'

'Ah, but you look just like a bal maid out in her finest on St Piran's Day.'

'Tis just my mother's garibaldi that she don't wear no more.'

'Then you dressed so prettily just for me?'

'Hah. What about you – them fancy pants an' yer red kerchief? Next I know you'll be sportin' one o' they hats the capun wears, an' givin' yourself his airs. You miners is all the same – so special you think you are.'

'We are special, Maisie. It's not every man that'll work night or day a hundred fathom down in the dark. Besides I could be a captain very soon.'

'That can't be true. You ain't but fifteen, an' why would Mr Scoble make you capun anyways?'

'It won't be Scoble's yea or nay, Maisie.' He takes her by the shoulders and holds her away from him. 'I found my father's lode, Maisie. I told you we been digging and I found it – my father's lode. The richest in Cornwall, Capun Clymo says. He took me to the duke and I'm going to get a lease. '

'A lease, what's that?'

'Permission from the duke so we can start a new mine, Capun Clymo and me. I will be rich.'

'What about your mates who helped you dig? What share do they get?'

'I don't know.' He stops and sits down on a rounded granite boulder and pulls her down to sit beside him. 'I had not thought of them. I'll pay them maybe, somehow. I shall ask the capun what to do.'

'Capun this and Capun that. You did not like him so much when he took up with your Ma. What's changed?'

Thomas scratches his head. 'I could not bear for him to take my father's place. But when I found the lode I did not know what I should do, so I asked for his advice. He has been good to me. He saved me from the noose, remember?'

'Only so your Ma would marry him. That's what they say.'

'Who says that?'

Maisie does not answer him. She just gazes into the distance tapping a booted heel against the rock.

'Maisie, tell me.'

She looks at him and takes his hand. 'Your Ma told mine an' she told me.'

Thomas gives a little shake of the head and thinks back to his trial. He did not question Mathew Clymo's motives then. He wrote to him for help and help he gave. Then he remembers writing in the letter: 'for the sake of my dear mother.' So the captain had made a bargain with his mother.

As if reading his thoughts, Maisie says, 'What Mathew Clymo does he does for himself alone. He's rich. My Pa is dying from working in his mine, an' he'll not take my Ma as parlour maid.'

Thomas nods. It is true. When his mother said she did not need a parlour maid he wondered why, for Jenny Tuttle is her friend.

'An' so the mighty Capun Clymo – what's he get from your famous lode?'

'It's not famous, Maisie. It must stay secret until we have the lease.'

'So we'll not be going to Australia then?'

'I do not know. Maybe not.'

'But we shall marry?'

'Of course we shall, and we'll be rich and live in a big house with room enough for all.' He laughs, jumps up, pulls Maisie to her feet and kisses her. 'Come, let's walk,' he says.

All afternoon they walk, hand-in-hand and barely talking, out across the open moor following the footpaths Thomas has known since childhood. Back in Penpillick he leaves her at her cottage door then walks back up through the village to the Clymo house.

This time he does not knock, but goes straight in to the parlour where he finds his mother and his stepfather both seated at the table. The captain is holding a letter. His mother looks up at him and he sees tears in her eyes.

'Thomas,' the captain says, 'the duke has written to me. Here, read.'

He takes the letter and reads aloud.

Dear Clymo, I regret that I am advised that it would be unwise to grant a mineral lease to Thomas Pascoe considering that my friend Sir Alexander tells me that he is in all likelihood to be arraigned regarding the question of the manslaughter of the Reverend Dippenden in Bodmin last year. You may wish to make your own provision with respect to this. However bearing in mind the exemplary manner in which you captained Wheal Emma until its loss to Mr Scoble, I will grant you a lease "in loco parentis" as it were on behalf of Thomas Pascoe. Payment for the lease will be the usual twelfth. I suggest you present yourself at the estate office where Mr Vivian will draw up the lease in accordance with your proposal. My advice to the boy would be to disappear forthwith and take ship to Australia perhaps. Unless of course he wishes to stand trial once more.

Yours

Bedford

Thomas sits dumbstruck. Maisie was right. Capun Clymo now owns the Pascoe Lode. His mother puts her hands to her face and wails, 'Australia, Thomas, Australia!'

33

PIECES OF SILVER

'THERE IS SOMETHING AFOOT, NELSON. I FEEL IT IN MY guts. But Loam will tell us, indeed he will.'

It is a bright Sunday afternoon and he rides out once again to meet his spy at the ruins of Wheal Venland. Loam is back on the drink, so Kit Robin says. Has been seen singing and even dancing in the Bedford Arms, the drunken fool. It will be that much easier to wring the truth from him, whatever that truth might be. Scoble slouches in the saddle deep in thought as the horse trots gently up the grassy lane.

It seems the Pascoe boy has settled his differences with his stepfather and is a frequent visitor at the Clymo house. This bothers him – his best miner, his money-maker back in the bosom of his enemy's family. But what bothers him more is that Clymo and the boy have been to see the duke, according to the porter at the Endsleigh gatehouse. And what business could they have with him? The fracas on the moor perhaps and his involvement in the death of Dippenden? But the boy's arrest is well forgotten, or so he thought. His bully boys – the only link to him and the crime are long gone, to Australia or so he hears. The only evidence linking him to that affair is the boy himself and why would he dig that up now?

He knows that Pascoe and his pare no longer spend nights clearing the tunnel where his father died. Did the boy find something that made him change his mind? Well, he can ask him, have it out with him tomorrow – that is if Loam doesn't tell him all he needs to know right now.

'Whoa, whoa there.' He reigns in his horse and stands in the saddle. There at the top end of the lane is the old mine dump and there, scrabbling up towards the crumbling engine house, is Loam himself. Scoble watches him as the miner stops, sits for a moment head on his knees, then turns and crawls the rest of the way up. 'I'd say he's in indifferent sorts, Nelson, wouldn't you? So much the better. Walk on.'

By the time he tethers the horse at the stunted ash at the foot of the dump, Loam has disappeared.

Scoble begins to climb and feels for the dagger beneath his riding coat. You never know when a drunk may turn. Last time he was here of a Sunday he nearly threw Loam down the shaft, but that would have been a waste. All in all, the fool has been an asset and worth every penny paid. He rounds the wall of the engine house and there is Loam sitting on a rock in the sunshine, swigging from a bottle.

'Arternoon Mr Scoble, sir. And how is you? Have a drink.' He wipes a dribble of cider from his moustache and waves the bottle.

By Christ he's drunk. 'Loam, you're drunk.'

'I is your Lordship. I been drunk since Sat'day. What of it?'

'You come into money, Loam, you feckless lout?'

'Secret sir. Tis secret. And I ain't no lout. I'se a Cornishman miner and I'se as good as any man.'

Scoble strides across the ruined engine house, and grabs him by the shirt front and lifts him to his feet. 'You're a drunken sonofabitch, that's what you are and there'll be no secrets between us. Hear me Loam?'

'I hears you Mr Scoble. Now you hear me. I said afore and I say it again, I don't like being swored at by you nor no man. Now you speak nicely to me an' give me one o' them guineas o' yourn, and I might let you into our little secret.'

'God's teeth, Loam your breath stinks like the devil's arse. Our secret? What secret? I'll really throw you down that bloody shaft this time if you don't talk.'

'Let go of me, then maybes I'll tell 'ee.'

Scoble lets the man go then steps back.

'Ahh, now here's a secret.' Loam taps the side of his nose with the bottle. 'Me bottle's empty and so's me pockets so give me money and the secret's yourn.' He giggles, and Scoble draws back as if to hit him but Loam collapses in a heap on the ground.

Scoble looks down at him, shaking his head. He takes a silver coin from his waistcoat pocket and holds it up between thumb and forefinger. It glints in the sunlight.

'Thass better Mr Scoble, sir. Bit o' silver. What about gold, eh? What'd you give me for gold?' He puts the bottle to his mouth and upends it and it clinks against his teeth.

'Gold, man? What are you talking about?'

'Gold, a face full of it, shinin' in the candlelight.' He staggers to his feet, jigs a few steps then collapses again, muttering. 'We is going to make him stinkin' rich, an all he offers me is a piece o' silver. An' me bottle's empty. Life is hard, ain't life too hard.' He lies back, his head against the rock and closes his eyes.

Scoble squats beside him and takes out his knife. 'Shall I slit your filthy throat, Jethro Loam?'

Jethro opens his eyes, 'Shlit my throat and you'll never know,' and closes them again.

He shakes him by the shoulder, puts the knife away then takes another coin from his pocket 'Look Loam, here's two crowns. Now talk to me, damn you.'

Jethro sits up, and spies at the sun through his upturned bottle. 'Golden, 'tis all golden.' He drops the bottle, sighs and holds out his hand. Scoble puts the coins in his palm.

'Like I told 'ee afore, we been working nights clearing the end where John Pascoe was kilt. We broke through more'n a week ago, broke through we did.' He closes his eyes again. 'Face was all golden in the candlelight.'

'Golden? What do you mean, man, "all golden"?'

'We cut it rich, richest I ever see. Go down there an' see for yourself if you don't believe us. Come settin' day, come Friday, we'll bid on her. Hah, silver, two pieces of silver.' He studies the coins in his hand, pockets them then lies back once more.

'I will see for myself, be sure of that. And if what you say is not the truth be sure that you will pay – and not just silver.'

Jethro just smiles then shuts his eyes. His mouth drops open and he begins to snore.

Scoble gets to his feet and, with a shake of his head, turns on his heel and leaves the miner sleeping in the sun. 'So,' he says to himself,

'I was right, something is afoot or rather underfoot.' He grins and in his mind's eye he tries to imagine what Loam has described. Gold, the face of a tunnel all in gold – his gold. What would that be worth? He has no idea. Clymo said there was no gold at Wheal Emma, no gold in Cornwall. Perhaps he was lying and has been cheating all along. Why not? They found a gold nugget at the Carnon mine after all and that's a tin mine just so why not gold in his, yes his, copper mine?

Oh, he is going to be so rich. He must get down there underground and see it for himself as soon as possible – though not today as Kit Robin's gone to Dolcoath to fetch his family. Tomorrow then, when the man is back. He mounts his horse. 'Home Nelson, home boy.' He'll open one of those bottles of vintage claret Hocking sent him when they took ownership of Wheal Emma. He'll celebrate.

But damn, he has forgotten to ask Loam what business the boy and Clymo have with the duke. Well no matter – with gold at Wheal Emma his worries are over.

34

FOOL'S GOLD

HE SIGNS THE LETTER WITH A FLOURISH, FOLDS IT AND places it in the envelope addressed to James Sanderson. He has asked him to find twenty thousand pounds to sink a shaft on the Pascoe Lode. He has little doubt that Sanderson will succeed. The price of copper is on the rise again, the City's Adventurers are flush with cash and Cornish mining is all the rage. Why only last month two Liskeard ladies found a stone of copper on their land at Caradon and sold the property to a Plymouth lawyer for the better part of eight thousand pounds.

No, once it gets around that he, Mathew Clymo, one of the best respected captains in the county, has found the mother lode, he'll be swamped with offers. No need to raid his funds at Bolitho's Bank. The Pascoe Lode will rock the county and the city too once mining starts – he sees it now, brilliant, shining in the flare of his tallow. He should go down again, just to make sure that it is real and not some dream brought on by weeks of fossicking on Dartmoor. The day core will all be at the workface and he could descend unseen – just sit there feasting his eyes on the sight of it. Yes, he will go down. He has no right of course; Wheal Emma is not his mine and Scoble will be enraged but he'll never know. The man so seldom ventures underground and Kit Robin is worse than useless as a mine captain. The miners will be cheating the both of them blind. It's a wonder that Wheal Emma still makes money but what does he care now?

Leaving the remnants of his lunch he calls out to Grace, 'I'm going out now.' He grabs his mining bag from the hook behind the door and walks up the hill, past the mine until he's at a vantage point above the engine house and the attle dump. He turns and studies the scene below – the smoking chimney stack, a dozen bal maidens breaking copper stones, bal boys wheeling barrows of rock from pile to pile, and in the sorting sheds children picking copper from waste on wooden screens. Thomas is right: there should be no children working here. A top-hatted overseer brought in by Kit Robin strides about the place, stopping now and then to harangue one worker or another. As always, Old Harry sits on his stool smoking his clay pipe. Above the hiss of steam and the swoosh of the great beam engine drawing water from the bottom of the mine, he hears the clank of a kibble brought to surface and dumped of its load. The overseer disappears into the engine house; Mathew scrambles down across the dump and with a nod to Harry enters the shaft. He breathes deep – oh the smell, the dank air, the sweating timber, and that sulphurous metallic stink that to him means money. He slips from rung to rung with practised ease, stopping on the third sollar to take his mining hat from his bag and jam it on his head. He lights and fixes a candle to the hat with a lump of clay from the bottom of the bag and continues his descent. A loaded kibble rattles up the shaft beside him but otherwise the only sounds are falling water and his own breathing. He is excited now that he is back underground. It is so familiar – he realises how much he has missed it these past months. Reaching the 120 fathom level he stops and listens. He hears the faintest echo of a shout from far below, but nothing from the darkness either side. He heads off down the crosscut, every twist and turn familiar to him. He stops to look at John Pascoe's marks upon the wall that Thomas showed him as they dialled the end. Strange man he was – half miner, half scholar, and his son is just the same.

Mathew shrugs and carries on into the darkness, sniffing at the scent of new-cut timber and knows he is almost there. And then he sees the rubble pile of the fallen roof with a path trodden up and over it. He scarcely breaks his pace, scrambling up and ducking double below the back. He stops to finger the drilling grooves that were the cause of John Pascoe's death – a foolish man for all his learning. Greed got the better of even him. If he had brought his discovery straight to Mathew he'd be living still. But then Grace would not be his, nor would she be carrying his child. Now, by default, the Pascoe Lode is his as well.

Mathew Clymo skids down the pile and there it is before him. Taking two candles from his bag, he lights them and fixes them with

226

drips of tallow to ledges in the wall each side of the face. Then he sits and stares, watching the flickering light reflecting off brassy crystal faces and iridescent minerals. So rich – it's just so rich, and all of it is his to mine.

Scoble sits in the counthouse studying the month's production records. But his mind is elsewhere. Where is Kit Robin, damn the man? He was due back from Dolcoath on Sunday and it's now Monday afternoon. He'll dock his pay but that won't get him underground, today, right now, which is where Scoble wants to be.

He tries to imagine how a face of gold would look. He takes out his pocket watch, turns it over in his hand feeing its warmth – a rock face made of this stuff? He shakes his head. Could it be true, or is it just the maunderings of a drunken fool? But surely Loam would not lie to him – he never has before. But the only way he can know for sure is to see it for himself and that means climbing down that filthy shaft.

He could go down alone, why not? He would have to count the levels to 120 fathoms. Surely he could find the end where Pascoe and his pare have worked so many nights. He sighs, gets off his chair and turns to the two clerks, who have been sitting silent on their high stools copying figures into the cost book.

'Tell Captain Robin if he comes, I am gone down the mine to the 120 fathom level and he must meet me there.'

They nod in unison, and when his back is turned exchange a look. He takes his coat and goes into the dry which stinks of mud and sweat and sodden flannel. He hangs his coat next to his canvas jacket, trousers and miner's hat – oh yes, he may not be a miner but they have equipped him well. He puts them on then, as an afterthought, takes his dagger from inside his coat and slips it into his belt. The bal maid scrubbing the floor on hands and knees looks up at him but doesn't speak.

'Candles, woman, get me some,' he shouts over the clank and hiss from the engine house next-door.

From a wooden box beneath the bench she takes four candles and hands them to him without a word. He hangs three by their wicks from a button on his jacket just as he has seen the miners do. The fourth he sets in a lump of clay from a bucket by the door, and sticks this on his hat. Dressed for underground, he starts to sweat. At the shaft head he stops before he sets foot on the first rung of the ladder, and looks around. Old Harry lifts a hand in salute.

'Tell Captain Robin he'll find me on the 120 fathom level.'

The old man nods.

Scoble descends into the darkness, stopping at the foot of the first ladder to light the candle on his hat. His nostrils wrinkle at the smell of burning fat. He must count the levels now, one every ten fathoms so the twelfth will be 120. Halfway down he stops, already soaking wet, his hands already sore from gripping the greasy rungs. He hears the pulse beating in his ears – beating fast as if he were climbing up, not going down. But he is not out of breath – he is afraid, alone in the dark. But he calms himself; there are men below him and he has nothing to fear down here – it's his mine after all. Then he hears a faint sound from above – a knock, yes and there it comes again. Is it the sound of boots on wood? Kit Robin? Looking up, all is blackness. He waits for the sound to come again but all he hears is the trickle of water running down the shaft.

Cupping his hands around his mouth he yells upwards, 'Captain Robin, is that you?' He waits, hears his own faint echo but nothing else. He looks down at the next ladder, takes a deep breath, and continues his descent.

'Twelve,' he says to himself and looks around. A tunnel on his left, another on his right, darker holes in the darkness. Now which way, left or right? He unties a candle, lights it and holds it high. There, the right-hand passage floor is well trod with boot marks in the mud. He checks the other side – nothing. So, right it is. He follows the tunnel's twists and turns until it forks, looks again at the floor, turns left. This is it, soon he'll see the gold.

He begins to hurry; another fork but this time both sides are well worn. Damn, which one? He tries to hold his sense of direction, as he would if he were riding Nelson in mist out on the moor. Yes, he's turned left once, so now it must be right and here are wheel marks in the mud – barrows coming from the face? This way then. Bang! He reels back clutching his head, the roof is lower and he has to crouch to carry on. Ten more paces – surely it must be soon. But then the ground beneath his feet is gone. With a cry, he falls and lands face down in utter darkness.

A bar of sunlight illuminates a man curled on sacks on the filthy cottage floor. The man rolls over, licks his lips and groans. It is Jethro Loam and he feels very ill. The sacking stinks of vomit. Clutching his head, he sits up and groans again. What day is it, what time? Past noon it must be for the sun to strike just so. Yesterday, yesterday was Sunday; he drank, he danced, he sang, he drank again. Today is Monday, yes Monday. He crawls to his feet – he should be with Thomas Pascoe and Henry Hopeful Down, working their pitch on the North Lode, down two hundred fathoms.

Oh God, yesterday he told Scoble. Scoble knows. Fool that he is, worthless drunk. Lord Jesus save him. Forgive me Lord, for I have sinned. He staggers to the door, and outside is near blinded by the sunlight. His gut heaves as he runs crouching to the village pump, ducks his head and works the handle, water streaming off his head and shoulders. Shaking himself like a wet dog, he stands erect and looks around – nobody. What should he do? Too late to go down the mine.

He remembers now – Scoble said he'd go see for himself. Perhaps it's not too late to find him, tell him it was all lies and drunken ravings. He must find him. Hand on his stomach he heads up through the village to the mine, where he sidles round the counthouse to the shaft head.

'Harry,' he mutters, 'Scoble about?'

Harry Rowse looks up at him, takes the pipe out of his mouth, and jabs downwards.

'How long since?'

'Five minnit, mebbe less. 120 fathom, by hisself.' He sucks on his pipe. 'You goin' down then, Jethro Loam?'

Jethro nods.

'Bit late in the day. Summat goin' on then? I sees Capun Clymo go down earlier.'

'Clymo? You sure?'

The old man rolls his single eye. 'Think I don't know Capun Clymo when I sees him?'

Jethro runs his hands through his hair. Thomas has told the capun what they've found – so the capun's gone to find him and then they'll go look at the Pascoe Lode. But he must find them first to tell them Scoble's already on his way. He takes to the ladderway and is a hundred fathoms down before he stops for breath. He stands bent over, hands on hips, chest heaving. His thighs and calves are burning and he wants to vomit. But he clambers on to the next ladder and half runs, half slides down it. He pauses for a moment on the 120 fathom sollar, cocks his head and listens. Scoble must be already there, gloating over the Pascoe Lode thinking it is gold, the fool. He dithers. Should he face him now? No, he had better find the others and have Thomas and the capun and Henry Hopeful Down beside him. He continues climbing down.

Ten minutes later he is stumbling along the drive towards the working end, where he should have been all day. He hears the ring of steel on steel and hurries on. He rounds a bend and finally he sees them – Thomas at the face holding the drill and Henry swinging the hammer. He looks around – no Capun Clymo. 'Where is he? Where's the capun?' he shouts.

Henry, about to swing again, turns and rests the hammer on the ground. 'If it ain't Jethro Loam. Where you bin all day then? Sleepin' off the drink, I'd guess.'

Jethro shakes his head, and still panting asks again, 'Where's the capun?'

'How must we know? Last I heard he was to Dolcoath.'

'No, I means Capun Clymo. He come underground an hour or so ago. I thought he'd come to fetch you to the 120 fathom end.'

'He's not here, Jethro. We've not seen him at all,' Thomas says.

'Mr Scoble's gone there too.' He stops and looks from one to the other. 'I'm sorry Thomas.' He pauses and studies his muddy boots. 'The

230

drink got to me again on Sat'day an' I told him everything.'

Henry drops his hammer and grabs Jethro by the shirt front, almost lifting him off his feet. 'You useless vagabond. What you do that for? We agreed – no word to no one till settin' day. Now you've gone and told, we'll never win that pitch.'

'Put him down, Henry.' Thomas tugs on Henry's sleeve and Henry drops the man. 'So, Jethro, Scoble and Capun Clymo are both up on the Pascoe Lode right now. Is that what you are saying?'

Jethro nods. 'Must be if they ain't down here.'

'We'd best get up there Henry, all three of us. Lord knows what will happen now.'

In the guttering light of three candles it looks as if Mathew Clymo is at prayer. He is sitting on a rock, elbows on knees, resting his chin on his steepled hands. He stares unmoving at the face in front of him. He wishes he could paint so that he could commit this image of buried riches, of wealth made manifest, to canvas and hang it on his parlour wall for all to see – 'The Pascoe Lode'. He sucks in a breath. Thomas Pascoe: what should he do about his stepson now? After the reading of the letter the boy stood silent, pale, just staring at him. And in the widening of those eyes Mathew saw the sudden doubt, and knew – Thomas suspected he'd made an arrangement with the duke. He would have spoken but the boy just turned away and left the house. He has not seen him since.

Grace sobbed in his arms, 'I'll lose my son, I'll lose him.' Mathew tried to comfort her but he had no words. He lay awake that night for many hours but the choice was stark – either Thomas must stand trial once more or he must flee and flight must mean Australia. But surely he would do well there? Mathew has heard much talk of rich gold diggings at Bendigo and Ballarat and copper at Burra Burra, of Cornish miners wealthy beyond their dreams. And Thomas, with his understanding of stones and strata – surely he will find success. But Australia is so very far and so very few come back, rich or poor. And Grace will grieve. But she will grieve much more and so in truth will he, if Thomas Pascoe's end is a hangman's rope.

No, the boy must go and soon. He will take himself to Plymouth and buy the boy a first-class passage on the next sailing.. And he'll set Maisie's mind at rest by finding a cottage for her parents and let Grace take Jenny Tuttle as a maid. It will cost of course, but once mining starts here on the Pascoe Lode and the smelters' buyers, hungry for such easy smelting copper, outbid each other, Mathew will make his second fortune. He'll send a sixth part of the value monthly to Thomas in Australia. With stuff this rich, one twelfth to the duke and a sixth to Thomas will leave nine twelfths to pay for costs and still provide a most handsome return to himself and his Adventurers. He sighs and rises to his feet, and holds a candle close to the face. He shakes his head in wonder. As he turns away he hears the sound of boot-steps and then a shout from beyond the rock fall.

'Capun Clymo, is that you?'

He knows the voice of Henry Hopeful Down. 'Tis I indeed, Henry. Who's with you?' But before an answer comes he sees a light atop the fall, and then his stepson's face.

'Thomas,' he says.

The boy stops and stares at him then says, 'Capun?' He clambers down the rock pile to the face and stands looking at it. Behind him comes Henry, and then the skinny form of Jethro Loam.

'It's quite a sight ain't it,' Jethro says. 'I told Mr Scoble it were gold – Lord forgive me, it could well be by the look.'

'You'm a fool Jethro Loam and no mistake,' Henry says.

'Why are you here, Capun?' Thomas asks.

Mathew is silent. What can he say? That he is gloating over what is not really his, yet has fallen in his lap?

'Capun?'

'I have written a letter to London to ask for funds, and I wished to verify that what I said is true – that this is the richest copper lode in England.'

Thomas nods then turns to Henry Hopeful Down. 'Forgive me Henry, but I did not tell you that here we stand beyond Wheal Emma.

232

The capun has obtained a new lease from the duke to mine my father's lode.'

'Thomas, I did not plan this. The duke decided,' Mathew says.

Thomas just stares at him.

Henry takes off his hat, scratches his head then gestures at the face. 'So that ain't Mr Scoble's then.'

'No. And we'll not be bidding for it at Friday's setting day.'

'So it don't matter I blabbed to him?'

'No, Jethro, it doesn't, Thomas says. 'But where is he now? You said he would be here.'

'Scoble here?' Mathew says.

Jethro nods. 'When I come down, old Harry said I weren't but five minnits behind him and he were coming here.'

Standing in the candlelight in air fast growing stale, with the stink of burning tallow in their nostrils, they look from one to the other.

'He must be lost,' Mathew says.

Scoble clambers out of the shallow pit and sits hatless and shaking on the edge. He has managed to find and light one candle but even so his sight is half obscured by blood flowing from the cut above his eye. He does not know which way to go nor even which way he has come. He is lost, and begins to shake with fear and shock. He feels for his knife – yes, it is still securely sheathed beneath his belt. He takes deep breaths to calm himself and rubs the blood from above his eye.

Then he hears the echo of a shout from the passage beyond the pit. Feet dangling, he edges round the rim of the pit on his bottom and once on the other side, stands up, still shaking. He holds the candle well before him and this time watches where he puts his feet. He hears another shout and step by careful step, head bent low, retraces the way he came. It seems to take an age but finally he finds the fork and this time he turns right. Following barrow wheel-marks, he turns right again. Here the floor is well worn, and once he sees the new-cut timber, he begins to walk with confidence. Then before him broken rock fills the passage. He stops, looks up and reflected off the roof he sees the glimmer of candlelight. On hands and knees, Scoble crawls up and over the rock pile – and there below him are Jethro Loam, the oaf Henry Down, the Pascoe boy and Mathew bloody Clymo, all with their backs to him. Beyond them, glittering in the candlelight, a face of gold. He can scarce believe his eyes – gold, just as Loam has said. He shuffles down the heap then slowly stands.

'So Loam, you spoke the truth then?'

They turn as one. 'We thought you was lost, Mr Scoble,' Jethro Loam says.

'I met with a small accident – fell down one of your filthy holes. But now I'm here.' He touches the cut above his eye. 'And I want to know what is going on. I want to know why you, Clymo, are here in my mine.'

The four miners look from one to the other.

'Who will tell him, then?' Jethro says.

'Tell me what? That that is gold? You told me that already, you drunken scum, and now I see it.' He points at the face and shouts,' You think I'm blind?'

Mathew grins. 'Gold? Gold? Loam told you this was gold?'

'Loam did – and I know enough of mining to see he told the truth.'

Jethro sniggers and Mathew laughs out loud. 'It's not even fools gold, Scoble. It's copper, and only a fool would believe a drunk. You're no miner. Just look at yourself. You should not be down here without your nursemaid.'

'Clymo, you bastard, get out of my mine before I kill you.'

'I'm not in your mine.'

'You are. Of course you are.'

Mathew shakes his head and smiles. 'No I'm not. Your mine ends the other side of that pile of duds behind you.'

'What?' Scoble takes a pace towards him, then wipes his hand across his brow where blood starts flowing from the cut. 'What do you mean?'

'Ask Thomas.'

'Well, Pascoe?'

'My father dug beyond Wheal Emma. He found this. The capun has a lease from the duke himself.'

Scoble looks from Mathew to Thomas and then yells at Jethro. 'Loam, you lying turd. You knew of this and did not tell me.'

'I did not know – and if I had I would not have said. And I'm no turd nor any of them other things you likes to call me. Like the capun says, you ain't no miner, you're just a fool.' Jethro drags a hand down over his moustache and spits on the floor.

'Spit at me would you, you filthy scum,' Scoble screams and with a movement so fast they barely see it, he draws his knife and drives it up and under Jethro's ribs.

Jethro Loam gasps, his mouth drops open and his eyes go wide as slowly he collapses to the floor. The candle falls from his hat, sizzles in a puddle then goes out. Scoble stands at bay, bloody knife in one hand, his candle in the other.

'You've killed him,' Henry Hopeful Down whispers. 'You've killed our Jethro Loam.' Then with a roar he lunges out to grab at Scoble's neck. But Scoble ducks and turns beneath his arm and scrambles up the rock pile. Henry grabs his foot, but the man kicks him in the face and then is gone.

'Follow him Henry, we'll see to Jethro,' Mathew shouts.

Henry crawls over the rocks and begins to run, but hampered by his height he cannot catch the fleeing Scoble. Then, just yards before the shaft, Scoble stumbles and falls to the ground. He scrabbles for his candle but cannot find it. Henry is almost upon him when he ups and runs again, charging towards the darkness of the shaft.

With a look behind him Scoble leaps on to the sollar, grabs for the ladder, misses it entirely and skidding on the wet wood floor crashes through the brattice work. With a wailing shriek he plunges down the shaft.

35

BURIAL

A ROBIN IS SINGING IN THE CHAPEL GRAVEYARD AND there is the smell of new-dug earth. With hands folded and heads bent, the miners stand around the open grave – Caleb Chapman, Henry Hopeful Down, Jakeh James and the captain, Mathew Clymo. They shared his first day underground – they and poor Jethro wrapped in linen, lying down below. Thomas watches them beneath lowered brows, until the minister catches his eye and Thomas bows his head. The minister intones, *'Let us go forth in the certain hope of being reunited with our brother Jethro Loam at the end of time. Go forth with God's peace and may the Almighty bless you now and forevermore. Amen.'*

'Amen, Amen, Amen,' they murmur, and turn away as earth thuds down upon the body. But Thomas stays watching as the grave cloths are hidden piece by piece with falling soil. First his father, then the Reverend Dippenden, now Jethro Loam and William Scoble – how many more will die for the sake of the wealth his father found beneath the ground? He sighs and feels the prick of tears then he too turns and follows the little cavalcade up through the village. Catching up with Caleb outside the Bedford Arms, he hears him say, 'Well I hope for Jethro's sake there's still good cider at the end o' time.'

And Jakeh James replies, 'Be sure of it, green grass and cider and the sunshine – that's heaven. And no more slaving in the dark and spitting black till the day I die.'

Thomas passes them and stands beside his stepfather. 'Capun,' he says, 'might we two have a talk?'

'Of course we may, Thomas. But first let us join the others and drink to Jethro Loam.'

'Yes Capun.'

The drinkers, already spilling on to the street, make way for them and once inside hands pass them a glass of cider each.

'To Jethro Loam,' Henry shouts, and they raise their glasses, 'To

Jethro – a miner and a Cornishman. May he rest in peace.'

'He was a good man in the end you know,' Thomas says. 'He warned us Scoble was on his way.'

'It's a sorry story, Thomas, a very sorry story. But let us save our thoughts until we are alone. We have much to talk about.'

Thomas nods. 'I'll wait for you outside.' He goes out into the sunshine and stands gazing down through the village past the Tuttles' cottage, past the cottage where he grew up, and down to the bridge and the stream where he and Maisie played as carefree children. He is grown now; he has seen men die.

He watched Jethro die cradled in the capun's arms, watched the life in his eyes flicker for a moment then fade away. 'He's dead,' he said to the capun.

'He is. God rest his soul,' and the capun passed his hand down over Jethro's face and closed the staring eyes. They left him there in darkness, slight as he was but still too great a burden for the two of them to carry to the shaft.

They met Henry Hopeful Down returning. 'Mr Scoble's gone,' Henry said. 'Fell down the shaft. We'll have to fetch his body up.' But William Scoble found his own way up to grass – his shattered corpse lifted in a rising kibble and scaring the daylights out of old Harry Rowse when it tipped out at the shaft head all broken bones and bloodiness.

Thomas shakes his head. Before that there was the Reverend Dippenden and his own father – all these men, good and bad, killed for what lay at the end on the 120 fathom level.

'Penny for them, Thomas.' The capun claps him on the shoulder. 'Shall we walk?'

Thomas nods, unspeaking, and they walk beside each other up the hill out of the village, not pausing at the Clymo gate.

'Come,' the capun says, and takes him to the engine house and up on to the bob plat where they stand looking out over Wheal Emma. The great beam engine is stilled as a silent measure of respect for the passing of a miner. No maidens work on the dressing floor and the bal boys are all gone home.

Thomas gazes southward to where the summer sun shines on the English Channel. He remembers the smell of Looe harbour the day they rode on Bill Burrows' cart for a visit to the sea, and the tide was out – salt, mud and seaweed and the putrid stink of rotting fish on the quay. 'Tide is out', his father said, then explained how the tide moved with the waxing and waning of the moon. Later they watched the fishing boats go out, and Thomas wondered how it would be to sail upon the sea.

He turns then towards his stepfather. 'What do you advise, Capun? Must I cross the ocean to Australia or should I stay?'

'Yesterday, as witness to the deaths of Jethro and Mr Scoble, I had to see the duke with William Smale the constable. With that business done the duke asked after the case of the Reverend Dippenden. The constable said the magistrate will shortly issue a warrant for your arrest.'

Thomas shakes his head and runs his hands through his hair. He takes a few paces before turning back to face the capun. 'I am innocent but I will not go back to Bodmin Gaol. So I shall take ship. I am decided.'

Then, pointing down towards the shaft, he shouts 'And Capun, you are welcome to the Pascoe Lode. It's yours. I want no more of it. Too many men have died.' He turns away to hide the tears.

Mathew nods and is silent for a while, resting his arms on the wooden rail and staring at his mine. At length he says, 'Thomas, you have made a wise decision. You will find a new life in Australia. But the Pascoe Lode is not mine. It belongs to you and your family, to our family and it will provide for you wherever you may be. You shall have a thousand guineas a year for as long as we bring copper to grass. Oh – and I shall pay your passage. You shall sail first class.'

Thomas looks up at him. 'Thank you, Capun. That is more than generous. Maisie Tuttle will be pleased.'

'Maisie Tuttle?'

'Yes, Capun. She will come with me, and we shall marry once I turn sixteen next month.'

Mathew claps him on the shoulder and shakes his hand. 'Indeed, indeed. Congratulations. I shall pay her fare too. You'll be on board ship and married by the captain?'

'That is what I have thought. But Capun, I have another favour I would ask of you.'

'Ask on boy, ask on. I am in a generous mood now I have my mine back and you no longer think that I would steal from you.' He chuckles. 'Do not look so surprised. I saw it in your face when you read the letter from the duke. You thought I had connived with him to steal the Pascoe Lode.'

'I did think that – and I am sorry.'

'Well, never mind that now. What is this further favour you would ask?'

'Capun, I did not dig out the 120 fathom level by myself. Without poor Jethro and Henry Hopeful Down I never could have done it. I cannot repay our Jethro but, if he will, I would have Henry come with me to Australia. He has been my workmate, teacher and my friend since first I went down underground. I would not leave him here a tutworker. He deserves a better life.'

'Henry is his own man and I cannot speak for him. But if he wishes to go with you then we will buy his passage also.'

'Thank you, Capun. And now I have a question. I know you lost Wheal Emma when Mr Scoble and his friends bought shares in Cornish Consols. How is it that you have it back? I mean – who owns Mr Scoble's shares now that he is dead?'

'No one as yet. He has no descendants nor can we find a will. I talked it over with the duke and we agreed that I should run the mine again. I have already called a meeting of the Adventurers and I do not doubt they will confirm my re-appointment. Particularly as it means we can mine the Pascoe Lode without another shaft. The duke is most content that we shall not destroy more of his pheasant shoot.'

'Is that all he thinks of – pheasants? I should steal one then you would have no need to pay my passage to Australia.'

'Transportation is no joke, Thomas.'

'I know that Capun. But I was thinking that I am to be transported – banished from my home – from all of this.' He waves an arm to embrace the mine, the village below and beyond that the patterned countryside. 'All because my father discovered copper. It is unjust.'

'It is indeed. But Thomas, you are not a convict, and you and your family will be rich just as your father planned. Is that not enough?'

'I do not know, Capun, I do not know. And how shall I tell my mother that I must leave?'

A shaft of light from the setting sun shines through the open parlour window illuminating the copper crystals from the Pascoe Lode that now grace the parlour dresser. Thomas and Mathew sit either side of the fireplace, boot heels on the fender. Grace stands before them, her back to the empty grate. They are silent while the distant creak and hiss of the beam engine and the rattle of a rising kibble drift in on the evening air. She looks from one to the other.

Finally Mathew speaks, 'He must go.'

She shakes her head. 'No, Thomas, no, you will not go. I cannot lose you. There has to be another way. We can hire that Mr Purdue, or if not him a whole raft of lawyers. We are rich enough now with this new find of yours, are we not?'

'Money will not help us this time, Grace. Thomas has no witness. It will be his word against the law and the law is cruel and almost sure to win. It is a risk too great to run. The duke tells me that if he is gone to Australia before the warrant is issued they will not pursue him. So I must buy his passage directly, tomorrow even.'

'Australia, Australia. Why must it be Australia? I cannot bear the thought.' She puts her hands to her face, covering her eyes.

Thomas rises from his chair and takes her hands and folds them into his. 'The capun's right Ma. I cannot stay. Besides I was already thinking of Australia even before we found the Pascoe Lode. So many miners have gone. I thought it might be a better life. And who knows, one day we might return. Come, do not cry.'

'I am not crying, I just cannot bear my thoughts. And what chance of your return? None that I know of have come back. And it is a convict place. How will you live? And what of shipwreck? Have you thought of that?'

'It is a danger Ma, I do know that. But I face danger every day I work

241

my pitch below. And we shall not go to the convict colony at Botany Bay but to South Australia where there are rich gold and copper diggings.'

'Rich, rich? We are rich already. What need have you of gold or copper?'

'Oh Mother, I am a miner. I know nothing else. Besides if I stand in court again I must either lie on oath or admit that my action caused the death of the Reverend Dippenden. And I will not lie. It was an accident but how will I convince a jury without a witness? Please, Ma, please understand. I will not be locked in Bodmin Gaol again.' He drops her hands and hugs her to him.

She rests her head against his chest and sighs, 'Oh my son.' She looks up, kisses him then frees herself from his embrace. 'I shall go to bed and take my sorrow with me.'

They listen to her footsteps on the stairs and on the floor above then hear the creak of bedsprings as she lies down.

'It is hard for her, Thomas,' Mathew says.

'Hard for me too, Capun.'

'You're not afeared then?'

'Capun, I was afraid my first day underground. I soon grew out of that. I was afraid when Scoble rode me down and again in Bodmin Gaol. And I was more than afraid at my trial when I thought I must surely hang. And trapped atop that rock fall on the 120 fathom I near soiled myself with fear. So I'm no stranger to it. But no – a voyage to Australia holds no fears for me. It will be an adventure, will it not?'

Mathew smiles. 'Aye Thomas, I guess it will.'

36

FAREWELL

 SHE SHOULD BE HAPPY, BOWLING SOUTHWARD IN Mathew's new four-in-hand on such a sunny day in June, but she is hard put to restrain her tears. Two years ago she lost John Pascoe. Now she must lose her son. He sits in front of her, upright beside her husband, he top-hatted, reins in hand. Next to him the bulk of Henry Hopeful Down part blocks her view. Mathew bends now and then to say a word or two to Thomas, words lost in the clatter of the horses' hooves and the rattle of the wheels. They spent last night in Tavistock and tonight they'll stay in Plymouth. Tomorrow, Thomas and Maisie and Henry Hopeful Down take ship. She can scarcely bear to think of it.

She turns to Maisie sat beside her. 'Maisie love, you'll look after him?'

'Of course I will, Mrs Clymo. You know I will. And we'll have Mr Henry too.'

She nods and whispers. 'I'll miss my Thomas so.'

She looks away to the west, past Kit Hill with its engine house atop, and knows that there beyond in the hollows on the edge of Bodmin Moor lies Penpillick, the mine, their home – none of which her son will ever see again. Nor will he know the child now stirring in her womb. She clasps her hands across her belly. For the past fortnight Thomas has lived with them in the big house. It was a thing she so desired but it is being ripped away. Tears well in her eyes and streak across her face, blown by the summer breeze. She cannot bear it but she knows he has to leave. She has accepted it.

She heaves a sigh and turns once more to Maisie. 'Your Ma and Pa will miss you too, Maisie.'

'They will, but leastways they have their cottage back now Mr Scoble's dead and gone. And Ma's not on the dressing floor.'

'And the capun's got his mine again so he's a happy man. I suppose I should be happy too.'

The carriage rounds a bend and there spread below them is Plymouth. Even from here she can see the vessels anchored in the Roads. One of them will be the ship that will bear away her son. She puts her hands to her face and stifles a sob.

Grace does not really cry until, standing beside her husband on the dock, she sees the mooring ropes let loose and the *Ramillies* slip away. She hears the sailors' shouts, the cheering of the little crowd and the cry of gulls and she knows these sounds will stay with her for the rest of her life. There they are, Thomas, Maisie and Henry Hopeful Down standing at the rail, waving and blowing kisses while the tears stream down her cheeks. Mathew puts his arm around her. 'There, my love, don't grieve so. I am sure it's for the best.'

But she just sobs the harder, burying her face in his chest. Finally her crying eases and she turns to look again at the ship. She sees sailors barefoot in the rigging, and watches through her tears as sails unfurl, and the *Ramillies* picks up way and heads out to sea.

'Goodbye, my dear son,' she cries. 'Goodbye.'

37

SOUTH AUSTRALIA

'WALLAROO,' SAYS THE SAILOR POINTING. 'THAT SMOKE, that's Wallaroo.'

'Wallaroo?' says Henry Hopeful Down. 'What strange name is that, Thomas? What place are we coming to?'

'I do not know Henry. At Port Adelaide they said the Burra Burra mine is finished but there is mining work at Wallaroo and a new copper strike at Moonta which is near.'

'That'll be right,' the sailor says. 'Richest strike in Australia, they say. You ain't the first Cousin Jacks we've brought here nor will you be the last, I reckon. But you don't look like miners to me, if you don't mind a sailor saying so.'

Thomas looks at Maisie and smiles, fully aware of how pretty his wife is dressed in the smart outfit she bought in Plymouth the day before they sailed. He admits too that he and Henry, in shirtsleeves and bronzed from three months at sea, the mine pallor long gone, are better dressed than they have ever been, thanks to Mathew Clymo's money. 'Well,' he says, 'whatever we may look like, we're just Cornish copper miners from Penpillick.'

'Penpillick?' says the sailor. 'I ain't never heard of that before.'

'And where is Moonta then?' Maisie asks, gazing shoreward.

'No more than ten mile south o' Wallaroo – just about there.' He points again.

'Could be the moon,' Maisie says gazing at the flat shoreline, her eyes shaded by the brim of her bonnet. 'Look at it – there's nothing there.'

'Ain't the moon, Missus. Not unless there's sheep grazing on the moon.'

For the last few hours the they have been sitting on the hatches of the schooner *Daphne* enjoying the sun's heat and gazing at the long, low coastline of South Australia. There are no towns or villages, no greenery nor any sign of life. The only breaks in the monotony have been occasional outcrops of red earth cliffs. Now, as they approach the coast they can at last see buildings, a chimney belching smoke and greenish-grey scrub along the foreshore.

'You'll be stopping at the Globe then?' the sailor asks. 'It's the only hotel in town.'

There is a bellow from the captain at the wheel. 'Ready about. Jump to it, jump to it.' Sailors leap to their feet and take their stations at ropes and windlasses. The ship heels and with a great flapping of canvas comes about and heads towards the shore.

As the schooner slips into the harbour the three stand at the rail watching the bustle on the waiting dock. 'Well Maisie, my love,' Thomas says, 'It's been a long old journey but here we are at last.'

A day later Thomas and Henry Hopeful Down stand on a slight rise overlooking the Moonta mining camp. At first it seems all heat and dust – a chaos of milling miners, hucksters and hangers on, lost in the haze of a vast plain which stretches to the horizon. But gradually they begin to pick out familiar sights – piles of rock and stones scattered amongst the twisted scrub, small shafts or simple holes in the ground, some with horse whims raising ore in kibbles; boys at picking tables sorting attle from green copper stone and there in the middle of it all the unmistakeable beginnings of a Cornish engine house.

The sounds too are familiar: the pounding of hammers on a dressing floor, the creak of windlasses and whims, the clatter of rocks tumbling from kibbles and above all the voices – they recognise the voices. The shouting of drunks staggering out of a liquor shack could be coming from the Bedford Arms, the cries of lads wheeling barrows are the same as those at Wheal Emma, and the bellowed orders of an overseer are those of a Cornish captain.

'Cornish miners one and all,' Henry Hopeful Down says.

'Aye,' Thomas says. 'Let us take a closer look.' They pick their way down through the confusion until they reach the foundations of the engine house. They stand and watch as a pair of stonemasons lay block on block. A voice from behind them says, 'And who might you two gents be and what do you want?'

They turn, and Thomas holds out his hand. 'I'm Thomas Pascoe from Penpillick and this is Henry Hopeful Down. We're miners, maybe looking for a pitch.'

'Are you indeed. Well, I am Captain Hughs. We need good miners. Are you two any good?' He shakes their hands.

'We brought more copper to grass than any other pare at Wheal Emma,' Thomas says.

' Hm, well, tell me what you think of this.' He takes them across to the dressing floor beside the shaft where men are breaking rock.

Thomas picks up several stones and studies them. 'Bornite and black copper what some call chalcosine, and here is bright pure copper.' He bends to pick up a piece of shining ore. 'The same as what we mined at Wheal Emma. Your mine is truly rich, Capun.'

'Indeed. This comes from eighteen fathom. If you would you care to take a look and make a bid come Survey Day, come back tomorrow and I will take you down.'

A miner's head appears out of the shaft. He climbs out, black-faced, panting and coughing and takes a long swig from his water bottle.

'Fall on twenty fathom, Capun. Joe Sidley's trapped. Like be kilt.'

He stands beside them chest heaving, and Thomas smells the familiar stink on him, black powder, sweat and sulphur. There is a difference though: this man is dry, bone dry and panting still with thirst. 'I'll fetch the boys, Capun, and we'll get back down there.'

'Yes, do that, Jacko.' The captain turns to Thomas. 'Well gents, I must go down and see what's to be done. No doubt I'll see you on the morrow.'

They shake his hand and make their way back to the horse and dray they hired in Wallaroo. 'Back to Wallaroo?' Henry asks.

'Yes, let's see how my Maisie liked her first day in Australia.'

Henry takes the reins on the hot and dusty road back to the town. Thomas sits bowed and silent, the smell of copper mining in his nostrils still. He sees again the face of dead Jethro Loam in Capun Clymo's arms, remembers the thud of the clod of soil his mother dropped on his father's linen-wrapped body, looks at his hands and sees the blood of Reverend Dippenden. He heaves a sigh, and raises his head and gazes all about him.

Far, far away to the north, beyond the plain, a range of hills are blue in the distance. What lies beyond them and beyond again? Why would he break his body in the darkness once more? He has money. This land is vast. He could go prospecting for himself. With Maisie and Henry at his side he could do anything.

Then, as if in echo to his thinking, Henry points off to the east where sheep are grazing in the grey-green mallee scrub.

'Must be a thousand head o' sheep in that there flock,' he says. 'Man told me at the Globe last night there's more money in sheep than mining.' He looks at Thomas. 'An' sheep don't kill a man.'

'Nor do they Henry, nor do they.'

GLOSSARY

ADIT – a level tunnel (usually driven into a hillside) in order to give access to a mine, and used for drainage or the hauling of broken ore.

ATTLE – waste rock.

BACK – roof of any underground opening.

BAL – a mine (from Cornish 'pal' a shovel, and hence a digging').

BAL MAIDEN – a woman or girl employed at surface on a mine, generally in the dressing of ore.

BEAM ENGINE – a type of steam-engine much favoured in Cornwall for use in pumping and winding on Cornish mines. The power from a large cylinder set vertically in an engine-house was transferred via a massive rocking beam or bob to the pumps in the shaft outside.

BLENDE – zinc sulphide.

BOB PLAT – the wooden platform on the outside of the engine house over the shaft pumping rods.

BORER – a steel rod with sharpened tip used for drilling shot holes in rock.

BRATTICE – timber partition work in a mine, e.g. dividing a shaft between ladderways and hoisting.

BUCKING – the breaking down of copper ore on an anvil to about 10mm in diameter by bal-maids using small hammers.

CORE – work shift as in 'day core' and 'night core'.

COST BOOK – the system of accounting by cost used on most Cornish mines and the books themselves in which these accounts were kept.

COSTEAN – a linear trench dug at surface to expose a vein or lode.

COUNT HOUSE – the mine office.

CROSS COURSE – a lode or vein which crosses the principle direction of mineralisation.

CROSSCUT – a tunnel or passage at right angles to the direction of a vein or lode.

DIAL – a compass like surveying instrument used to map underground openings. Hence to 'dial' a drive.

DRESSING – the concentration of copper or other ores contained in the rock excavated from a mine. Carried out on DRESSING FLOORS.

DRESSING FLOORS – an extensive area at surface on a mine where the various processes of concentration of ore took place.

DRIVE – a tunnel excavated on the line of a LODE as the first stage of the development of a STOPE.

DRY or CHANGE HOUSE – the building within which miners changed their clothes before and after going underground. Some were heated by steam pipes connected to the engine boilers.

DUDS – waste rock.

END – a working place underground.

ENGINE HOUSE – a building designed to contain the steam engine on a mine or other works. When forming part of the framework of a beam engine, these were particularly strongly constructed.

FATHOM – six feet.

GARIBALDI – a lady's tight fitting jacket favoured by Bal Maidens on feast days.

GOOK – a Bal Maiden's bonnet.

GRASS – the surface at a mine – as in 'they came to grass'.

HEADFRAME – the tall construction set over a winding shaft which carried the sheave wheels over which the winding ropes ran.

HORSE WHIM – a winch with power supplied by a horse walking around a circular platform applied to an overhead winding drum.

KILLAS – shale.

KIBBLE – a large, strongly-constructed, egg-shaped, iron container used for ore and rock haulage and hoisting.

LEVEL – a working level underground e.g. '60 fathom level' – the horizontal workings 60 fathoms from surface.

LODE – a linear area of mineralisation underground. Generally vertical or near-vertical, and often extending for considerable distances along its strike.

MUNDIC – arsenic sulphide.

PARE – two to four miners working as a team.

RAISE – a shaft driven upwards between two or more underground levels.

SETT – the legal boundary within which a mine could extract minerals.

SETT – one of the components of timber framing of an underground opening where it ran through loose ground.

SHAFT – a vertical or near vertical tunnel sunk to give access to the extractive areas of a mine.

SOLLAR – a platform set at regular intervals between ladders in a shaft.

SPALLING – the breaking of large rocks at surface with long-handled hammers.

STOPE – an excavated area produced during the extraction of ore-bearing rock. Often narrow, deep and elongated, reflecting the former position of the lode.

STRIKE – the long direction of a lode or rock formation.

TAILINGS – the waste, sand and slime from a mine dressing floor, not containing workable quantities of mineral.

TALLOW – a candle usually made of animal fat.

TRIBUTE – the system of payment whereby groups of miners (pares) bid against one another for contracts to work sections of the mine for a percentage of the value of the ore raised from that area. Hence 'tributer'.

TUTWORK – a system of payment whereby groups of miners contracted to work on a 'payment by results' system at previously agreed rates – usually for shaft sinking or driving levels. Hence 'tutworker'.

WHEAL – a mine.

WHIM – the winding gear used for hauling from a shaft consisting of a power source and a winding drum. See HORSE-WHIM.

WINZE – an inclined shaft joining two or more underground levels.